Penniless Souls

Penniless Souls

Lost Compass Love Book 2

Eve Gaal

Dedicated to Women:
Especially if someone hurt you or made you cry.

Acknowledgements

The funny thing about being a woman is that we have a lot more power than we think. We have something they want, and we can cover it up, walk out or spill a drink on the one wanting it. We can laugh with them or at them. We can take it as far as we want, then try something new or go with the flow. It's how we roll. Sometimes we don't trust ourselves. We don't like our own choices. We're embarrassed about the way we handled a sticky situation. That happens to everyone. It's the hasty reaction that can cause more trouble than it's worth. No matter what, they can't buy or steal your soul. It belongs to you.

I know this because I've hurt both physically and mentally. I've catered to the wrong voices and watched the pain make me feel less. I had scars, bruises and cuts. I cried, and no one listened; well, no humans anyway. My soul was still there, but it needed help. It needed saving.

My journey to God came through literature. Writers, who didn't believe, cast their souls into either the real or proverbial fires of Hell. They painted lovely pictures and used strong language, giving me examples, of how **not** to live. As an impressionable and naïve young woman, their anti-establishment poetry pushed me into the arms of grace. I'm convinced, Amazing Grace saved my soul. I also believe that all writing, good or bad, comes from the Almighty. Even if you don't accept any of it, it doesn't matter, because He listens to you. He listened to me and I am grateful.

Not only did he listen, he also provided me with my husband's enduring love, caring and fascinating friends, exceptional readers with extraordinary taste and a publisher for this book. For these miracles and more, my heart is filled with boundless gratitude. Thank you.

"We can make our plans, but the Lord determines our steps." Proverbs 16:9

Prologue

Ever since modern casinos replaced coins with little slips of paper, the fake sound of cha-ching fills the smoke-filled air in surrealistic dreams, where few win, most lose, but almost everyone pretends they're having fun. Players wear lucky hats and keep a good luck charm or a fortune from a cookie in their wallets. They strike a poker face and study the odds, thinking life's a crap-shoot anyway. All members of the human race, pawns on a giant chessboard, knocked around by destiny.

Outside of a gaming house, on legal documents, these are referred to as uncontrollable Acts of God. They include hurricanes, fires, earthquakes, floods, disease and violence. Which begs to ask the philosophical or rhetorical question: how do happy, healthy people manage to evade depression and loss? How is it, their child is spared from autism? Why did their house remain standing during a wildfire? Why did the bullet ricochet off the building, hitting someone else? There must be a trick, akin to counting cards. A practical guide to parenting based on the mathematical theories of probability. An answer every mother of a teenage daughter wants to know, regarding control and the perfect timing for letting go.

* * *

Early one Tuesday morning, Penny Murray found herself on the Las Vegas Strip inside a behemoth casino, where John, her husband of 21 years, needed to pick up a check. His last and final paycheck for a February spent in the seedy opposite of the luxury surrounding her. While waiting, she thought about the check. It reminded her of the little slips of paper the slot machines spat out after someone won a jackpot. Faux coin sounds mingled with tinny, clinky chimes, rattled around in her head. She thought about their upcoming move back to California, and how their time in Sin city didn't prove to be fun at all. Especially, after the nerve-wracking incident at the local airport that had made her blood-pressure orbit. *She thought about what all of it had meant. Everything, it seemed had a reason. Predetermined by fate or merely random, she wondered, thinking of the last few weeks and the unexpected joys and dark lessons that clung to her like desert sand.*

Cha-ching—the repetitive sound surrounded her, driving her mad with anticipation. *They had to get out of Vegas,* she thought, swinging short, shapely legs onto a bar stool and wondering why picking up a check took so long. Her eyes focused in on a middle-aged, heavy set woman playing a five-dollar slot machine. The woman wore a hot pink, polyester sweat-suit with worn sneakers. Maybe those clothes had fit her once. A tight bra accentuated her unpleasant back fat. Every few minutes, a cherry symbol gave the woman three dollars, and one time she even had a big ten-dollar win. Poor lady, Penny thought, wondering why the woman kept feeding money into the stupid machine. '*I'm going home lady,*' Penny whispered to herself, turning away in disgust. '*And I suggest you do the same thing.*'

Something kept that woman glued to that cushioned stool. Her motives had to reach well beyond the obvious desire to win. What made one person lucky and why did others lose? Penny began to judge and analyze the situation. Perhaps the monotonous motion, consisting of pushing the same button, comforted that lady in an odd sort of way. Maybe she needed blinking lights, Day-Glo neon and the maddening sound of phony coins. Perhaps her cat-filled, dilapidated home begged for a tractor to make a path to her bed-bug infested mattress. Or worse, her husband had left with some floozy he met one night at a club, and her deadbeat children lived in another state. Penny figured, the loud chimes and casino noises drowned the woman's pain, replacing her solitary and bored life with not-so-cheap thrills, thereby placating her soul.

Cynical and sad about the recession, a bankruptcy and a year full of nothing but trouble, Penny didn't enjoy watching people lose their money. She doubted her instincts were far from the truth. Life in Vegas had taught her many strange and unusual things. *Anyway, you sliced it, she hated to think it, but that woman in hot pink looked like a born loser.*

A scream filled the air. The woman playing the slot machine shouted and bounced up and down on her stool. It sounded like a knife had plunged into her buffet-filled intestines. The reason became apparent rather fast. There, on the monitor, lined up and flashing, ringing violently with ear splitting sirens and notifying everyone within a mile, this underdog looking woman had won a jackpot. Glowing ruby sevens–pulsated almost sexually–as a crowd gathered. She turned around beaming, revealing a row of coffee-stained, crooked teeth. The slot attendant came over and paid her twenty thousand dollars faster than a winning horse pulls into the lead at the Kentucky Derby. Minutes later, the woman called two or three people on her cell phone.

Maybe, Penny thought, *the woman didn't have a problem with hoarding after all. Maybe she had family members who loved her, and they were coming to get her right now. Hopefully, they'd take her to the dentist on the way home before stopping at a hair salon to have a root touch up.* Penny had to admit, watching the entertaining commotion felt like suspended animation. The harder she stared, the more her heart pulled her back into the blissful scene.

Oddly, Penny's viewpoint changed. It didn't happen fast, but when her cheeks blazed, it seemed obvious she felt ashamed for her preconceived notions. While staring at the cheering crowd, something deep inside began to twist around, creating a certain kindness towards the plump woman in pink. The more Penny watched, the more she realized the woman must have lived a hard life, earning wrinkles and age spots, one miserable day at a time. Time seemed to stand still. The contagious smiles bouncing from one face to another in the casino, gave Penny hope. Where was John? He needed to see this. Twenty thousand would really help them right about now.

An hour later, John still hadn't returned with his check and the winner had left with two security guards. Though she thought about going to the parking structure to see if he was at the car, she remembered his words, "Penny, wait here or I'll never find you." So, she waited, and thought about the events that uprooted them, bringing them to this gambling mecca in the middle of nowhere.

Chapter 1

When they married in Hawaii, so many years ago, John Murray had vowed to love, honor and cherish her forever. Through sickness, health and all the other stuff that came and went in their lives, he had managed fairly well. At this moment however, he didn't know what to say. After all, people lost their jobs everyday, but somehow, he never thought it would happen to him.

She sat there like a queen from an illustrated book on ancient civilizations. Her auburn hair, now a natural looking shade of red, made her look younger than her years. Sparkling eyes, the color of fresh Key limes, focused beyond the curtains. Her underlying mood, made his heart twist into a massive knot. Normally, she had a friendly, expressive face, but now it looked frozen and the warmth in her cheeks appeared drained and pale. *Worry made him wonder what she was think-*

ing. It looked like she focused on the drought, outside in the yard. Maybe, he had hoped, she stared at the sprinklers. The local California water company had told him to adjust his timer. His ears tried to listen for the spray hitting the side of the house. Maybe, she wanted him to adjust them, so they wouldn't hurt her delicate zinnias.

The striking, good-looking woman he adored, to the deepest part of his soul, usually had the answers and the best ideas. This time however, like those sprinklers, he had come to a wall. This time, he really needed help and her silence only made it worse, because deep in his heart, he knew the truth had nothing to do with lawn irrigation or zinnias. He waited for her to speak.

"Did Lani leave?" Penny asked, without moving her head to look at him.

He glanced at his watch and grumbled an affirmative answer, before his eyes moved to her adorable ears. Perky, little soft ears, with cushioned lobes, he enjoyed kissing.

"Well did she?"

"I said, yeah, sorry."

"Stop being sorry," she demanded, in a curt tone that reminded him of the way she spoke to their daughter Lani when she did something wrong.

But he couldn't help it. "Sorry."

Sighing, she turned into the room. "Look, it's not your fault, we'll figure it out. We've figured other things out in the past, so maybe we'll get lucky and do it again."

John didn't think luck had anything to do with it. Was she being facetious? The heaving of the shoulder and an additional sigh, told him her mind kept zipping through some pretty deep stuff. Sometimes, when the going got tough, she still managed to fall into her fantasy world where dreams became reality, and everything eventually worked out. Though an endearing aspect to their relationship, it didn't add anything solid to his side of any argument. Most often, he'd simply agree, supposing that she'd work it out in her mind. She had a magic touch which in most cases, worked in their favor, but this time, she sounded painfully hopeless. Unless he hawked some of the junk in the garage, so he could make a few bets on a horse race, he didn't see luck entering the picture.

He wasn't sure, but thought he noticed red-rimmed eyes and wet lashes, indicating the severity of her displeasure. Wearing vulnerability like a hat fashioned from invisible straw, something he rarely saw, confused him, making him feel helpless. Like a man in a leaky rowboat without any oars. She was more than simply his other half. She was his rock and that rock had become seriously upset. Anything he said only made him feel foolish. He didn't know what to do, or say, to make things right. When she sniffed, he noticed her nose had turned a rosy shade of pink.

The last time he saw her like this was at her dad's funeral. He couldn't fathom how any of this could even vaguely be similar to a life and death situation. His eyes watched her turn back to whatever was happening outside. The sprayers outside had stopped. He could hear the gentle hum of air-conditioning streaming through the vents. *Think, he told his brain. Somewhere inside there might be an answer. After all, no one has died.* But his brain redirected everything to his heart.

"Babe, I love you." Maybe she just needed reassurance. The timing seemed awkward, so he looked down at his scuffed work boots.

"I know you do John, but sometimes love is not enough."

Inside his chest, he felt his ticker beating like a Cuban conga drum. "What does that mean?"

"You tell me," she replied with an angry tone to her usually lovely voice. "I quit my job at The Globe to raise our daughter and thank God, she's going to college. We both saved and scrimped for our little girl but now this...crap." She paused for emphasis, waving her arms towards the window. "I don't even know what to say John. Without a job, we're going to lose our house. This recession hit Riverside County hard. The people across the street just went into foreclosure and there are five houses for sale on Lime Street."

"I know Hon. I applied at six different sites and even asked Hans about being an apprentice at his cabinet shop. Construction is at a huge stand-still right now." The dialogue came to a standstill too. He listened for the sprinklers, still hearing nothing. A minute later Penny pointed out the window.

"Someone's at the Brown's house right now. I hope they mow the lawn."

"Did you hear me? There are no construction jobs available. Like you said, it's a recession."

"I hear you, but tell me what exactly happened at that cabinet shop?" She turned towards him, wiping her face on her sleeve.

"Hans fudged around trying to tell me he wanted a younger apprentice, without actually saying it. I think that's what he meant. Heck, nice guy and everything–but when he gets going, I have trouble understanding him. Guess it's that accent. Anyway, I'll keep looking, I promise."

Her voice now an octave higher and louder, "I know he's nice John, but nice isn't helping us, is it?"

Man, how he hated arguing. "What do you mean by that?"

"It means–having beer with the old crew isn't going to solve this problem."

Ouch, her sarcastic little comment hit below the belt. He had to admit the drinking buddies made him feel better about almost everything. Maybe he could turn the emphasis around and see how she liked it. "Well, you can go back to the paper."

Disgusted, she rolled her eyes. "John, in case you haven't heard, there is no paper. It folded up, gonzo. Adios, bye-bye."

He knew that and felt bad for saying anything about it. "Wasn't it sold to a new publisher?" He wanted to hug her, but she didn't look approachable. The difficulties and economic turmoil slamming the nation for two or three years were crashing onto his family like a wayward tornado. He needed to think of something fast. *Think harder, he repeated to his inner self as if sending an elf down a corridor to open a few doors full of ideas.*

"No, John the Globe is gone. Absorbed by the internet and that monstrosity we are subscribing to, which, as you know, is located over eighty miles from here. Nowadays, major metros eat community papers for breakfast. I'm sure you don't expect me to commute over one-hundred and sixty miles a day."

He went to the window and placed his hand on her shoulder. "No, of course not, but I also want you to know I'm with you all the way dear."

"I know that," she whispered. "Any other bright ideas?"

He searched the street and stared at the lawn. Their flowers looked fine but the lawn at the Brown's house looked completely burned out. A colorful, blazing red foreclosure sign popped out of the dry grass like blooming tulips. *There it was–a red sign that popped up in his mind with a plan.*

"Not really, but I heard there's a bunch of new construction in Vegas."

She moved away, causing his arm to fall from her shoulder. "And?" It looked like she had swallowed something disgusting. Even her nose wrinkled, as if an obnoxious odor had filled the room. "What does that have to do with anything? We don't live in Vegas, John."

"You wanted ideas, Hon," he said, pausing and trying to figure out what else he should add to the squabble. "Can I repeat one more time that I love you Penny?" He had run out of options but knew his feelings were in the right place. He rarely went to battle with her and like a good husband, generally chose the side of least resistance. Sick of fighting, yelling and wondering why everything had turned to shifting sand, he waited for her tone to subside.

"Sure, repeat it all you want, but love doesn't pay our bills."

"Didn't love get us through everything before?"

She put her head down and began to sob. He placed an arm around her, pulling her near, so he could kiss away a salty tear and perhaps calm her down.

"Penny," he said quietly. "Didn't your mom talk about patience and faith?"

"Yes, but..."

"With a little bit of planning, it will all work out. I promise. With your imagination and my desire to work hard, we can do anything." More tears rolled from her radiant, now sparkling eyes, onto cheeks flushed with emotion. "Can you trust me?"

Quietly, she nodded and placed her head back on his shoulder. "I have so far," she mumbled without conviction. *It felt like a white flag of surrender. The type of submission that reminded her of submissive women in advertising campaigns of the fifties. Without a job or money, she had only one thing left. Fortunately, it was something valuable, something called love. The Murray family had loads of it. Love for each other. Love for strangers. Love for nature. For God. And, they were grateful for everything they ever had.*

They both heard the garage door open as Lani's car drove up the driveway. "Let's not fall apart in front of Lani," he whispered, pulling her toward the hallway and into the family room. A large portrait of a Hawaiian goddess in front of a volcano loomed above the fireplace. A New Zealand artist who met Penny after he had completed the picture had done the oil painting. Strangely, the woman in the painting looked identical to a younger version of Penny. John pointed at the framed artwork. "What's with the crying? Remember you're like the goddess Pele. People are supposed to fear you."

Penny wiped her eyes with the back of her hand before smiling impishly at John. "Let's tell her we're going to Vegas."

Chapter 2

Lani whispered into her cell phone when her mother walked into the room to pull shades, turn off lights and most importantly to kiss Lani's cheek.

"Go to bed Honey," she said, leaving the room.

"I've got to go," Lani said to her friend before clicking the phone off and throwing it on the couch. "Wait mom, come back."

Penny popped her head back into the family room. She glanced around, into the dark shadows to find her daughter's face. When she hit the overhead light switch, Lani turned toward the wall. Her shoulders were shaking, and she was crying.

"Lani dear," she took a step closer and moved toward the fireplace. Two large chairs flanked a giant couch below the painting of Pele. Lani sat in one of them. "What's going on Princess?"

"I don't know mom," she sobbed. Huge tears rolled down her cheeks and Penny noticed her eyes were completely red. It looked as if she had spent hours crying.

"What happened?"

"I don't know. One minute I'm the prettiest, sweetest girl in the world and the next–my best friend is pregnant–from him.

What did I do wrong?"

Did her daughter just say someone the same age, is pregnant? Penny recalled some of her own dramatic memories and sat down on the couch, so she could be near her daughter. Watching her little girl suffer broke her heart, and she worried she might say the wrong thing. "Oh Lani, you didn't do anything wrong. Men can be fickle."

Giant sobs spewed forth after the word 'fickle' and she looked up at her mother. "It's more than that mom. Tim said he wanted to get…married after I finished college. We had made some basic plans. He was going to ask dad about it at…at…Christmas."

Married? At her age, Penny shuddered and felt *like genuflecting or praying immediately. The Lord sure works in mysterious ways, she thought, with*

19

a thankful, overjoyed heart. "Oh honey, I'm so sorry." Penny reached out to caress Lani's arm. "Now, now, please don't let anyone do this to you. Tim isn't worth all this pain. He's just a guy. You'll find a better guy." *Someday in the future, like the distant, far off future.*

"Mom? Didn't you hear me? I love Tim and we were going to get married."

Though this information came as a huge surprise, Penny tried remaining calm. For one thing, she was tired, and it was late. "I understand. Love is hard to explain. There are many different types of love and your old mom knows a little bit about this subject."

Tears dripped from Lani's eyes. You and dad have the perfect marriage and I want someone like him. He's so dependable. Mom, you really lucked out."

"Yes, that's true, but it wasn't always like that. I had to go through a lot of soul-searching to make sure I was doing the right thing," she smiled. She continued to caress her daughter's arm, hoping the repetitive motion might calm both their fears.

"What do you mean by different types of love?" Lani asked with a gentle sniffle.

"Well for one thing, I know you love chocolate ice cream."

Lani smiled and reached over to embrace her mother. "I love you mom."

"I know," Penny whispered into her daughter's chestnut-hair. "The love of your family is different than the love of a man. When the right one comes along you'll know it. Maybe not right away, but if you're patient, the answer will be right here in your heart." When she said the word 'heart', she moved a hand to her chest for emphasis.

"Really? I thought Tim was special. He said he loved me."

"You're a big girl now Lani, I don't have to tell you this, but sometimes people say words without backing up what they mean. In other words, they say things but don't understand how important the words are to the person listening. The words are hollow like an old log eaten by wild termites. People can say anything they want to say, but actions speak louder than words."

Lani smiled again and as she processed this information, her face took on a look of comprehension. She sat up, arranging stray hairs, pushing a few strands behind her left ear. "You mean actions like the time when dad went all the way to Hawaii to find you, when you were lost?"

"Well, that certainly put tons of positive points in his favor," Penny said with a small laugh. "Come here, let me hug you."

"Yeah, thank God he did that."

Penny squeezed her daughter, thinking about the strange turn of events leading up to Lani being born in Hawaii. "Now, let's see–how about you spend some time at Aunt Bess'? She has an amazing guest room."

"What? Why?" Lani stretched out the word 'why' and her face looked horrified as she pulled her arms away from her mother. She stood up and went to the window. "I thought you're on my side."

"I am."

"Doesn't sound like it."

"Please dear, think of it this way. You'll get your mind off Tim, while your father and I go celebrate our anniversary in Vegas."

Lani's red-rimmed eyes looked sad again. "You're leaving me with Aunt Bess during Christmas break?"

"Yes, but we'll be back Christmas day." Penny stood up and turned out the lights. "Now put on your jammies and go to bed. I'll bring back an extra-large tee-shirt as a souvenir, for you to sleep in."

Lani hugged her mother. "Okay, but I'm not thrilled about this."

"Trust me; it could have been much worse."

"How?"

"That stupid Tim could have gotten you pregnant, instead of Emily."

Chapter 3

When the doorbell rang, she ran to peek through the curtains. A cop car stood at the curb. Thankful the lights weren't blinking, she hurried to the door to open it a crack. Penny pulled the lapels of her worn-out pink robe closer to her chest, as shivers ran up and down her spine. John had left early to talk to a construction manager and Lani wasn't home. A policeman asked her name before relating a deeply disturbing story.

"Ants?" Horrified, she brushed her hand through her hair and tried closing her gaping mouth.

"Giant fire ants ma'am." The officer looked down at his shiny shoes. "After being released from a medium security prison for men, his bones were found in the Mojave Desert."

The granola she had for breakfast began to churn.

"Okay, well that's sad and everything but I hardly knew the man and I also don't know what this has to do with me." She wanted to shut the door and take a shower. Twenty years ago, she–*almost*–and the key word in her mind was *almost*–had a fling with an airline pilot. Now, she couldn't care about his bones–dead or alive. Her eyes darted to his clipboard holding a manila envelope. "Are you sure it says my name on your papers?"

"Yes ma'am. I plan to leave you some documents. Can I come in?"

Hesitating, she stepped aside for him to enter. When, pointing towards the dining room table, she realized she might have made a mistake. Wearing a dark uniform, black leather boots and a formidable weapon, he towered over Penny, making her nervous. Her mind did a quick inventory of possible weapons: flowerpot, chef's knife, frying pan. "Yeah, come in" she mumbled.

"Seems the victim didn't have a next of kin and his ex-wives didn't, and I should emphasize, they still don't want to have anything to do with him." As he ambled to the table, Penny could see that he'd be easy to outrun. "Guess both of them filed restraining orders. Now that Mr. Losegg has passed away, that leaves you, because he had a trust fund naming you—-only you—as the beneficiary."

"Captain."

"Excuse me?"

"You said, Mr. Losegg, that's all. He was a Captain." Astounded, while also being grossed out, Penny tried to appear calm in front of the heavy-set officer. He wore a tight shirt pinned with a blinding gold badge. Perspiration dripped along his hairline. Something didn't add up, but she nodded and accepted the letter. "Doesn't the government reclaim funds from criminals?"

"Not sure ma'am. I think we took back the money he owed the government, but these funds are in a private account. The sum of what's left is yours now."

"Thank you," she said with a sigh, glad John wasn't home and thanking God Lani was in school. The oddest things happened when she found herself alone. As if any of this mattered. Dan Losegg could leave her the world and she wouldn't want it. That creep had ruined an entire hard-earned vacation. He almost had her killed.

Sweat trickled down his neck, creating spots all over his shirt.

"Can I get you a glass of water?"

"No thank you ma'am. If you could just sign on the dotted line to show receipt," he said, reaching towards her with his pen.

She signed her name quickly and noticed the officer's vacant, but professional expression. "Just bones?"

He smiled, tipping an imaginary hat. "Yup, be careful out there." Her eyes continued to assess his bulky frame when he turned to leave. A reassuring calm came from deep within, making her forget her fear. This man, the strangest of messengers, huffed and puffed in the warm morning sun all the way to his patrol car. Only after she saw him drive away, did her attention settle on the envelope in her hand.

Ants? What the heck? She ripped it open and found a handwritten letter and a bank statement with directions to a safe deposit box in Nevada. A small key on top of the statement lounged securely under several pieces of clear tape. Maybe, she ought to find a comfortable place to sit down before going further. She returned to the dining room table and sat, wondering why she could hear her heart beating like a lost drummer boy from a holiday song. Quivering fingers read from pages written on a yellow legal pad.

'Hi Penny', it said on the top of the letter. 'If you're reading this then I'm not around anymore. Who cares, right? Anyway, there's so much I wanted to say to you, but first, let me say, you're one of the classiest dames I've ever met. I never forgot how I hurt you. Leaving you in Hawaii and then almost pinning a drug shipment on you was low class. You are so sweet, and I know you're older and wiser now, but I'm sure you're still the angel I remember. I'm truly sorry. Better late than never, right? I spent more than ten years in prison thinking about all the ways I'd want to apologize, and this is the best I can do.'

'They took back most of my drug money, even though I invested most of it and yeah, some of it might have been laundered. The government found all my hiding places. Trust me—nothing I'm giving you is bad money. (Carson Rheingold is my parole officer and can verify everything.) I've had to prove this money was my money before anything went nuts in Hawaii. The small amount I have hidden in the Mojave is mine, but now that I've croaked, it'll probably be lost forever. Everything in my bank account is yours. Rightfully yours–no strings attached. Most important of all: Please find it in your heart to forgive me.' It was signed, Respectfully, Dan.

The attached statement showed his name and her maiden name, Penny Himmel as account holders. She focused on the bottom of the page, but her hand shook, and she blinked several times as if she had forgotten how to read. She counted the zeros to make sure, before almost falling off the chair. Snatching up the paper with the key, and the letter, she hurried up the stairs to shove the offending envelope into her underwear drawer. When she let go, her fingers felt cooler.

It wasn't true. It couldn't be true. He had always lied to everyone. Penny felt convinced this was another one of his whopping charades. Dead or alive, this guy had been evil to the core. No wonder the ants came to get him. She cringed at the thought of him and immediately turned on the shower. Trembling inside, her entire body shook, thinking Dan had stalked her from beyond his dusty desert grave.

Two million dollars, the bank statement said. Captain Dan Losegg had left her two million dollars. Sure, when chickens have lips, and pigs fly. Accepting any of this as truth, she felt, would guarantee Hell. There had to be a way to forget this morning ever happened. As she lathered up with soap, her tears mingled with the warm water. Maybe if she scrubbed hard enough, the entire fiasco would go away. She had to convince herself the last hour had been one of her outlandish nightmares. *And that disgusting cop, she figured, had to be a harbinger from the dark side. No way, she thought. Satan can go right back to his inferno down below.*

Chapter 4

Lani sneezed, wiped her eyes and said, "I can't stand being allergic to everything."

"You're not allergic to everything," her mother admonished tenderly. "It's just pet dander and cat hair. Your aunt Bess has two cats."

"So, remind me why we're here again?" Lani sneezed into a tissue. "And why does everything smell like cat urine?"

"We're traveling and you're healing. As far as the cat goes—well–I don't smell anything bad."

"Healing?" Is that what a broken heart is, a disease? Lani wanted to scream at someone—anyone. First Tim—now her parents–wanted to dump her at her aunt's stinky house which might as well be an asylum. "Mom, I'm old enough to get a job. I'll get my own place."

"Young lady, we've been through this subject a hundred times. Why do you want to wear me out? It's a recession. Jobs are scarce, and you haven't finished college. Besides, your dad and I prefer knowing you're safe."

"Emily said you're just trying to control me."

Penny rolled her eyes. "You want to be like Emily?"

Lani pouted and *thought of her friend suffering from morning sickness.* She quickly answered with a resounding, "No way."

Penny recognized the rebellion in her normally sweet child, and though Lani wasn't a teenager anymore, she would always be her baby. "She tapped a hand on Lani's knee. "Keep an open mind angel. Things have a way of working themselves out in the long run."

Seconds later, Aunt Bess burst into the room with a tray full of snacks, ice-cold cans of soda, glasses, napkins and chocolates. Following behind her aunt, way down near her feet was a fluffy looking white dog that immediately jumped onto the couch and tried nuzzling onto Lani's lap.

"Get away, dog." Lani remarked with a slightly aggressive sounding tone. Pushing the dog away, she sniffled and said, "Can't you see you're a curse?"

"I really think it's the cat dander," her mother interjected, politely. "Look at all these nice snacks your aunt put together for us."

Lani didn't feel like snacking on cookies and chocolate when her head felt like exploding from nasal congestion caused from a house full of stupid pets. To think she would have to spend the entire week locked up with these insane creatures was making her sick to her stomach too.

Never missing a beat or an insult, Aunt Bess made a sad, questioning face before looking down at her dog, "Curse?"

Time to change the subject, Penny thought. She tried to make a noise by clearing her throat and popping the top on a soda. Foamy bubbles filled the glass, gurgling and distracting Aunt Bess from more of Lani's negative comments.

"It's such a hot day. I figured we needed something to cool us down. Speaking of hot, when are you and John leaving?" Aunt Bess asked smiling.

Lani picked up a napkin and blew her nose.

"Next week, Bess," Penny replied, after taking a nice long drink from the leaded crystal glass.

"I've got the guest room fixed up for you Lani. I changed a few things and added some shelves. Plus, now there's a bigger bed. I hope you like it. Do you want to take a look?"

"No, maybe later," Lani said, pushing away the dog that kept trying to sneak back onto her lap. When she sneezed, the playful dog jumped off the couch, hid under the coffee table but kept wagging his tail.

Bess continued to smile and Lani noticed her mom staring at the carbonation in her soda. *This was such a strange situation. To Lani it felt like a fight or flight moment in her life. An effervescent bubble, that could sink or rise to the top and burst at any moment.* She *looked up at a painting in an old walnut frame depicting a romantic couple in a rowboat. They were floating down the river of life. If she didn't do something at this instant, her entire life could essentially be ruined, washed away like the uneven shoreline in the impressionistic painting. It was a crucial turning point. She felt no one at home cared about her opinions, even while her teachers treated her like a grownup. At nineteen and a half, girls should have some rights regarding their pet peeves. Still, she hung to the precipice of her dignity and tried allowing her mother and her father's sister to chat in peace. Obviously, they didn't care if she died from her allergies as long as everything happened with good taste and refinement. In their eyes, she was still a little girl and they kept referring to her as a child. Lani didn't have any other options and now here she was, caught like a trapped animal–because they weren't about to let her stay home alone.*

"Bentley, leave Lani alone," Aunt Bess said, reaching for the dog that was now on his hind legs, trying to poke his tiny muzzle under her dress. "He's such a sweetie, Lani." Picking up the dog, her aunt placed him on her lap and tried calming him down. "Don't worry my dear; I'll keep him out of the guest room while you're here. I can also run to the pharmacy for some allergy pills."

Lani stared at the stupid, fur ball sitting contentedly in her aunt's lap. Bentley stared back with jet black, beady eyes that seemed to want to challenge Lani to a dual. When she sneezed, the dog began to bark like crazy. The determined canine jumped off Bess's lap and ran around the room faster than any dog she had ever seen. *That mutt could be part greyhound, thought Lani.*

Aunt Bess got up and clapped her hands, yelling for him to be quiet. Meanwhile during this melee, her mother stood and picked up her purse. *Oh gawd, that defining moment had arrived. Lani leaned back on the couch feeling defeated. She felt as if she was going to be institutionalized in a home for the mentally unhinged. Discarded, pushed to the curb by her family, like a* worn-out sofa that only needed attention, such as new upholstery. Abandoned, displaced from her room, with its lavender painted walls–and worst of all–her friends, she felt the tide pulling her out to sea.

"Bess, we'll stop by on Tuesday morning. We're leaving at nine."

"What?" Aunt Bess shrieked over Bentley's continuous barking, accompanied by Lani's sneezes. "Bentley," be quiet she shouted in a kind-hearted way. Aunt Bess didn't scold her dog. She treated the dusty mop looking dog like a member of the family.

"We'll see you on Tuesday," Penny repeated, reaching towards Bess and giving her a hug.

The dog ran around and around the dining room table like a crazy racehorse. A tiny pink tongue hung from his lips and drool flew in the breezes he created. Aunt Bess gave Lani a quick hug and went back to clapping and yelling at her dog. On Tuesday, Lani would begin a new chapter in her life–a life that included a very rambunctious dog and two cats that might kill her. Her boat capsized on a deserted island. *She felt like a hostage, held against her will, a caged captive, in a strange place filled with unusual wildlife.*

Chapter 5

Lani sat in the park with her nemesis Bentley at the end of a long, royal blue leash. The least she could do was take the stupid mutt for a walk. After all, Aunt Bess had been nice to her and let her pretty much do anything she wanted to do within reason. Freedom had a price and walking the dog seemed like a pretty good deal. The fresh air outside the house helped her allergies. Even though the spoiled dog drove her nuts, as long as they weren't indoors, her breathing felt better. Bentley began pulling the leash and growling when a ball bounced into his line of vision. Seconds later, a guy ran over to fetch the ball. Bentley barked and carried on as if his life depended on it, exposing his fangs, drooling and making a fuss in the quiet midday afternoon. Bentley acted very different from a dog simply wanting to play with a ball. This unusually antisocial outburst was some sort of communication or form of defense that Lani didn't understand.

Looking up at the towheaded guy she yelled above Bentley's obnoxious noise: "I'm sorry, he's not my dog."

"That's okay," the man replied, coming over to befriend the jumping, growling canine by attempting to pet it. When he splayed his fingers so that Bentley could smell them, she cringed.

"Watch out, I think he's Satan."

"Satan? Ah, come on," he laughed. "You must be referring to my kid brother." A few moments later, Bentley seemed to come around, allowing the stranger to do a little petting. Like greeting a long-lost friend, the dog sat back on the grass, spread his paws up into the air, hoping for a belly rub. "What a cutie," the guy said, rubbing Bentley. "Is it a poodle?"

"I have no idea."

"Hey Dickhead," a voice came from around the tree. "I'll catch you later," and with that comment, a similar looking blonde guy threw a baseball mitt onto the ground next to Bentley before running away.

The guy rubbing Bentley's stomach waved at the younger boy and looked up at Lani. "See what I mean? Now it's my turn to say I'm sorry. That's my brother and in case you were wondering, my name's not Dickhead."

"To be honest, I wasn't wondering, but I'm glad it's not your name. Can you imagine it on your name badge?" Bentley sniffed the guy's legs, knees and crotch. "I guess he likes you."

"I love dogs," he replied, trying to calm the dog while petting him vigorously. "Look at him now." Bentley's eyes were closed. The dog surrendered to pleasure and almost seemed to smile. "My mom works at the animal clinic."

"It's my aunt's mutt." She yawned, suddenly feeling bored or maybe as relaxed as Bentley. "Hope we didn't ruin a good baseball game or something."

"No, we were done playing," he answered, reaching for the leash. "May I?"

"What, keep him?" She asked, pretending to have a serious look on her face.

He laughed at her question and pulled the leash from Lani's fingers. "No, I just want to let him run for my ball."

"Go for it, I hope he'll run away," she said dryly, as she crossed her arms in front of her chest.

"What's his name?"

"Bentley," she yawned again but had to admit, she enjoyed watching the dog run ten feet after the ball. *It made her think of people who always raced around after the same old things, only to come back to the place they started. Life was a game of fetch, she reasoned. Go get this and that and then come home to where you need to have a garage sale in order to get rid of all the things you've accumulated. Like the big sale, her parents had after coming home from their Vegas Anniversary trip. They sold almost all the furniture in the house. The circle of life, she thought, stifling another yawn. This time they left for a long time and now her future looked bleak.*

"Sweet. I like that name," he said tossing the ball.

"You would. A Bentley is a fancy car." *It was one of those possessions people raced after. People like her parents. A gleaming end-all, the big prize laden coach, offering heated leather seats, power windows and a laundry list of options. The Bentley,* and similar luxury vehicles came after a long line of dreary, boring sleds in the parade of life. A lifetime filled with pink slips, registration fees, insurance, license plates and havoc.

She had heard the stories: the first car–a manual transmission, came with deep bucket seats, but also had a leaking sunroof. They also owned one that overheated too many times. It had impressive wood veneer and air-conditioning. Dad drove a small dinged up truck for a while and of course, he used it for his work. They also bought a practical family-sized car after she came into the world, but someone stole it. The boring car story went on and on and around and around, like a whirlpool.

Someday they'd be a reward for completing that circle. For putting up with lying mechanics, bad brakes and expensive tow truck drivers. If not at the end of the circle, perhaps the gaudy trophy in the middle. Though it seemed like too much trouble, her parents deserved the best. Even if all of it reminded her of those chocolate cream donuts that almost shouted: this is too sweet, it's too much, don't do it and it wasn't worth all the trouble after all.

"Yeah, I've heard about those cars," he said.

Distracted by her thoughts and returning to the moment. "What?" she asked feeling a chill in the air, which meant the sun was setting and her aunt expected her home for dinner.

"Hey, Bentley, come here." Bentley came running to him immediately. "You're a good dog, aren't you Bentley?" The dog pranced around happily, and the young man slipped the leash onto his sneaker, so Bentley wouldn't leave. The beige and snow-colored fluff ball acted as if he had known this man all his life. Finally, the dog nestled into the grass right next to him, placing a little white paw on his ankle while watching nearby birds. It seemed Bentley had made a new friend.

Lani wanted to get up and leave, but her options were somewhat limited. Going back to Aunt Bess's too early would mean she would have to set the table, maybe even chop vegetables for a salad. "Are you a twin? You look just like your brother."

"Nope, he's tall for his age. I'm in college and my brother's a high school freshman."

"Oh," she said, wondering if she should just leave and remove the leash off the guy's foot or if she should ask for it back. Even though she loved the feeling of being free to talk to this guy or anyone else for that matter, it still felt strange conversing with a complete stranger. The air had started to cool and evenings at her aunt's house required a sweater. "I've got to go home and eat dinner now," she said, standing up. "I think it's getting late."

"Late? It's not even five yet," he said, petting Bentley.

"I don't care, it's getting dark. I really should go. Can I have the leash?"

He stood up, handed her the leash and the ball. "Well, maybe I'll see you and Bentley out here tomorrow. My name's Pete."

"Maybe," she answered, turning to go and pulling on Bentley who didn't want to leave. This neighborhood was now her home. Bentley had made a friend, and, in all likelihood, they'd see each other again.

"Bye Bentley."

The circle continues, she thought. Tomorrow they'd be more cat hair and dog spit. She yawned. "Come on dog, I'm sure you'll see that dude again. Now let's go, so we can get warm."

Chapter 6

One week in Vegas began as a test. They would celebrate their anniversary, check into the work situation and then decide if they could live there.

The week before Christmas made her remember her time in Kauai. Lush and tropical, it always rained in Hawaii. Penny leaned against the headrest, watching clouds drift over the desert. *She calmed herself looking at the horizon, knowing she had nothing to worry about because Lani was spending the week with John's sister. In the event they were moving to Vegas, Bess had mentioned that her house was big enough to have Lani around all the time. As an aging spinster, Aunt Bess kept to herself by keeping busy with crafts and managing her array of fluffy pets. Still, Penny thought she must get lonely now and then. That's where Lani could provide a little human interaction, maybe even companionship.*

The good news was that if they decided to make the big move, Bessie already had a couple of tenants in mind for their house. In the unlikely event of a financial meltdown, she did have that secret envelope in the bottom of her dresser. Not that it mattered, because she didn't believe Dan's paperwork amounted to an anthill of coffee beans anyway.

She had to think positive. They could do this with or without those dubious promises, even if the clouds burst upon them. If this short anniversary trip worked out and John found some leads for a job, they'd immediately be heading to Vegas. But that would be in the New Year, after the holidays, and it meant they would live in Nevada for an undetermined, perhaps long time.

"Do you think the weather will hold up?" She stared far ahead, noticing cumulous thunderheads in the sky.

John stared straight out the windshield at the deserted highway. They had passed many strange rock formations, borax mines and piles of tumbleweed before coming to an area where train tracks crossed the road. "Look at that sign, a closed cavern."

"Stalactites are limestone. Right?"

"I think so. Honestly Hon, I don't know much about that subject."

"Stalagmites are the ones on the ground. They form into a column. Sometimes they meet in the middle. Isn't that cool?"

"You mean like us?" He smiled, but his eyes scanned the skies.

"Yeah exactly, nature can be romantic. So, speaking of nature, do you think it will rain?"

"It looks okay right now," John answered. "Don't forget it's December and the desert gets flash floods. Did you see those puddles about ten miles back?"

"No, were they big puddles?"

"Just small ones, but those gray puffy looking things up ahead are either filled with rain or we're going to be eaten by a swarm of giant locusts." He reached over and tried to tickle her but she pushed his hand away.

"Very funny—your fingers don't look anything like locusts."

"You're a wise woman, but now you're expert on entomology?"

"Yes and no," she answered, smiling and looking forward to her anniversary trip. "I'm fascinated by ants. They work so hard and never give up." *John's question about entomology reminded her of a recent online search she had done about man-eating ants. Her basic research indicated that army ants and driver ants are carnivores, but they don't march around anywhere near the Mojave. Ants in the United States are usually fire ants, Harvester ants or the well-known carpenter ants. She concluded that Dan might have met up with some dermestidae also known as larder beetles, skin beetles and leather beetles. According to the website photos, she noticed the black ones could be confused with a type of ant.* "Locusts look similar to grasshoppers. I'm pretty sure it's raining over there. John, hello? What's wrong? You stopped listening to me."

"What dear?"

"Are you worried?"

"About the rain?"

"No, I mean the job market."

"Oh that. Not really, I think my mind wandered when you mentioned that ants work hard and never give up. I know we won't give up. If we can handle moving to Vegas, then everything will be fine. They're having a giant building boom right now. It's like the fastest growing city in the nation, maybe even the world."

"Yeah, I know. I'm just wondering if you like the idea of working there."

"Sure. It's moving that sucks. If we're really going to do this, we'll have a yard sale, which should bring in a little bit of extra cash. You know I like to work. Just like those ants, you mentioned. I'm a carpenter and they need carpenters like crazy. The money's supposed to be great." He reached over taking her fingers into his right hand. "Now stop tormenting yourself over what might or might not happen and start enjoying yourself. We're not moving yet. This is just an anniversary trip, and I intend to make sure my bride is still happy, even after twenty years of marriage." He squeezed her hand and smiled. "Do you think maybe you can forget some of our worries and focus on having fun?"

He crossed over bumpy railroad tracks. The road seemed to stretch out in front of him forever. It all sounded so promising. It, being the intangible call of the open road, which pulled them into unknown directions, where opportunities waited like mysterious fillings in a brand-new box of bonbons. "Sure," she whispered. "I want to enjoy our vacation." *But even in the best selection of chocolates, from the most expensive chocolatier, there were those disappointing ones that stuck to your fillings.*

"Good, then shut up and be happy."

"Wow, remind me why I married you?" she chuckled, thinking about his anniversary gift that she had wrapped in a romantic, island-motif wrapping paper, decorated with red hearts and tropical palm trees. Hidden on the floor behind the passenger seat, she thought it was the perfect present. A beer stein etched with the words 'Happy Anniversary, John.'

"Because you loved me more than some drug smuggler."

"Ouch," she laughed. "Thanks John, guess I'll never live that down. You know he had a few positive traits. For example, he was a pilot and a damn good looking one too."

"Whatever," John smirked, rolling his eyes, but he kept staring at the road in an effort to stay safe. *The first time he heard about that pilot, he had run his pickup truck off the road. Now he had a small scar, as a subtle reminder, to drive with cau-*

tion. She didn't have to remind him. Each time he looked in the mirror, he saw the physical evidence of her foolish behavior. He knew all about it and remembered the entire incident as if it were yesterday.

"Well it wasn't like you were on your knees proposing or being all dreamy-eyed. Mr. Pilot on the other hand, wanted to whisk me away to the islands...." She loved getting his goat and teasing him about his failure to appear romantic, but after two decades of marriage, she figured he'd drop the subject soon."

"I know, but haven't I made up for it?" Small drops of rain began to hit the windshield.

"Yes, you have..." she said without hesitation, as a large SUV sped by, sending more water onto their car. "That big gray cloud I pointed out a few minutes ago, has moved right over us." She had to agree about him making up for everything. An exemplary father, his gentle nature brought kindness everywhere. Though predictable, he remained caring and compassionate whenever difficult issues arose. On special holidays, he tried being romantic, but his idea of romance ended up more lumberjack meets handyman about the house. Instead of Valentine's Day chocolates, he'd make an end table out of a log and carve their initials into the bark on the side.

He also tried to preplan things, never letting anything jeopardize her safety. Being a type of Renaissance woman, he rarely had to rescue her. He never had to untie her from the train tracks, but in case anything bad would happen, he knew she'd be prepared. He changed the light bulbs before they exploded, sprayed for spiders, made sure there were batteries in the smoke detectors and took precautionary measures to protect his family. He planted a rose bush under her favorite window. Long stems, he'd pull off the thorns and place a dozen on the breakfast table. He made heart shaped pancakes on Sundays. He made sure her car had enough coolant, oil and gas. He was a protector, a provider and her knight in practical, paint-splattered jeans.

More puddles filled the road. Every time a car passed, muddy water splattered onto the vehicle. John slowed down to below the speed limit and turned on his headlights. Visibility was poor, and the rain had become heavy. The clouds that were high above them in the morning, were bouncing along on the ground.

"Watch out John, there's a big puddle up ahead."

"I see it, but I can't see much. Can you believe this crap?"

Penny looked out the side window and saw huge parcels of desert turning into lakes. The water poured down in sheets and John hummed along at a snail's pace. "We should have stayed home," she said, with a serious tone. "Maybe we should turn back."

"Please shut up." John sounded annoyed. "I don't like this either, but we've gone more than half way through the Mojave Desert and you want me to turn around? Just be quiet. You know I can do this."

"Wait, what's that?" Penny asked, pointing ahead?

John slowed down noticing a giant rain filled sinkhole had swallowed a small economy car. The brake lights were on and it looked like the car had sunk into the hole only a few minutes before they had arrived. Though hard to see what, or who, was in the car, John decided he'd take a look. He pulled over to the farthest side of the puddle, parked and turned on his hazard lights. "I'm going to see if I can help."

She watched John wade to the car. Water around him soaked him above his ankles. The small car seemed to be descending into what looked like a ten-foot deep pond. A few seconds later, John returned, breathlessly notifying her that a woman and her child were in the car. He needed Penny's help to push the car out of the water-filled pothole. Reluctantly, Penny stepped into a whirlpool of water, mud and swirling desert soup. Her shoes, clothes and hair were drenched, but as soon as she saw the screaming baby through the fogged-up window, she knew her clothing didn't matter.

They both tried pushing and pulling the vehicle and nothing happened. Penny yelled at John that she'd be right back. She trudged back to their car, grabbed his gift from the backseat and quickly un-wrapped the packaged stein.

"What are you doing?" John shouted, as the rain came flooding down all around. "I need your help," he shouted, watching his wife slog back and forth through the churning water.

Penny held up the stoneware stein. "This is your gift," she mumbled, hoisting herself onto the trunk of the slippery car. Getting a grip on the antennae, she pulled herself up to the rear window and motioned for the mother to move the child away from the back seat. Afraid of slipping, she held on with one hand, while she slammed the back window with the heavy stein. At first, nothing happened but Penny continued hitting the window with all her force, finally breaking the rear windshield. Penny poked her head into the vehicle. "Please let us save you," she said to the scared looking young girl and her sobbing baby. Both appeared to be shivering. "Let me finish hitting more of these shards off so the two of you can fit through the window. "Cover the baby's face for a second. Don't worry we'll give you a ride to wherever you're going." As she tapped on the sharp edges of the glass, she felt the car fill with more water. The weight of the extra water kept pushing it further down, into the sinkhole. "John," Penny yelled. "I'm going to hand you this baby."

Once they had returned to the safety of their own car, John and Penny introduced themselves.

The young girl called herself Mirage and the baby's name was Cleo. "Are you going to Vegas too?" Penny asked the mother, who tried to console her crying child. She looked in the glove compartment for napkins to dry the child's face and handed them to Mirage. "All my towels are in the trunk. I hope this helps."

"Yes, thanks for saving me," Mirage replied through chattering teeth. "I live in Vegas." Mirage kissed little Cleo's arm. "I'll never forget you rescued my baby." A few minutes later the clouds moved again, and the rain subsided. Sunshine paved the road the rest of the way through the desert. The smell of caked mud and wet diaper made for a once in a lifetime experience. After dropping Mirage off at her apartment complex, Penny had joked with John that she hopes none of it would be an olfactory omen.

"Our car smells like limburger cheese."

"What's that like?"

"Stinky. On a scale of one to ten with ten being the foulest thing you ever took a whiff of—that's what it's like. Green mold churned with rotten gym socks and unwashed athletic supporters."

"Honey, when have you ever smelled an un-washed athletic supporter?" He held up his right hand. "Wait. Please don't tell me."

Chapter 7

Outside of the drama caused by the flooded road and rescue, the anniversary trip had been fun. Penny and John had stayed right on The Strip. John's sister, Bess had played in a yearly poker tournament and the room, food and even a couple of shows had been comp'd. Even though the sun had come out, they rarely ventured outside of the enormous resort hotel, except to walk to a musical revue. The luxurious swimming pools at their resort had a tropical theme, reminding them of Hawaii. The entire trip had been a wonderful sensory experience filled with colorful memories and spectacular food. Nothing came near either one of them that seemed even remotely malodorous, making the idea of a temporary move sound like a wonderful idea. In fact, Penny seemed to have had a complete shift in her attitude and looked forward to the upcoming adventure.

Once back from the anniversary trip, they had a meager Christmas and informed Lani of the decision to return to Vegas. She called Aunt Bess and told her they planned to go immediately, before they changed their mind.

John's sister had recently helped them also find a tenant for their home. With a tenant paying rent, things looked promising. It would be enough money to pay their mortgage, home taxes, insurance, and the general upkeep of their home, allowing them to take a good look at the huge building boom in Vegas. His friend Hans put him in touch with one of the major contractors. They told him he didn't need to interview, as long as he had a clean track record and recent pay stubs, they'd hire him on the spot.

The Magnifique Hotel and Spa was undergoing construction near the McCarran Airport. The site sat close to Flamingo road and all the newest Las Vegas attractions. A few blocks away, there were several apartment complexes with what sounded like reasonable rents, but before deciding, they also wanted to look at small homes on the outskirts of town. Maybe check out an open house or two. With his background and experience, John looked forward to getting back to work.

"Sure, was nice of Bess to help us out." John said without taking his eyes off the road. This time the weather felt warm and sunny. Not a cloud in the sky, it looked like the perfect day for a long drive through the desert. "Lani isn't too happy, but she'll get over it."

"Tell me about it. As her mother, I don't think I've ever heard her grumble as much."

"Yes, you have. Remember all those nights she kept us awake because she didn't want to sleep in her new crib?"

"True. But now she's a college sophomore."

"She'll always be our baby."

"Our big baby."

Penny had grown tired of Aunt Bess being so ever-present in their lives. Cloyingly sweet, her personality a caramel filled nougat that embeds between molars and doesn't go away. Like her brother, her ways were kind, helpful and well intentioned. Without a spouse of her own, she made sure to be involved in everything they did. "Yeah,

you've got a great sister," Penny muttered, looking ahead, worried about possible road hazards.

The Mojave Desert had long stretches of open
road with nothing but sand, tumbleweeds, rocks
and sage as far as the eye could see. Mountains encircled the entire way from California to
Nevada, in a lace framework that transformed
the stunning views by changing hues every few
minutes. Her background as a graphic artist
made her appreciate the sandstone hills that
changed from lavender to plum, and later to a va-
riety of shades in the peach or coral spectrum, reminding her of a color chart. Selecting paint sam-
ples for most projects seemed difficult anyway,
but these colors changed in an instant. There
wasn't one hue that outdid the others. They were
gorgeous, especially when clouds brought in the
mysterious, darker shades.

Famous songs and poems wistfully praise and
yet warn, about how the Mojave Desert lures
like a dangerous and fickle beauty. Unsuspecting
tourists hike into canyons for photo-ops of dramatic vistas or try reaching incredibly desolate
cliffs with changing weather conditions consisting of blazing heat, gusty winds and monsoon

downpours. Penny had an ominous feeling about those who survived and those who didn't, especially after hearing about what had happened to Dan.

Sharing photos might be a survivor's dream but what about those who didn't make it? As in the skeletal remains that had nowhere to run? No bathrooms, no hospitals, no police stations or even fast food restaurants. Those skeletons may have had a few tales to tell–their advice to those passing through–would be to do it quickly. But dead men had no tales. At least that's what she'd heard, and yet here she was thinking about the caves underneath the mountains where smugglers hid treasures while facing enormous obstacles to hide ill-gotten loot–not to mention the gun-toting bad men lurking in the shadows waiting for innocent travelers. Her mind wandered, imagining Dan gasping for his last breath while deadly ants or perhaps beetles snickered, licking their tiny chops at the base of the scenic panorama. An echo filled the cave she pictured in her head that sounded like "I'm sorry Penny," repeated over and over, undulating like the end of a scratched vinyl record. Soon however, a bumpy stretch of road and John's reassuring voice brought her out of the daydream.

"Remember the last time we went on this road and that giant puddle?"

"How could I forget? We rescued some woman and her little child."

"You rescued her, Penny. I was in shock and didn't even know what to do."

She smiled, pulled down the visor and looked in the mirror. He always set himself up for one-liners. "Might be a man thing."

"Yeah, maybe," he replied, cracking a smile.

Where had their smiles disappeared to? —she wondered, her eyes now back on the horizon. "I wish Lani was here to back me up." The tension of the last few months had not only created conflict, but also it kept them from enjoying the things they used to enjoy doing together. Christmas came and went with a tabletop tree. John didn't even put lights on the house. The neighborhood looked bleak and so did they.

"Wait, I agreed with you."

"I know, but it's nice to have a witness."

"I'm your witness. I mean it. I have seen you handle unbelievable stuff. Don't forget I was in

Kona where you proved you were superwoman. Why do you think I had to marry you immediately?"

Penny laughed. Immediately? She had gone through a minor hell to get him to pop the question, which had taken years and a crowd of supportive, risk-taking friends. "That's not why you married me."

"No, but it didn't hurt knowing you're a goddess."

"You like those take-charge types, huh?"

"Well, I don't know. On you it works. When you make up your mind to do something, then everyone should just get the hell out of your way." She was special when he married her all those years ago and now she had blossomed into a tough woman and a great mother. "I'm not saying you're a bitch—because you're not."

She laughed again, deciding to play along. "Does that aspect of my personality bother you?"

"Are you kidding? I love it. I love you."

Still the sweetest man in the world–still a great husband and father, though slightly shy and sometimes forgetful, she was very glad they had found each other. "Watch out for that bump.

Speaking of take-charge types, remember Tina and Ron?"

"How can I forget?"

"They bought a home in Henderson and they both worked for the newspaper in Vegas."

"Seriously?"

"Ron might have retired by now, but last I heard Tina heads up the entire advertising department—or did anyway."

"Oh God."

"I know, funny huh?"

"No, I mean yes, I mean oh God."

"What's wrong?"

"We're out of gas."

Chapter 8

"You do realize, it's 115 degrees out there and when I turn off the engine that will be the end of our air-conditioned comfort?"

Penny yawned. "Yes dear. I'm starting to think that we can't get through this friggin' desert without something bizarre happening. As a responsible adult, aren't you supposed to buy gas before you move your wife all the way out of California, to Vegas?" It was scorching hot outside and she knew walking wouldn't get them very far. *The irony, she thought. Less than ten minutes ago, he had called her superwoman and a goddess.* "I'm thinking you want me to snap my fingers and magically realign the entire universe or something?"

"Well what the heck? I filled the tank. Unless we have a leak, or the heat is making it evaporate. We're getting very bad gas mileage."

Ashamed of the truth, she clenched her teeth, squinted and wrinkled her nose. "No, I'm sorry," she remembered letting Lani take the car. "It's my fault. I let Lani take the car to the store yesterday."

"What store? The store is two miles from our house."

"Not the market. I let her take it to the big mall."

This time, John scrunched his face into a scowl and took a deep breath. "Right. That's twenty-five miles, times two, which equals about 50 miles worth of gas we could definitely use right now." She hated his tone. Both of them clearly remembered the nightmare storm they had gone through on the anniversary trip.

"Settle down it's not the end of the world."

"It might be. I'm still getting over the last time we tried driving this road."

"What does that mean?"

He envisioned a worse case scenario and it showed on his face. "Ah let me see.... Woman raped–husband stabbed by wayward trucker in desert–film at eleven."

Penny rolled her eyes but knew he could be right. "Look that's imaginative, but highly unlikely. And you always tell me I'm living in the fantasy world." Penny took her cell phone from her purse and tried getting a signal. "No reception."

"Does any of this seem familiar to you?"

Of course, it looked familiar. Did he mean December of last year or did he mean twenty years ago when she had wandered away from a fancy resort on the island of Kauai? Back then, her flip-phone needed a charge and it rained buckets. On top of all that, she had kept walking without a plan, or a map. "Stop it John. We're in this together. It's not as if I'm lost on an island all alone. I have you and a truckload of stuff in the trunk."

She watched him pucker his lips as if he had taken a bite from a lemon. *When she thought of her belongings in the trunk, she also thought of the ominous and most likely, phony letter with the key she had stuffed into her overnight bag. She still didn't want to tell John about it. He'd freak out. First of all, if there was even a shred of truth to the money, why would she consent to move, leaving the comforts of home? Major freak storm, but that would seem like a reasonable question. Secondly, he'd wonder about how well she knew the pilot. Discussing their relationship wasn't an option right now, or ever. She had to think of Lani and Lani's college tuition. She had to figure out where they were going to live. There was too much drama on her plate without adding Dan's bullshit into the mix. Maybe they'd be an opportune time later...to bother John with the contents of the letter. Maybe, she needed to forget the whole thing. Looking at the contortions on his face made her think she better get him tipsy before she mentioned it.*

His fist hit the steering wheel, his tone filled with sarcasm. "Well isn't that great? There's no room back there, so at least they can't stuff our bodies into the trunk."

"Just wait until the next car passes by and we can flag them down for help. Here comes a car now."

John could see two fast moving cars approach from behind. They looked like they were speeding, weaving and playing some sort of game, racing on the empty road. "Well, here it goes. I'll get out and wave them down," he said glumly. The minute he opened the door, oven-like heat filled the car. "Oh man, this is brutal." He stood and waved at the first car which quickly sped past them, while the second car honked and passed the first car, coming dangerously close. Dust swirled around John who burst into a coughing spasm. He couldn't see anything for a moment. "Did you see that?" he asked with more coughing. Tears stung his eyes, creating tears. He wiped his face with the back of his hand. He sneezed and coughed again, then wiped his face with the bottom of his tee shirt.

"Here take a sip of water," Penny suggested, handing him a bottle. "It's warm but better than nothing." Meanwhile, she pulled a magazine from her bag and slowly flipped through the pages while waiting like a princess, for a chariot to come to the rescue. Her mind however, wasn't on the glossy pages of flashy clothes or the articles. The wheels were turning. She had to think of something and she figured the less she moved, the less she'd feel the heat.

John took a long sip and the dust finally settled. "That shit is horrible. Why does coffee get cold, but water always gets hot? Wish we had coffee." He chugalugged the entire bottle as if it were an ice-cold, craft beer. "Ever wonder how these Joshua trees make it out here?" He rambled on and on for another hour, working into a frenzy about scorpions and the lack of facilities. A few cars passed by quickly and John waved at all of them. Quietly turning pages, Penny listened to her husband vent. "I think we could definitely fry some eggs out here on that rock. Do you have a spatula in the trunk? Oh, look a lizard." Clearing his throat, he announced the next car.

"Good. Hope they're nicer this time." But they weren't nice, and they didn't stop. Five or six vehicles drove right past them. John's shirt stuck to his back and perspiration dripped down his cheeks. He returned to the car and got in, wondering what to do.

Penny had begun to formulate an idea, because his macho-way obviously wasn't working. It was time for her to take control of the situation. "Okay," she said throwing the magazine into the backseat. She unbuckled her seat belt and with a sexy flourish, she pulled off her top. "It's my turn."

"Penny, sit down and put your clothes back on."

"Forget it. It's hot and I need to help. Did you ever think that maybe these people didn't stop because you are sweating all over the place? Would you want a drenched, clammy guy in your car?"

"Ah, I hate to break it to you, but you'll be sweating too."

"Not as bad as you. Plus, it's not as obvious without my shirt.

Don't worry sweetie, this bra looks like a white bathing suit top."

"Hon, let's not go crazy." He shook his head and couldn't believe that she had removed her shirt. "Penny, you look great, but don't forget you're a middle-aged woman."

A few seconds later Penny squealed, "Too late," while vigorously waving her shirt. A black sedan drove up and parked behind Penny and John's vehicle. It appeared to be a luxury limousine with a chauffeur. "Check it out John, I think we'll be traveling in style."

Chapter 9

Julian Diszno yelled into the phone. "Just shut up you stupid slut. You won't win. I gotta go." He made sure the call disconnected by pressing several times on the bottom of his phone. A barrage of curse words flew from his mouth in a medley of Bohemian languages.

"What's wrong Boss?" Ray asked. Both well-dressed men sat in the back of a private coach heading for Las Vegas. Ray had dull looking small eyes. His biceps bulged through an expensive silk suit. As a personal assistant with a background in European law, he doubled as security to the famous painter who owned several homes in various countries. Right now, they were traveling from his Rancho Mirage estate in California.

"Number six. Bitch is divorcing me and wants to sue for alimony. You met her at the Getty museum." He sighed. "Alia-she's the tall one, remember?" He looked sentimental about the entire fracas and sounded melancholy, as if recalling the wild times, they had shared in bed.

Ray nodded but laughed again. "Why do you let these bitches bug you so much? You do everything for them. You bring them here. You help them make money. They should worship you."

"They do Ray. It's the ones I marry that make things difficult. I'm still paying child support to someone I married fifteen years ago, and I don't even remember what she looks like." Rough acne scars and stubble gave Julian a dark, swarthy complexion. "And the kid, do you think I've ever met this kid? Never. Can you imagine some sorry-ass, son-of-a-bitch teenager is wondering where their Pappy is?" With his right thumb, he picked at a morsel of prime rib still wedged in his molars from the previous night's meal.

Ray continued to chuckle.

"Don't laugh. Once a whore always a whore, I guess. I keep messing up by mixing business and pleasure." He sighed again but returned to picking his teeth.

"Sorry, but it is kind of funny. What do you want, they're women?"

"Yeah, I know. You're the smart one. Single and proud of being able to do anyone, any time...."

"As if, being married ever stopped you from dipping your stick into the white or chocolate fountain...." Ray knew everything about Julian. He also knew that he didn't have a ton of respect for marital bonds. He didn't discriminate either and treated women like chattel. Tall or short, thin or chunky he didn't care what race or creed as long as the hormones were working long enough to get him off.

"That reminds me. I have a gallery showing of my art in Geneva next week. I'm flying from Vegas to N.Y on an International flight. Do you think you can get Sonia a seat next to me?"

Money had helped refine some of Julian's latest conquests, but the attachments were over before a relationship could develop. "Sonia?" Ray whistled under his breath... "chestnut hair with killer legs? Sure. I'll call Lufthansa as soon as we get to the Strip."

"Thanks." Julian grumbled, adjusting his pants. At five feet seven and three hundred pounds, his tailored slacks fit a skoosh tight in certain areas, especially after a big steakhouse dinner. "Don't forget we're picking up those sixteen-year olds at McCarran International."

"You should call them 'fresh product," Ray admonished, with a sneaky looking smile. "They all received instructions, new clothes and stilettos. I hope they are ready."

"Hell. That last one, from Moldova was a failure. Have you heard of these activists enacting new laws around here? As if that would make any difference? These women want to make money. We just show them the easiest way. But that last girl—um what's her name-Helena or something. She really wants to get me and there's no way to prove anything. Besides, most of the time I'm painting, like an innocent Bambi in my studio."

"Boss, no one's going to believe her testimony. Besides, isn't she flying high on coke all the time?"

"Helena's on everything and blames me for it."

Ray laughed and pointed at John and Penny's sedan on the side of the road. "How would you feel about an older, redhead, boss? Most of her clothes are already off," he snickered.

Julian stared through the tinted glass and pushed a button to lower a window behind the driver, so he could get a better look. "Hmm…," he savored the view as if biting into a cream-filled pastry. "She has some mileage on her but I think redheads are sexy don't you?"

"Probably a dye job, but the real ones make us the most money."

"That's what I'm thinking, plus she has cute tits." He caught his reflection to check his teeth and adjusted his graying hair. "George," he alerted the driver. "I think we need to stop behind that car."

The driver made a U-turn and parked behind Penny and John's vehicle. Ray continued his conversation with Julian. "So, what did Alia find offensive about living in a mansion? You gave her everything. Didn't she come from some disgusting place with a well and a goat?"

"I have no idea what her problem is. She shops at Gucci and all the best stores and eats caviar or whatever she dreams up any time. Last week she wanted to try some fancy spa truffle diet and she already looks like a bag of chicken bones."

"She does have that skeleton-like look, but Julian you can't deny she has a few well-placed curves on that rack and tons of thick, sexy hair. Now she even speaks English. I bet that's the problem, right?"

"It's part of it," Julian sighed. "Guess you can't tell those curves are fake, thanks to the best plastic surgeon in Beverly Hills. Even though she had plenty of hair, she wanted extensions. You have a valid point about her language skills. Three years ago, she didn't even know what human trafficking is, and now she's developed some holier than thou attitude. I should just send her scrawny ass back to that God forsaken place she came from, so she can fetch water in a pail again."

"Didn't you bring her parents out last year?"

"Yeah those blasted potato farmers." He shook his head. "I'm screwed." The car stopped abruptly. Julian opened the door slowly. Shocked at the sudden blast of desert heat, he wanted to move fast, but ended up wobbling across the asphalt with short, slow steps like a cat about to snatch its prey. When he reached Penny, he extended his thick fingers towards her. "Julian Diszno at your service," he wheezed, sounding out of breath. The gravel under his slippers and a small gust of wind made him appear unbalanced. He grimaced, pulling her delicate hand into his as a greeting but also to keep his balance. "Have you ever heard of Dante Charles Gabriel Rossetti?"

"The pre-Raphaelite painter?"

He snickered and looked up into the cloudless sky, wondering what spectacular luck he must have to bring this vision to him in the middle of nowhere. "Yes," he nodded, immediately intrigued with her brilliance. "La Ghirlandata, maybe even his Helen of Troy," he mumbled. A look the famous artist, Rossetti had captured on canvas, stood in front of him. The big soulful eyes, the porcelain skin and the imperfect red hair tossed by gentle breezes. "Please follow me."

Chapter 10

Staying with Aunt Bess wasn't quite as bad as she had originally envisioned. Having Bentley around reminded her of school friends who looked like they listened but didn't talk too much. Every day Lani would take him to the park, and every day she'd meet Pete under "their" gigantic oak. He usually sent his brother on some sort of ridiculous errand and this time, Tyler came running up with a handful of daisies. "Here dickhead," Tyler said, handing the bunch to Pete.

"Thanks bro." Pete replied, before handing Lani the flowers. "Happy one-month anniversary," he said. Tyler rolled his eyes and grabbed Bentley's leash.

"Ooh-la-la. I'm out of here. Can I walk your dog around the park?"

"Sure," Lani answered, sniffing the bouquet and sneezing.

"Come on pooch." Tyler pulled on Bentley and they ran down the green out of Lani's field of vision. The park had giant oaks, leafy sycamores, tall eucalyptus and a few weathered Augustine pines around the perimeter. As California parks go, it lacked the distinguishing feature of ubiquitous palm trees. Instead, this park had a wholesome Midwest vibe. The type of park built for family picnics instead of touristy photo-ops. Instead of bougainvillea, the hedges looked like English privet. Had Lani closed her eyes and opened them later, she could have felt transported to anywhere, U.S.A.

"That's so sweet but does your brother do all your dirty work?"

She looked at Pete's face and then back at the flowers. "You're quite a romantic." They sat on their jackets. She placed the daisies against the trunk of the massive tree.

"There's more. I wrote you a poem too." Pete reached into his pocket and pulled out a wrinkled piece of notebook paper. It's called 'My Kite'."

Lani blushed. "Kite? Like the ones in the air?" When he nodded she added, "No one ever wrote me a poem."

"Well, I did. Here it goes." He held her hand and began to read.

"You're sweeter than honey, dripping with per-fection,
My heart is beating, bursting with affection.
Your hair, your smile, your eyes hold me tight,
Hopelessly wrapped like a wayward kite.
High in the branches on top of the tree,
Rain and wind try pulling it free,
Wood on wood makes it want to stay,
But nothing on Earth can pull it away.
Because my dear Lani...it's meant to be...."

When he finished reading, he pulled her hand to his lips. "I love you Lani."

She smiled at his words and yanked the paper from him to reread the poem. "Does this mean you feel stuck? My mom says she feels stuck. Isn't that a bad thing?" Lani thought of all the recent arguments at home. She knew her parents had had a few tough months paying the bills. She also remembered her mother talking about how being a wife and mother had taken her away from her career. Sometimes her mother lashed out in protest, saying she felt trapped and stuck, similar to Peter's kite in the poem.

"No," he took the poem back, folded it and shoved it into a pocket. "Your mom and dad are different from us. It's not that kind of stuck. I can't imagine another day without you. I'm glad they've left for a while. You need to learn some independent thinking."

She held an index finger to his lips. "Hey, I love my parents, so don't say another word."

"It's not that." He took hold of her hand again and held it tight. "Hear me out. I joined the Navy for five years and learned so much. Our ship went to places I didn't even know existed. We spend a few hours in school and they do their best to teach us stuff, but they can't teach us everything. And your parents are probably super interesting and intelligent, but they can't show you everything."

"Pete, it's not like you're going to teach me everything either."

"I think you're naïve, that's all."

"Is that bad?"

"Not at all, but it can be dangerous, and I care about you, that's all. So, when are they coming back?"

"They have temporarily moved to Vegas, so they can pay our bills. Dad's going to work in construction. They want to travel back and forth to see me of course, but from what I can tell, they're going to be living there for a few years." She wondered why goosebumps traveled up her arm and butterflies stirred in her stomach.

"I want you to know that you don't need them to pay your bills. Someday, I want to take care of you. I want to be with you forever."

Forever? This was getting weird. Was he dreaming? Lani felt uncomfortable. She pulled her hand free and looked around for Bentley and Tyler. "Where did your brother take my mutt?"

"Who cares?" he turned her face towards his by holding her chin and then stared into her eyes. "I don't think you know how serious I am about you."

Serious? Oh-oh. She sighed and picked up the daisies. *Pete was nice and super good looking, but she had to finish college. There wasn't time to waste with some heavy-duty relationship. Besides, her parents would kill her if she ended up preggo like Emily.* "Look, it's only one month. Why don't we take things a little bit slower? You're kind of freaking me out." One thing she did learn from her mom was to be honest. Besides, if he really loved her, he'd be able to handle it and he'd wait for her to finish school.

Pete looked away and wiped a tear from his eyes.

"Don't cry. You know I care about you," she said pursing her lips into a sensual looking pout. Your poem is beautiful."

"Thanks."

Silence hung over them until they heard Bentley barking in the distance.

Lani stood and dusted the grass off her pants. She picked up her denim jacket, shaking it a few times before slipping it on. When Pete stood up, he put his hand under her jacket pulling her close. His hand lingered on her waist and moved to the small of her back pushing her close to his chest.

"I love you," he whispered into her ear.

"I know," she replied. "I love you too but I'm just…."

He cut her off by putting his lips on hers. They had kissed before, but this kiss had passion behind it. This kiss spoke to her heart and told her he really did want her entire body and soul. Except, she knew, she wasn't ready.

Gently, she pushed him away. "Sorry, but I couldn't breathe." *Was it the jacket that had made her warm?*

"Oh." He looked out of breath himself and embarrassed.

"No, it's okay. Just give me some time. Can we do this slowly and see if things work out?"

"They will work out. Don't you believe in fate?"

Bentley ran up and jumped on Pete. His leash hung loose behind him. "Where's Tyler?" They asked in unison. Bentley's tail wagged quickly, and he barked at Lani as if he wanted to say something.

"Do you think something's wrong?" She asked.

"Not sure. He's your dog but my stupid brother should be holding his leash. Let's go find out."

They followed Bentley across the park where National Forest grounds full of mature trees and bushes edged a paved parking lot. Three men dressed in dark clothes hung around looking at the ground. One stood on top of Tyler, shouting curse words at him.

"Leave him alone," Pete yelled as loud as he could, his voice reverberating, bouncing off the giant trees.

The inked up, leather dressed men looked scary. Though they may have heard Pete, they continued beating Tyler. They were tall and looked like stereotypical convicts. Bald heads, black pants and jackets, multiple tattoos and various piercings made them look seriously foreboding. These were not high school students or even local residents. They looked meaner than hungry wolves. Tyler's mouth was in the dirt, and a motorcycle boot stood on the middle of his back. Bentley barked and growled. The little lap dog looked like it wanted to bite the one hurting Pete's brother. As Pete ran up to the scuffle, the one standing on Tyler moved aside and let him get to his feet, but he kept a hold of him by clutching his ear. "Who is this you little prick?"

the swarthy man asked Tyler, before shoving him aside. One of the other crazy men acted as if he wanted to kick Bentley with steel-toed boots.

Tyler wiped mud from his mouth but said nothing. The man put his hand to his head, scratched it as if confused. He pointed at Lani asking, "And a chick too? Since when do you bring your family, nut job?" He growled with a sinister sounding snarl. And then, glancing at his evil friends, he waved an arm towards their bikes and said, "Let's get out of here." Seconds later, the men jumped on their motorcycles and rode out of the parking lot, leaving dust and fumes in their wake.

"Tyler, are you okay?" Lani asked, seeing a small drop of blood on his arm, trickling down from a cut on his chin. He looked at the ground where Bentley stood at his feet and like a wayward child filled with shame, he couldn't look into her face. He patted Bentley's head as Lani pulled on the leash, as if to remind the pup they had to leave. "Did you know those guys?" She asked."

"Unfortunately, he does know them. Don't you?" Pete muttered through clenched teeth.

"What did you do wrong this time? Not selling enough?"

While dusting himself off, Tyler nodded.

"I got to go." Lani felt the rage rising in Tyler's brother.

"Settle down Pete, they're gone." She didn't know what was going on, but a deep-rooted instinct told her she needed to leave.

"Yeah, dickhead," Tyler finally spoke. "Don't worry; they thought she was my sister."

Peter noticed Lani wanted to run home. "See you tomorrow? Right?" Pete asked, with pitiful, looking hound dog eyes. He tried smiling at Lani, but anger had turned his entire head into a shade of boiled radish. Red-faced and embarrassed by his brother's shenanigans, his hair stood straight up like a stalk, and what appeared to be hives stretched the length of his throat.

"Sure," she replied to Peter, but she remembered his tears and now observed those pathetic eyes. For the first time in a month, she wondered whether she knew anything about him at all. "Come on Bentley." Lani pulled her aunt's dog by the leash and they raced most of the way across

the park. A breeze had strewn the daisies all over
the grass.

Chapter 11

Penny and John sat in the limo across from Ray and Julian. She sipped a diet soda. Cool relief washed over John after she had slipped her top back on. During stressful times, he had a habit of pulling inward, to meditate or to beg for God's assistance. Either way, he had an undeveloped second sense that seemed to know when trouble lurked around Penny. Maybe the weird suit and the bold tie on the swarthy looking guy called Ray, made him feel guarded. The apparel alone appeared to be odd, based on the simple fact that the temperature outside hovered above the nineties.

"I love your accent," she said to Julian, sounding like a hillbilly from the Ozarks. "Are you French?"

"No, I'm not French but I speak several languages."

Ray smiled. "Haven't you heard of the great Julian Diszno?" he asked in a haughty tone. Ray removed a silver flask from the inside of his jacket and took a swig from it before pouring some of the unknown substance into his own can of soda. Not wanting the condensation to drip on his trousers made him hold the can away from his legs. He held up the small pocket decanter and offered some to Penny who turned it down.

John stared out the tinted windows and hoped they would get to Vegas soon. Not only ugly, these guys were suddenly condescending too.

"Diszno? Do you mean the world-renowned muralist who uses architectural elements combined with surrealism?" Mouth agape, she was impressed, and it showed. Luckily, there weren't flies zooming around in the coach or she would have caught several in her mouth.

Julian nodded with a chuckle. "You do know me?" He seemed surprised. Maybe she wasn't a hillbilly after all. This woman had heard of Rossetti and she had heard of him too. He winked at Ray.

Her mouth now dry, she closed it, gulped a sip of soda, swallowed and began to ramble. "I majored in art and used to be a graphic artist." She nodded in the affirmative. "I'm one of your biggest fans." She turned towards John. "We have two or three of your latest coffee table books. Don't we, Hon?" John nodded but didn't smile. Worry pinched the corners of his eyes. "In the newspaper business I used to be so busy with deadlines and even though I worked on a computer, forms kept piling up, getting heaped into my in-box. Art is not supposed to be stressful, is it?"

It was a rhetorical question and she didn't let him answer anyway. "I worked for a newspaper but I'm sure you've heard that some of them went under because of the net." Suddenly self-conscious, she looked at John, hoping he'd say something. This man was famous and revered in all the art circles, museums and galleries. Penny's heart pounded with enthusiasm for the famous artist she had idolized her entire life. She licked her dry lips, took another drink and continued talking. "We're moving to Nevada, so my husband can find construction work at one of the hotels. He's a carpenter. I'm hoping to find work too, but it might be difficult right now. You know, with the economy and all."

Julian looked at Ray again. Ray nodded and they both smiled at Penny. "My dear, I believe you have come into my life for a reason."

Penny felt flattered at the way he said, 'my dear'. Not only did it appear personal, but also the accent had elevated it to something intimate. She was riding in a limousine with Julian Diszno! If only those idiot college professors who had thought of her as trouble, could see her now. "Well you certainly came into our life in a nick of time," she joked. "Thanks for saving us."

"Did you study Miro and Mondrian?"

"Of course, and I also studied architecture, fashion and bookbinding. But painting was my favorite."

"Interesting." Julian nodded and looked at Ray, who smiled like one of those ridiculous Cheshire cats. This drunken cat looked like it might have morphed up on a sixties brew of heroin. The more he drank, the more his smile looked crooked and his teeth looked yellow. Ray not only held his soda far from his body, but John noticed that while all his fingers wrapped around the can, his pinky stood standing up in the air. "Picasso, Dalì, Magritte?"

"Oh definitely… and Pollock, Kandinsky, Warhol and you of course…."

John yawned and tried not to stare at the wrinkles in the fat man's linen shirt.

Julian loved getting compliments. Fascination twinkled in the famous artist's eyes and his body language indicated a restless excitement. He grinned and looked back at Ray. Now his eyes changed to pleading like a dog at the breakfast table-waiting for-bacon-to fall-to the floor. But he waited and didn't say what he wanted to say.

Instead, Ray felt the tension and spoke up. "Where are you going to live in Vegas?"

Her index finger pointed at John and then her hands turned outward as she shrugged. "Not sure—yet. We have a couple of comped nights from his sister, after that, we have to find an apartment to live in. Ask me next week," she said with a wink.

"The reason we're asking is because Julian's looking for an artist to paint murals for his new studio."

The sound of the road blended with the soft sound of a violin concerto streaming through the automobile speakers in the background. Penny's eyes became the size of hubcaps. Enormous, smoldering, emerald-green hubcaps, while her jaw slowly mouthed a question. "Are you serious?"

Julian nodded. "I'm doing a modern-art designed studio and spa hotel. The name of it is **The Oasis**. At my age, it's hard getting on ladders. What I need is someone who knows my style and can interpret it onto the bare walls of the property." He gestured with his hands and stared at the concept in his mind. "There won't be architectural elements because the magnificent building is finished. It's strictly painting."

Bare walls? This sounded like a dream come true. She didn't want to appear too eager but knew her eyes and emotions had already given her feelings away. Yes, she knew his style. She had taken classes on architectural design. She had even written a paper on Diszno, twenty-five years ago. At the time, he was a budding graduate from the Royal Academy of Art. The media referred to him as L'Enfant terrible and a child prodigy, who had cre-

ated incredible designs by age ten. A reckless play-boy, he had dated royalty and Hollywood stars. He parked his yachts in secluded cays, where no one could find him. He'd show up with a young starlet to the Cannes Film Festival. Tabloids would show him sunburned in the Mediterranean without a shirt, his lips glued to someone beautiful, most often famous.

She looked at John who had tuned out everything. Once the name Miro had come up, he zoned out, staring out towards the tranquil views of the shimmering Mojave.

"I don't have any problem with ladders," she stuttered. She thought back to those old front-page photos of this man and how he had changed. Once a type of Zeus commanding hearts, now he looked like a repulsive, shapeless blob. His swollen chin full of baggy skin rested on top of his expensively tailored clothing. Dark circles rimmed bloodshot eyes. Where decades ago had been a dark, waxed moustache under a large commanding nose, was now, white stubble and thick fleshy lips.

Ray smirked. "Sounds like she'll do it boss," he said.

The lights of Vegas flickered up ahead and the limousine drifted onto the highway, leaving the dry, dusty desert behind. Penny looked forward to a new chance, at a new life. Things were looking up. Her mind wandered, and she imagined her name flashing in pink neon and white lights on the Las Vegas Strip.

"Yes, it would be an honor to work for you Mr. Diszno."

"Julian. Please call me Julian. I hope you enjoy art rather than think of it as work. Don't worry, I plan on paying you and I even have an apartment you can live in."

Huh? Did they just win the lotto, or did she wake up in a parallel universe? She mumbled a prayer of gratitude. "Okay, that would be…wonderful." She inhaled and wondered what had happened for a miracle to happen in the middle of nowhere.

"The apartment is only a one bedroom on the tenth floor but it's right off the strip. It's clean and has an excellent view. If you really know my soul and can interpret my designs, then your pay will increase every week. We'll start at one thousand a week and I'll double it every month. After all, you'll be like a muse," he chuckled. "Is that all right?"

Amuse? His accent made it hard to understand his words, but she got the drift. He would pay her well, for something she loved to do. As the glittering lights beckoned up ahead, Penny shook her head in agreement and finally exhaled. Though he had only listened to parts of the conversation, John also exhaled. Something about that ride gave him a clearer idea about what his wife had meant, regarding the putrid smell of limburger cheese.

Chapter 12

Pete had called Lani every day. Aunt Bess heard Lani yelling into the phone. She also noticed that Bentley didn't get to go on his regular daily walks. "Oh, Lani dear, can you take the dog out?"

Lani didn't want to make a spectacle. "My allergies are acting up today. Can I do it later?" She whined and sniveled; her nose congested from a combination of crying and cat dander.

"Sure, but the sun is setting. Why don't you go now? You'll be back before you know it."

Lani felt like screaming inside. Her aunt wore a ruffled, polka dot blouse and had a matching bow, in her frizzy, at-home-colored hair. The woman sounded as chipper as a television game-show hostess. "Okay," Lani mumbled, finally agreeing. "Let's get out of here," she said under her breath, as she grabbed the leash.

Of course, Pete sat there, under 'their' favorite oak tree in the park, smiling from ear to ear. Fortunately, Tyler didn't seem to be around. Pete stood up and ran to Lani. "Hey Bentley," he said, petting the dog. "How's my favorite pooch?" Afterwards, he attempted to hug Lani who pulled away with a scowl.

"Leave me alone," she snapped, with an obvious angry tone, spittle flying from her lips. "I'm not in the mood for surprises. First, tell me, why obnoxious supremacists from some gang, almost killed your little brother. I don't want to talk to you about anything, until you can tell me what happened the other day. Call me sheltered or whatever, but this…this was a first." Her facial contortions turned her skin from ivory to fuchsia and her sinuses still sounded blocked.

Checking around, he had to see if anyone else had heard her screaming. "What?" He didn't blame her for being angry. Several days had passed, and he had hoped that maybe she had lightened up from all the bitchiness he had experienced over the phone. "Can't we put this behind us?" He put an index finger to his mouth while she continued to yell. "Hey pipe down. I love the passion and you're adorable in a troll-like sort of way, but what do you mean 'a first?' "

"I don't know. Usually this kind of thing happens on the six o'clock news, not with the 'normal' people I hang out with." She lifted her arms, dropping quote marks in the air with her index fingers when stating the word 'normal'.

"Well la-dee-da. Welcome to the real world, Princess. Things happen, you know?" Pete brushed his hand through his hair. "Why are you mad at me? I didn't do anything. In fact, I protected all of us."

She turned towards him and her eyes seemed to be casting flaming arrows, her brows arched, "From what? That's exactly what I want to know? You want to be in a relationship but don't think being honest is important? Just forget it. Forget everything." She wanted to run home but knew that Bentley still needed his walk.

"Those idiots are not important, but you are important. Trust me, the less you know about those guys the better." He took a deep breath before reaching over to pet Bentley again.

"Why? Is your stupid little brother selling or buying drugs from those psychos?" She watched Pete plop down onto the grass next to the dog.

"It's not just drugs. It's way more than that and I'd rather not discuss it. Wish I didn't know. It's one of those deep dark secrets that are better off being buried in a bottomless hole." Pete looked sad and frustrated. He yanked on the grass and then he pulled on his hair. "You're an only child, right? So you don't know what it's like to have a brother? Can't you be on my side? I thought you loved me too?"

He watched her blink dazzling, and now sparkling with moisture, hazel eyes. "Deep and dark secrets, huh?" The pain within her heart made her knees buckle. Deflated, she crumpled onto the grass on the other side of Bentley. "As in, you'd have to kill me if you told me?"

Pete attempted a small smile. He could tell the blazing beauty's wrath had settled into embers. "No, but almost." God, she was so exquisite, her face an emotional piece of statuary. Her angelic face, whether happy or all riled up like a mischievous elf, he could stare at forever. But how could he fix this, and smooth it over, so she'd understand he had nothing to do with his brother's creepy friends. He couldn't stand another minute of her being upset with him, and he knew he would do anything, say anything or promise anything, to make her want his love. As the rosy cheeks faded and her facial coloring returned to normal, he felt he had a chance. "I think you're too young to die."

"Very funny, but not what I wanted to hear. Now I have to know. Spill it Lovecraft."

Pete's smile quickly disappeared. Maybe because she used his last name, he shuddered to think he'd have to dish the dirt and tell the truth. "Look my brother is involved in all kinds of bizarre shit. Let's forget it—please?" He moved closer, acting as if he wanted to kiss her.

"I can't," she gently pushed him away. "Do you know I had nightmares about those guys twice this week?"

"Will you kiss me if I tell you all about it?"

"Maybe," she whispered, but she didn't sound convincing.

His mouth longed to touch her peachy sweet lips." Gawd, gawd, gawd," he mumbled, looking askew through the branches of the trees. His insides were churning. He felt torn about what to say, and what to do. "Try and remember that what I'm telling you is about my brother. I don't have anything to do with what he's up to." He nervously pulled up a blade of grass and began to shred it into mulch. Then he popped the green shreds into his mouth, chewing like a crazy goat before swallowing all of it.

She patiently pet Bentley who had stretched across her lap. "I'm listening." *This should be interesting she figured, slowly crossing her ankles. And if this idiot thinks she'd kiss him after he chewed up the grass where Bentley had relieved himself, he had another thing coming.*

"You didn't spend too much time at our school before it got out for summer recess, but do you remember Cindy?"

"Do you mean that Goth girl? The one with stringy hair, bad attitude and black clothes that matched her jet-black lipstick?"

"Yeah, her. She works in Vegas now, goes by the name 'Sin'."

"That sounds fitting. So, what does she have to do with anything?"

"Tyler, my stupid brother, makes money on girls. Those guys you saw, they buy virgins from him for a thousand bucks each."

Lani laughed. He had to be joking. "You are such a liar. No one **buys** girls," she said, swinging a fist at his arm. "Besides, there's no way that…that Cindy was a virgin," she stuttered, *thinking that the girl she remembered didn't look like she was even born a virgin.* "Not since I met her, anyway."

He sighed, shrugging his shoulders. "I'm not kidding. It's the horrible truth." He grabbed both sides of his head with his hands and closed his eyes for a few seconds allowing silence and traffic noise from across the park to reach his ears.

Comprehension slowly descended onto her heart with a massive thud. *It couldn't be true, and yet, here was this guy telling her otherwise. A handsome guy that she was falling for, telling her it was real.* She tilted her lovely face and looked into his eyes. "Seriously? You're telling me your brother sells girls?"

"Girls, coke, opioids, ecstasy, grass. Whatever he can get his hands on. No one would suspect him because he looks so innocent. The time they came to the park, those guys were here to collect on some drug run. Tyler didn't have the money. My brother has a baby face and looks almost ten years younger…."

She cut him off. "So, wait a minute, what do these girls do once they're—purchased?"

His throat felt constricted and he coughed a few times before laying out the truth and possibly his only chance at love. "Those nasty assholes–excuse my French–resell them to even bigger, more powerful jerks who give the girls…ahem…jobs." He kept clearing his throat and spitting up shredded grass and saliva. Was she pretending to be naive, he wondered before another attack of tickling coughs. Did she understand? The important part he omitted had to do with those bad men giving the underage girls sedatives called roofies and other narcotics, so they would comply with all their disgusting demands. He watched her tiny hands petting Bentley, move faster and faster.

"By jobs you mean prostitution?"

"That or a dancer, remember I said Cindy's a dancer?"

She had heard enough. Her parents would both keel over and die if they knew she talked to someone about this subject. Pete's crazy family contained more drama than an afternoon soap opera and certainly more than she wanted to be around. Such a shame too because she liked Peter and thought he was cute. Standing, she dusted herself off. "I have to go."

Nervously picking on another blade of grass, he looked up with pitiful eyes. "Please Lani–you wanted me to be honest."

"Whatever."

"Wait, whatever you do, never ever tell anyone I told you what my brother does for cash. First, they'd kill him and then the rest of us. These are very bad people Lani, like the worst, ever. Will you swear not to say anything?"

Pulling at Bentley and looking back at Pete she whispered, "I swear."

"Wait, what about that kiss?"

She turned around to leave and didn't want to turn back, lest she'd turn into a pillar of salt or something. "Bye Peter. Please forget you ever met me." She felt his eyes follow her steps out of the park. *He might be nice to look at but what happened to his brain?*

Chapter 13

Penny stared out expansive windows over the lights of The Vegas Strip. The apartment, in her estimation anyway, had to be one of the loveliest in the entire city. Contemporary furnishings and modern stainless appliances reflected the twinkle of neon lights. Day or night, everything sparkled, illuminating the gleaming white paint and the appliances. At night, multihued rainbows bounced across the ceiling. Custom tiled floors, luxurious linens in dreamy muted tones made her feel she had slipped into a dream. Everything seemed perfect. Julian had insisted on providing them with concierge services for everything. Like royalty, she had a car or groceries at her disposal any time. John could walk to The Magnifique building site, located only two bustling blocks away.

Her cell rang, and she quickly answered it with a smile in her voice. "Hello dear. You left real early. What time will you be finished?" She listened to him talk about his new job while running her hand through a fluffy, couch pillow. The first week he'd be training and learning new techniques. The company also wanted to make sure he had all the gear he needed. John sounded excited about the opportunity and she couldn't wait to get started too.

"I'll be going to the new studio today," she said. "Can you imagine? Bare walls? My fingers are itching to start painting." She looked out onto the busiest section of town and noticed traffic backing up in front of one of the luxury hotels. Famous name singers, magicians and ventriloquists were a few steps away. "He's sending that Ray guy and a limo. I'll be home by dinner and we can walk around and explore some neat places tonight. Maybe we can check out that wildlife habitat with the live cheetahs and komodo dragons. Or we can go see that shark exhibit." They were literally minutes from world-class dining and entertainment. "Love you more," she responded when she heard a knock at the door. "I think they're here. Wish me luck. Okay, bye." She disconnected her phone and put it on the counter. The knock sounded loud and impatient. Penny grabbed her purse and opened the door.

A young man about Lani's age stood at the door. He had one large pierced earring, various tattoos in comic book colors and a solid black tee shirt with a small, **Oasis Spa** logo. He stared at her for a few intense seconds, and then appraised her by looking at her from head to toe, before verifying her name.

She smiled and slipped on her sandals. "Yup, that's me. I thought Ray is coming."

"He's downstairs in the car. We have to hurry," he grunted without returning the smile.

She quickly locked the front door and followed the driver to the waiting car where Ray looked engrossed in something on his cell phone. The driver opened her door and Ray turned to greet her. She climbed inside the massive car and immediately realized she couldn't run back to get her phone. Shoot, she thought wondering why everyone seemed to be in a hurry. The car pulled away from the curb and Ray slipped his phone into the breast pocket of an ostentatious, shark-skin suit jacket. Under the flamboyant gray, he wore a red golf shirt. Penny wore a navy-blue knee-length skirt with a pink sweater set and low-heeled, comfortable sandals. Today she'd see the space for the murals and order the paint and supplies. She didn't think it would be grueling, but on her first day, she wanted to look nice. Once she began painting, she'd be wearing over-alls or Capri pants with tennis shoes.

"George, don't forget to stop at the airport first," he told the driver who nodded. Then Ray took off his sunglasses and peered into Penny's kelly-green eyes. "You're a cutie. Anyone ever tell you that?" She smiled, but immediately felt uncomfortable. "Awe come on, someone must have told you that?" He leaned closer and Penny didn't like his aftershave. "Too bad we don't have more time," he said with an ugly sneer as he placed his right palm on top of his fly.

Gross, she thought before rolling her eyes. This moron knew she was married. "That's funny but you must have confused me with some-one else. Remember John, my husband?" She scooted away and then crossed her legs. When she moved her legs, he ogled every inch of her exposed calves. Screaming inside, she berated herself and felt foolish for not wearing pants.

"Ah yeah, that stiff you're married to. I remember. What's a babe like you doing with that boring piece of shit?"

"Excuse me?" Penny couldn't believe her ears. The car stopped, and the driver mentioned something about being right back. Fortunately, Ray became engrossed in sending some text messages on his phone. Twenty minutes passed, and Penny kept staring out at the airplanes climbing into the sky. High above the planes she noticed small wispy clouds. Since Ray appeared to be a complete jerk, she didn't want to talk unless she absolutely had to say something important.

Twenty minutes felt like four hours, especially because of Ray's aftershave. Finally, George arrived with two teenage girls and their small battered suitcases. Dressed in torn jeans and cheap looking high heels, the two girls rode along in silence. They whispered to each other and giggled but didn't talk to Ray or Penny. The car hit potholes in downtown which made the girls lean into each other and smile, but still they didn't say anything. They fingered the locks and brushed the leather seats with long, manicured nails, while Penny wondered why no one bothered introducing them. Finally, the car stopped in front of a strip mall that sold souvenirs, pizza and auto parts. Next to the pizza joint the sign said, 'Day Spa'. The words 'Grand Opening' were painted with fluorescent colors on the windows. The car turned to go to the back of the shopping center where they stopped, and the two young women climbed out of the vehicle. Penny waved goodbye.

"Ray?" She whispered. He had dozed off. "Ray," Penny repeated at a higher decibel, as the car drove out of the parking lot.

"What?" He looked annoyed. "First you brush me off and then you give me the silent treatment. What do you want?"

"I just wondered why you didn't say anything to those young ladies."

"You did, huh?" He seemed amused and wiped a spot of drool off his mouth with his fingers.

He sure knew how to make her feel uncomfortable. "Yes, because it's my first day and I want to meet everyone associated with Julian's business."

Ray laughed, sticking his hand out, with the palm facing her in a type of stop sign motion. "Look Penny, don't try and meet everyone. Trust me." When he said the words 'trust me', he shook the same hand back and forth to emphasize his point. "Just do your job as the artiste you're meant to be." Obviously sarcastic, he stressed the word 'artiste' while rubbing his eyes and smirking. "Those bitches didn't talk to us because they can't talk."

Penny looked confused. "I heard them whispering. They can talk."

"Man, this one knows everything. You're quite a dame, eh?" he asked looking annoyed. Yeah—yeah, they can talk, but not in English. Capiche?"

"Oh, they're Italian?"

"No, those are fresh little Bulgarian chicks."

Chapter 14

Five years ago, Dan Losegg had crawled around under a boulder off National Trails Road somewhere in the Mojave, several miles from Amboy and miles from Hwy 40. His mind sharp, like the needles on the rare cacti bordering the cave, he knew navigation better than any GPS or online mapping system. After all, they didn't call him Captain for nothing. Plus, he had a plan. In his pocket, he had a list of coordinates. The pinpointed latitudinal and longitudinal markers corresponded to degrees, thus narrowing his search down to decimals. Sweat rolled into his eyes, but nothing could stop him. He felt confident and had no doubts, regarding the stash of dollars hidden among the rocks.

That morning had started right on schedule. He paid the Las Vegas taxi driver to take him through the desert and told him where to stop.

The remote site, a forgettable, flat piece of desert without hills or mountains. Far from everywhere, Dan didn't want to look suspicious. The train tracks were ten miles in one direction and the road meandered up and down through Joshua trees and scrub brush.

The cab driver looked happy with the large tip, although it might have been because he felt glad to dump Dan in the middle of nowhere. The agonizing stories of world travel and the excruciatingly boring tales about a one-of-a-kind Hawaiian shirt collection, wore on the hardworking driver's nerves. Most Vegas cabbies weren't accustomed to spending more than a few minutes with each client. This one sped away faster than a roadrunner trying to out maneuver a coyote.

Dan hiked for several hours before the tender, dew filled, morning air changed dramatically into what could also be described as the baking-mode temperature inside a Suzy Homemaker oven. Fortunately, by this time, he had found the mountain cave where he needed to dig. He wore boots and knew he didn't have cell phone reception. Doreen had promised to come by in her classic, red Cadillac convertible at exactly five

P.M. He had to hurry. Inside the shelter of the cool surroundings, he removed his backpack and pulled out his stainless water bottle. He took a sip and matched the rock formations at the entrance, with the ones he had marked on his wrinkled slip of paper. Everything checked out because he had thought of everything. He caught his reflection in the water bottle and congratulated himself for being smart and good looking too.

Next, he removed the small shovel and used his compass to line the door of the cave up to the coordinates. In front of him were several rock piles. He noticed an arrow shape design made with rocks, which might have been the work of scouts. He thought he'd wander in that direction, but also worried it could be a diversion. Another arrow and now an empty fire pit with charred remains sat close to the quadrants he needed. He sat down for another drink, when a lizard made him jump from a sitting position to standing upright. The sudden movement had caused him to hit his head in the low ceiling of the cave. Thumping his head made him lose consciousness for a few seconds. After reclining for a few minutes of solitude, he regained a foothold and continued his one-person endeavor. The numbers corresponded to the rocks nearby. Getting closer made his heart pound with anticipation. The bump on his head gave him a huge headache and caused him to be woozy. His fingers clenched the boulders around him, but as he stepped over a large rock, dizziness made him trip again, causing a strain of his right ankle. He just needed to keep going, but now he had agonizing pain in his head and his legs. He cursed his old worn out hiking boots and cussed at the poor reptile that had made him strike his head.

The cave narrowed. He had to go deeper into the darkest part of the cavern where he had to find a penis-shaped rock. But first, he had to sit down and rest. His water bottle didn't have a single drop. His Omega watch read four-o'clock. Doreen's instructions were to stop for five minutes, but not to wait.

Waiting wouldn't look good. If the CHP drove by, they'd wonder about a woman alone on the side of the road. He had told her he'd be ready to go at five. He told her he'd wave her down with his red bandana. He had to hurry. His leg throbbed, his head hurt. Everything seemed dark when he began to itch. He had planned for everything, everything except thousands of hungry fire ants that crawled into his boots, scattering all around his body and eagerly running up his legs. The flesh-eating beetles came much, much later, finishing off the sloppy work provided by a greedy, manic woman named Doreen.

Chapter 15

"The Magnifique Hotel and Spa will have four thousand rooms, ten restaurants, a shopping mall and a lake with a giant waterfall." The human resources woman holding the orientation pointed to an enormous map of the pie-shaped property located directly on the Las Vegas Strip. The artistic rendering made the proposed resort look gargantuan. In fact, it would be bigger than most of the other resorts in the vicinity. In the picture, it dwarfed the world-renowned, gigantic hotel casinos on both sides. Some of which had five thousand rooms on several acres.

John sat in a large theater filled with at least a hundred new employees and construction workers. In his lap, he had a thick pile of forms. A woman at the podium changed the overhead image of the map to another screen in her presentation. "If you are working on the design and build of the structures then you won't be required to return tomorrow. Today is simply an overview of the entire project. Tomorrow, all full-time employees will begin hospitality training. If you have any questions, please hold onto them until the end."

Though excited to be back at work, he squirmed in the comfortable theatre seat and couldn't wait for the meeting to be finished. He wondered why this woman's voice almost lulled him to sleep. Maybe if she spoke more about the waterfall and less about the time clock procedures he could stay awake. During the break, he attempted to call Penny, but she didn't answer. He went to find some coffee and had a sip but could see other employees filing back into the auditorium. He tossed the foam cup and hurried back to his seat as the lights dimmed.

Another map flashed above. "The monorail will eventually connect The Magnifique to the MGM and the New York-New York," she continued with a nasal sounding voice. Her laser pointer pointed to a fenced in lot on the map. "Until that time, all employees are urged to park at the airport. A shuttle will drop you off in front of the hotel." John felt fortunate knowing he could walk almost two miles from the apartment. To some employees that distance would sound far, but John felt, that walking seemed like a healthy option. Especially since he needed to work off some of the cheap, Vegas buffet food. On and on she droned about the extravagant features, the color of the luxurious carpets and the emphasis on service and elegance.

Though somewhat tedious, he knew that teamwork and cooperation would be necessary to complete a top caliber hotel with so many well-appointed, spa-like amenities. Naturally, every business in Vegas, on or off the Strip, elegant or shabby, shamelessly competed for those all-important tourist dollars.

"Please sign and date the insurance forms and drop them in the box near the exit. Part time employees are eligible for special coverage. If you are doing physical labor, please also fill out the life insurance form."

A hard hat illustration flashed on the screen. John looked at his forms. Insurance? He had worked on large buildings before but nothing over ten stories. The dangers involved in working thirty or forty stories high had never occurred to him. Dependents? Not for much longer–he thought. Lani kept maturing by the minute.

Two days ago, she told her mother she might be in love with some guy called Pete. As John signed the papers, it made him feel like he had accomplished something important. Lani Murray he wrote on the line for dependents. The next batch of questions asked for a beneficiary. He scratched his head and immediately wrote in Penny's name. Like a runaway freight train, the moment collided in his head with reality. Life seemed to take on a different tone. It chugged uphill. Reminding him about the serious factors involved. The hotel had reminded John of things he rarely thought about, including his own mortality. The meeting also reminded him that his daughter had become a grown woman.

Chapter 16

The limo turned onto a serene, palm tree lined driveway that meandered around a placid man-made lake. They were miles from the noise, the neon lights and the party atmosphere of Vegas. Everything seemed so tranquil and dreamy. There were no Keno numbers filling the air from overhead amplifiers, no loud mouth announcers taking bets on horse races, and absolutely no fake or actual jingling coins buzzing out of slot machines. Penny wondered whether they were going to Julian's private home or to a spa, but she didn't want to begin another conversation with Ray. When the car stopped, a young man dressed in a safari-style khaki uniform opened the door.

"Welcome to The Oasis," he said, with an inviting smile. He offered a hand to assist her out of the back seat. "We're serving lunch on the patio today," the young man added in his soothing voice. Ray quickly put on his sunglasses and buttoned his jacket.

"Follow me," Ray ordered.

Glad to be able to breathe fresh air again, she inhaled and smiled at the young man, before looking around at the exotic landscaping. "Would you hurry up?" Ray ordered with a touch of impatience. "There's a lot to do here. I thought you wanted to get started." She hesitated and slowly followed Aftershave Man up the tiled steps. Curious, she turned to look at the blossoming Jacaranda trees losing soft, lavender-colored petals in the warm desert breeze. Near the front door, a fountain with a nude statue of a voluptuous Venus reached towards heaven as water rolled through her fingers. The delightful chirps from long-tailed black birds, she interpreted as a splendid, personalized greeting from nature.

Mesmerized, Penny followed Ray into the building in slow motion, where a huge, wrought-iron staircase and marble floors added to the impressive foyer. An imposing hostess desk stood on the left and an archway led to swimming pools and sauna rooms. Penny gazed at the walls and up at the ceiling where Italian frescoes stretched around artistically placed skylights and painted cloud formations. "Wow," she said almost tripping on her sandals.

"Come on!" Ray said with an impatient sneer. "Haven't you ever been anywhere nice in your life? This is fairly typical in Vegas and that ceiling you're drooling over is covered in decals."

"It is?" Penny followed Ray into a large office where Julian Diszno happened to be yelling at someone on the phone. A red and gold parrot squawked and said something that sounded like '**Come here babe**'. Large potted palm trees filled the corners around a gorgeous picture window that looked onto a lake. Beyond the water, on the other side, were those magnificent, peachy and plum colored, desert mountains. Bougainvillea flowers edged the outside patio. Had she crossed into a daydream? The setting reminded her of some of the places she used to imagine in her fantasies, until Julian slammed the phone down, yelling at Ray.

"Where the fuck have you been all day?"

Ray sat down and pointed to another chair for Penny. "Boss we had to go to the airport. Remember?"

"Well you might as well take her home Ray. I don't have time for this bullshit today."

They kept talking as if she wasn't sitting in the same room. Though she noticed the tone of voice, she felt she had to focus on her goals. Not wanting to be invisible, Penny interrupted with a smile. "Julian, I'm excited to be here. Just show me the room for the mural and I'll go get some paint."

Julian looked at Ray and laughed. Then he made a serious face, pounded on the desk with the palm of his hand and laughed again. *It reminded her of a standup comedy show where the joke wasn't supposed to make the performer laugh, but he couldn't help it.*

"I thought you knew something about painting?" He could hardly get the words out as tears rolled down his cheeks and his eyes bulged out of his fat, ugly head.

At least, she thought, his emotions had changed from anger to amusement. "I do," Penny replied, feeling uncomfortable. *What in the world did she say that made them laugh hysterically?* A small voice in her head told her she probably wasn't going to be having lunch on any outdoor patio. *Stay confident, she told herself. You can do this.*

Julian continued to guffaw like a hyena and soon, Ray joined in too. "You do?" He wiped his face with his hand, drying it on his ample stomach before raising it in the air to silence Ray. Penny swallowed, attempting to smile, but her knees began to quiver. One of the parrots screeched before a quiet hush filled the room. She looked from Julian to Ray and decided to keep her attention on the dust particles that streamed across slivers of sunshine coming through the window slats.

"Fine," Julian grumbled. He stood up, violently slamming a drawer on his carved desk. "First of all, this is not normal paint. Come with me." He slipped on some backless velvet slippers and he motioned for her to follow. They returned to the lovely entry where they climbed the stairs. At the top of the stairs there were hallways going in several different directions. At the end of each hallway, there were enormous ballrooms. In between the top of the stairs and the ballrooms were corridors leading to private guest quarters, where workmen were in the process of adding final additions to cabinetry.

Electricians were installing graceful sconces to the walls. The upstairs floors were walnut, but most of the magnificent intarsia and detailed designs had drop cloths protecting them from the workers. Mosaic tiled bathrooms and French doors added illumination and a palatial feeling.

Julian stopped after opening the second ballroom. Obviously out of breath, he turned around and looked Penny straight in the eyes. "This top floor is fifteen thousand square feet." He grinned without showing his teeth in what looked more like a sneer rather than a smile. "We talked about murals interpreting my ideas," he whispered, pointing a finger at himself. "My ideas, he fumed a little louder. "Remember?" He smirked again but now it looked evil. He shook his head, making facial contortions, finally landing on what some would call a sardonic smile. Ray stood behind him snickering. "How many gallons of paint do you think you need to pick up on your way home?" He shook with convulsive laughter and Ray joined in for another complete chuckle-fest.

"Ray, why are you laughing? Our wee little muralist wants to go get the paint," he doubled over and put both his hands on his hips, as he tried to catch his breath.

"Alright, alright, I didn't realize...."

Julian cut her off. Now he sounded angry. "There's a lot you don't realize. If there are brains under that cute mop of red hair, you'll understand why you can't buy supplies and 'some' paint." He tousled her hair, like a father would a naughty five-year-old. "Why don't you let us get the paint and you can start on this tomorrow. Okay?"

He went down the stairs. Ray and Penny followed. They stood on the inside of the grand entrance and she could hear the fountain outside. Glancing up at the fresco on the ceiling, she imagined her fingers reaching for the heavens, when Julian's booming voice filled the cavernous building, bringing her back to reality. "Well?"

Startled, she wanted to run like a puma and never return, but she also knew that at at this point in her life, she had no choice. Though not an expert, she knew, from reading checkout stand tabloids, that celebrities could be narcissistic and arrogant. She had expected a certain level of self-importance, for the simple reason that Julian had developed a name, and a following out of nothing but the exact subject they were discussing, which happened to be paint. His condescending attitude however, came across as an offensive slap on the cheek.

"Okay."

Julian looked at Ray before he motioned towards the door with his chin. "Get her out of here."

Chapter 17

They met in front of a buffet restaurant for dinner. John liked the midcentury retro look of the hotel. It had a cartoon vibe that made him recall his sheltered childhood. *His dad would have loved this place, he thought, looking up at the sign advertising breakfast, lunch and dinner.* One block from the strip, the old place had two towering date palms in the parking lot. Surrounded by mega hotels, monorails and conference centers, progress had blossomed around the shabby, but inviting little property, called the Magic Carpet Motel and Casino. Rumors still circulated about how in its heyday, the Rat Pack had stayed there when they wanted to hide out from snooping investigative reporters and paparazzi flashbulbs.

Above the street, a flashing rose-toned, neon genie sat atop a blinking green rug. Though some of the bulbs needed changing, the attention getting sign still evoked cheerfulness and fun. Another sign advertised free shrimp cocktails and a three dollar and ninety-nine cent sirloin steak. The Enchanted Buffet served food around the clock for five dollars and ninety-nine cents. Located close to their fancy apartment building, they enjoyed the convenience of dining in less than ten minutes.

After they paid, and stood in line for a portion of food, they slid into a worn vinyl booth. Each laminate table had an imprint of a different Persian rug. The drink servers wore harem pants and tiny gem-embellished vests. Fake palm trees shivered in the corner of the air-conditioned restaurant.

On the way in, Penny had noticed the L on the word motel didn't light up, displaying Magic Carpet Mote and Casino. It made her think about the dust motes in Julian's office. Though old and seedy, compared to Julian's lavish resort, this place felt real, and oddly comforting. John must have felt the same way because he plopped into the booth as if he were at home in front of the television.

"You look tired Hon," John said, crunching down on a fried wonton from the Asian section of the buffet.

"The worst day ever," she answered after spearing a small sliver of ham onto her fork. The glazed ham came from the American section. If you wanted macaroni with it, you had to go to the Italian section or you could get classic, greasy fries from the French section. Not gourmet by a long shot, the place served enormous portions of comfort food in a relatively clean environment.

"Are you complaining about this buffet again?"

"No, it's fine. It's Julian, my new boss. He is so…" There were probably many juicy words to describe Julian, but at that moment, they had all slipped her mind. She stabbed another piece of ham. *How could she explain such a strange, haughty character?* "Eccentric," she finally stated. "Beyond anything I would have imagined, and that's saying a lot."

"The rice and the wontons are good," John replied, trying to forget the men they had met in the limo. He hoped she wouldn't go on about the ugly fat one while he ate. Trying to smile, he didn't want to lose his appetite. His day hadn't been stellar either. Besides, Penny had a knack for handling the odd or the peculiar. She had studied art with a bunch of bizarre art students. More importantly, she had always wanted to paint murals. "At least your day doesn't sound boring. We had orientation and…."

"John, I don't mean to interrupt, but can you listen to me for a second." She swirled her peas around and thought about going back for a ladle of beans from the Mexican section. Her eyes flashed like diamond-encrusted emeralds from Tiffany's. "You've seen pictures of the Sistine Chapel in Rome?"

John nodded with his mouth full.

"It's fairly small, right?" She put a few peas on her fork and chewed slowly.

"I guess. We've never been there."

"I know, I know—but I remember studying everything about it in art school. It took Michelangelo four years to paint."

"Yeah, so?"

"Don't you see? Julian wants three hallways, three massive ballrooms and at least ten bedrooms painted with murals and that's only the upstairs." Inhaling but exasperated, she took a sip of her iced tea. "Downstairs there are several changing rooms that lead to private saunas and Julian didn't mention painting down there, but I have a feeling he has plans for all of it. They did the foyer with massive decals, but I have to paint the rest of it."

His eyes followed her flourishing hand movements which indicated imaginary places on the ceiling. He wiped his mouth into a paper napkin, gazed around and noticed the chrome fire sprinklers above. The floral shaped sprayers stood out like thirsty camels on a deserted field of pale blue. The desert motif at the Enchanted Buffet stopped at the chair rails above the booths. When he looked into her face, he felt confused.

"Isn't this a good thing?"

"Are you kidding?" She shook her head and looked disgusted, as if he had flown down from another planet and spoke an alien language.

John squinted and scratched his head. "I'm confused and don't get mad at me, but I don't understand. I thought you liked the idea of painting on bare walls. Doesn't this guarantee a lifetime of job security? Once they see your work he'll want to hold onto you forever."

Penny put a hand to the right side of her head and massaged her temple. Her other hand gripped the side of the table. When John said the word 'forever', it filled the entire buffet area like a reverberating echo. An unusual lull in the restaurant's normal cacophony silenced even the hushed conversations at the surrounding tables. She strained to hear the slots, the voice of the Keno announcer. In the distance, Rimsky-Korsakov's Scheherazade played from speakers on an endless loop. *Men could be so dense. Forever was a long time to be away from her daughter and husband.* John slid from the booth to get dessert when her cell phone rang.

"Lani, settle down. What's wrong? I thought you liked Peter?

Well then, don't walk Bentley anymore. Your aunt has a backyard. Promise me you won't go back to that park."

When John returned, she had tears in her eyes. "Okay, goodnight dear. Thanks for telling us. We love you."

"What happened?" John came back with two chocolate chip cookies and a piece of pie, on an oversized plate.

"Lani called to say she's afraid of Peter and his brother. I miss her so much."

"Why what happened? Didn't she say she loved him a couple of days ago? If that sonofabasket even wrinkles her blouse, I'm going to kick his ass." He held up a cookie, offering it to Penny who didn't look amused.

She smiled and wiped her eyes with the back of her hand. "What if he owns a mule instead of an ass?"

"Whatever—ass is not a cuss word." He tossed the cookie back onto the plate. "Are you being dramatic, or do you think this is something serious? Did she tell you what's going on?"

"No one hurt her. I guess this Peter guy has weird friends."

"That's strange. They probably just had a fight."

"I sure hope this has nothing to do with drugs."

"God, help us."

"Good point." The entire incident reminded her about how she wanted to tell John about Dan and the inheritance, but every day seemed to get increasingly more complicated. Meanwhile, she felt guilty for holding out on him. While John hovered on a different wavelength, Julian demanded the impossible. And with Lani being far away, possibly in some sort of trouble, it wasn't hard to understand why she had a throbbing headache. "I need an aspirin," she said with a sigh. But it wasn't just her head and she knew it. It was everything. "Do you think there's a church around here?"

Chapter 18

Aunt Betsy had one of those annoying voices, the type of voice that could wake a slumbering ghost. "Lani," she shrieked across the room, "Why don't you walk Bentley?"

It took a lot more than the sound of her aunt's vocal acrobatics to make her sick. Most of all, she missed her mom and dad. Plus, she didn't want to go to that park anymore. Not since, she had found out about Peter's brother. She missed Peter too and her heart felt like it had landed in a wood chipper. Though, she imagined the noisy pulverizing mechanism turning, it hadn't completely shredded her heart into microscopic pieces; not yet, anyway. Things had to get better. Her heart felt more as if it were in the process of shredding—an active verb—rather than a painful memory of the past. Her aunt's timing impeccable, Lani could almost feel shards blasting around in the middle of her chest.

"Lani?" Aunt Betsy stood at the door to her room. With an outstretched arm, she held onto a brand new, red-leather leash with two fingers, as if it smelled like dog poop.

"I don't feel like walking right now." *Or talking for that matter, but Aunt Betsy didn't notice these things. Aunt Betsy took pride in being the textbook sister to her dad. She also wanted to be a wonderful aunt, as long as you liked homespun crafts, apple pies and patriotic songs about America. When it came to modern matters, she acted unobservant and illogical. 'Go crochet a dog blanket or something,' Lani wanted to add, but she yawned instead, hoping her aunt would get a clue.*

"But Bentley loves walking with you and you've missed three days." *Lani knew her aunt didn't mean to plead, whine or beg. It had to be a type of generation gap, because though unobservant, Betsy happened to be a nice woman with a scruffy little dog. Maybe the weird squeaky tone of voice came from a long lost relative. It had to be genetic. The woman probably couldn't help it.*

Though Lani had grown quite fond of Bentley in the last few weeks, she still felt it odd how Aunt Betsy insisted they should go for walks. No one walked anymore. *If she hadn't witnessed Aunt Betsy driving her sedan to the supermarket, she'd never believe her aunt had even heard about the invention of cars.*

"Lani, wait until you see the sweater I'm knitting for Bentley. You'll love it."

"Can't we just let him out in the backyard?" She turned toward the wall, inhaling the sweet smell of softener on the chenille bedspread. *Only Aunt Betsy would have a chenille bedspread, she thought. Her aunt had told her they called it chenille. Lani wondered what they made it from, to make it so soft. The summer like smell reminded her of cotton candy and bubble gum. Though she liked the smell and touch, it still looked old-fashioned. And did people still knit outfits for their pets? Ever since she came to live at Aunt Betsy's she felt trapped in a time machine. Back, back, back to some godforsaken year before her birth and perhaps farther back, before even her parents were born.*

Lani heard the leash fall to the floor. Seconds later, the restless little hairs on the back of her neck sprang into action when her aunt shook the bed by plopping her plump, polyester clad hips down next to her. "You don't have to feel like you're alone. Why don't you tell me what's wrong, dear? Maybe I can help."

Lani wanted to talk but couldn't, not to Aunt Bess, anyway. Maybe if she didn't smell like a mixture of violets, vinegar and cheap stretchy fabric. Tears rolled out of her eyes onto the pillow. "Leave me alone," she said with a sob.

Aunt Betsy patted Lani's arm, before heaving her body off the bed and turning towards the door. "I made your favorite salad today—the one with chicken and artichokes."

"I'm not hungry," Lani shouted, surprising her aunt.

"You miss your mom and dad, don't you?"

"No, that has nothing to do with it. Please leave me alone." She inhaled the softener on the bed and wanted to put Aunt Bess out of her mind. I'm sorry for acting like this," she said between small sobs.

Aunt Betsy picked the leash up off the floor and gently closed the door, thinking this would be a good time to call her brother.

Chapter 19

Penny and John crossed Flamingo road and turned on a side street near Hooters. There, amid throngs of intoxicated partygoers and fun-loving coeds of various ages, stood Christ the Redeemer church.

"I hope the priest will listen to my confession," Penny said to John.

"Why wouldn't he?"

"I'm thinking it's kind of late. Remember they usually hold confessions in the daytime? A few weeks in Vegas and suddenly you're a night owl," she said, cheerfully.

Before John pushed the door to the sanctuary open, he noticed a few scruffy looking homeless men and women loitering, chatting and eating near the side of the building. He grasped Penny's hand, to yank her inside. Inside the bright lobby, he saw a small sign that read, 'Parish Office.' He let go of Penny's hand and knocked gently on the door. "Hello, anyone here?"

After a few minutes, the door opened a crack. A gnarled, quivering hand rose to shake hands with John. "Hello, I'm Father Charles. Can I help you?"

"We're new in the area and hoped we could talk to you for a few minutes."

The priest smiled, glancing at Penny and addressing both of them. "I'm so glad to have new members, but tonight we have a soup kitchen dinner and our church is low on staff." He winked at Penny. "I'd love to chat, but maybe you can make an appointment with my secretary."

"When do you hear confessions?" Penny asked.

"Anytime but now; there's only two of us here. You may have noticed there are about fifty of God's children out there waiting for dinner. I really must run. God Bless you both. Hope to see you on Sunday." The door closed, and he tottered off. They heard his shoe soles shuffling away, moving towards the other side of the building.

"Make an appointment with me secretary," John imitated the priest's Scottish brogue.

147

"That's not nice, dear."

"What? We're here because we need help. Maybe not food, but our souls need nourishment too," John replied. His face showed disgust and disappointment. "Don't we rate as God's children too?"

"Aren't you being harsh? That poor old man is cooking dinner for hundreds of homeless people. Those folks didn't get scalloped potatoes with roast beef and chicken Chow Mein followed by apple pie at the Enchanted Buffet."

John looked peeved. He kicked the front entrance open with his work boots, pulling Penny into the hubbub of a crowded sidewalk filled with giggling, happy tourists. The contrast of emotion changed fast however, as they passed the side of the religious building, where a long line of sad, disheveled people hobbled like zombies down the alley, towards the church. Floodlights shined from a small window with aluminum shutters. From the sidewalk, they could see the unmistakable silhouette of the balding, short-statured priest. He gesticulated with his arms, motioning for the next person in line to step up to the window. John and Penny couldn't hear anything but cars.

Penny looked at her watch. "John it's almost nine-o'clock in the evening."

"I know." His shoulders seemed to settle down and he finally cracked a small smile, "What's with you and confession, all of a sudden, anyway?"

"Nothing," Penny replied with a yawn. Let's go home. I have a feeling tomorrow is going to be another crazy day."

Chapter 20

The guys at work had filled John's head during lunchtime with all the unusual things that happen in Vegas. These were bizarre, true-life stories that also happen, perhaps less frequently, elsewhere in the world. To an ordinary crowd in any other town, it would sound like hyperbole, but it wasn't. Every day, the guys at work wanted to make it a battle for one-upmanship.

First, there were desert snake stories and stinging scorpions. After they tired of those, there came the wacky tales about threesomes and cheating wives. John learned more about porno movie stars and pole dancers than he thought he should. The men he worked with shared their experiences regarding the best mail-order companies for ordering the strangest, most satisfying sex-toys and prophylactics. They piqued his interest when they gossiped about lesbian encounters, but the transgender soap operas made him question everything he thought he had learned in sex-ed. All his life he had assumed all men in work boots were heterosexual. He felt like an outcast, because none of the others thought marital bonds kept couples faithful or monogamous. After the first few weeks, he wondered whether he'd ever get used to hearing about any of it.

Even worse, he especially disliked the degrading tones they used to describe women. They referred to females as: whores, bitches or chicks. Never in his wildest dreams had he ever thought of calling his wife such horrible, disgusting names behind her back.

Now, after twenty years, in what most would call a successful marriage, he stood next to Penny in his boxer shorts. "So, what's the scoop about this confession? Let's hear it." The more he thought about it, the more he worried. After all, she hung out with her favorite painter all day, while his head was up in the clouds, safely tucked into a giant tower, like a male Rapunzel. "We miss a month of church and suddenly you've got things to hide from your husband?"

Tired and sunburned, his face hurt. His attitude didn't strike a conversational tone.

"It's late, can we discuss this tomorrow?" Penny asked, as she pulled back his side of the covers. She patted the bed, so he would crawl in next to her, hopefully forgetting all about it.

The more she thought about the money, the more she realized it is good news, as in a sort of windfall and a blessing. It had to be unveiled like a masterpiece, over wine and fettuccini. She attempted to change the subject. "Did you know Ron and Tina live in Henderson?"

"Who cares?" He grimaced, while keeping both hands on his narrow hips. Sometimes it seemed his mind could be set on one track which helped him with his job. He focused like a winning horse with blinders at the track. He'd know how many nails he needed for most projects and he'd stay the course, until he finished the work. Similarly, Penny knew that when an argument ensued, it would have to run its entire ugly course. Though she couldn't hide from such honest, loving eyes, she kept on going about Tina and Ron.

"What do you mean, who cares? Do you think we'd be married if she hadn't done all that creative finagling?"

"Finagle. That's a great way to describe it. All I remember about Hawaii is standing on the beach and holding the woman of my dreams. Okay, I'll give her some credit. Tina supplied me with that weird looking white shirt that made me look like a Latino bartender. Now, let's get back to the confession thing."

When he uttered 'woman of his dreams' she thought maybe she could distract him, so he'd forget all about it. "Am I still the woman of your dreams?" She puckered her lips and made a coquettish look with her eyes by batting her lashes, in a feeble attempt at sexiness.

"Penny," he sighed and sat on the edge of the bed. He looked so worn-out and tired. "I better say yes, or you'll get mad at me."

She sat up like a jack-in-the-box and sprang to attention. "What the hell is that supposed to mean? All of a sudden I'm not your dream woman?" It came out sounding like a snarl. Lately everything seemed like a snarl. Besides missing Lani, Vegas already seemed to be getting on her nerves, especially Ray and his lurid comments. Statistics proved that money problems caused most divorces. As empty nesters, it had crossed her mind that things could go either way. Fortunately, she had an ace in her bag that she hoped would save her marriage. The time had come to lay the supposed bequest on the line.

"Well, I have to admit that my dear little redhead has turned kind of bitchy these last few years." He tried being nice, but his voice quivered as if he feared retaliation. He rarely used words like that but the salty-tongued devils he worked with had rubbed off on him.

Surprised by his language, she countered with a few questions. "Bitchy, huh? Well, I'm sorry if my newspaper went out of business. I'm also sorry you lost your job. I'm sorry about all of it. I've done everything I can for this family and it's never enough. In case you don't remember, I literally took my shirt off to get the job I have now. Maybe there are degrees to bitchiness. My bold and compromising move also had something to do with getting this awesome apartment. What part of my bitchiness factor do you like? Or do you conveniently forget the important parts?"

John shook his head and looked sad. "No, I didn't forget," he whispered.

"Well, brace yourself for my big bitchy confession. Remember that pilot who flew me to Hawaii? I've told you a thousand times about that lying, two-faced scoundrel, the one who dumped me in Kauai? Remember?" She asked in a sharp tone.

John bit his lip and nodded his head.

"Well allegedly, he left me two million dollars. So maybe you can start being happy. We have money." She swung her arms into the air as if throwing confetti, laughing hysterically and pounding her fists into the mattress. "Hooray! All I have to do is go to the bank and claim it."

"Shut up. What is wrong with you?" He jumped out of bed faster than a fireman heading to a five-alarm fire and stepped into his dirty jeans. "Are you talking about that married scumbag from twenty years ago?"

She nodded, but her smile faded as she watched him dress. "One and the same dude, yup."

"I knew it," he spat the words. "So, you lied." He looked around, pulling his shirt from the laundry hamper.

"About what? Your bitch made you rich." She laughed again at the sound of the words.

"You know exactly what I'm talking about. No wonder you're acting insane."

"I am not lying."

"You said nothing happened between you two." He buckled his belt and retrieved his boots from the closet.

"Nothing did. What are you doing?" *What was wrong with John? She wanted him by her side when she signed the papers. She wanted to be able to return to California, to Lani and more than anything, she wanted a normal life again. She had a bona-fide ticket to freedom right there in the bottom of her bag.* "Don't you think it's a miracle? We needed money and now we have it."

"Money isn't everything. I'm leaving."

"Why? You're just tired. Please John, settle down and come to bed. Don't you think it's great?" *She attempted to smile but he looked away. Maybe it was all the grueling hard work he had been doing lately that had set him off. In twenty years of marriage, she had enjoyed knowing his reactions were usually reasonable and friendly. When she made a stupid mistake or overpaid for an item or burned his dinner, he had laughed off most of her errors. He, the sounding board to her wild ideas, had been her rock, her go to guy for everything from wrenches to spiders and all sorts of things in between.*

"Great that you slept with him and lied about it, or is it great, that it took twenty years for the truth to come out? No wonder you desperately wanted to go to confession." His face showed anger and disgust. The old scar on his forehead looked pinker than usual.

Penny didn't expect this reaction. As a fiery redhead, she considered herself the emotional spouse. "That's not what happened. I never slept with him." She got out of bed and stood by the door in her nightgown. Blinking back moisture, her eyes sparkled, remaining cool, jewel-toned emeralds. This couldn't be happening. "John, he meant nothing, and you know that. Don't leave."

"You know something? Those big green eyes have saved your butt many times, but maybe your luck is running out. This time, your creative thinking might have gone over the edge. Don't worry because I'm still Lani's dad. I love her." Seething, he took a labored breath and tied his laces. "She better be my kid," he muttered and shook his head, cursing under his breath. "Maybe you shouldn't confess anymore of your stories. I'm done with your bitchiness and lies."

"Wait," she tried to keep him from opening the door. "Even if I had slept with him, which I didn't, I think you should forgive me. A few minutes ago, you said I was the woman of your dreams. We've known each other a long time," she mumbled, wondering if he was seriously considering taking off and not coming back.

"Can't you forgive me?"

"Save your Jesus stuff. You know I'm a regular human being and you've decided to back up your load of dirt a little too late." His eyes looked wild and his nostrils flared. "This is beyond ridiculous. The truth is probably lodged somewhere in the dictionary between cow-shit and horseshit." He grabbed his wallet off the nightstand, pushed her gently away and pulled open the door. Here's a newsflash for you baby: people, especially airline pilots, don't just leave two million dollars to women they didn't sleep with. I've had enough. See-ya." He slammed the door and his last words were, "You are such a liar."

Chapter 21

He'll be back, she thought, sinking onto the bed. Though usually cool, he had lost his patience with her before. Minutes turned into hours and she wanted to hear his knuckles on the door. She listened to strangers hurrying through the hallway and after a while, she focused her attention to the traffic below.

The city that never slept had yellow and white taxi cabs from one end of the strip to the other, forming a yellow conga line under neon lights. It all seemed to be a never-ending party to visitors from faraway places. The sidewalks were full of people getting out of shows, milling about and laughing. What just happened? *Did her party just come to an end?*

She thought about Dan and the money. She thought about him dying in the desert because of ants or some sort of bugs, and the thought made her skin crawl. All she wanted to do was tell John the truth and instead he had grinded his work boots into her soul. The same work-boots that had kicked open the church door carried her husband away, taking him all over this bustling town. Sighing, she thought of work. Simply thinking of the unending workload made her tired. Ray had said he'd come get her a little earlier, so she could get a head start on her mural. She had to get a few hours of sleep. Seconds after her head hit the pillow, the phone rang.

At first, she thought John had come to his senses. After all, where did he plan to sleep? What did he want her to do? They had very little money. Spending money on things they didn't need would be unwise. Hoping to hear him apologize, she pushed the answer button but instead of John, she heard Aunt Betsy's frantic voice.

"Penny, is my brother there?"

"No, not right now—ah—he just stepped out. What's going on? Is everything okay?"

"She's gone," Aunt Betsy screeched like an owl.

"She?" With her mind on John's sudden absence, she thought she misunderstood. "Who, Lani?"

"Yes. Yes. That's what I'm trying to tell you if you would listen for one second."

"Hold on, don't be upset with me, I'm listening. How long has she been gone?"

"I haven't seen her since yesterday and the cops just left. They took a report."

"Oh Gawd," Penny said quietly. Aunt Betsy's voice quivered. Her uneven breath made it sound like she might have a heart attack.

"Please calm down, Bess. You know you have high blood pressure."

"I can't calm down. You told me yourself she's always saying, don't have a cow. Well pardon me while I have a cow. Listen, she left with that Peter fellow and I'm sure you don't want to hear this, but she took all her things. My dear, I feel responsible and this is weighing heavy on my heart."

"Lani's a big girl Aunt Bess. She'll be fine."

"I'm not so sure. I mean Lani's an angel, but she told me a few things in confidence about Peter's brother that would make you nuts. I guess he's a bad seed and now she's involved with their family."

"Has anyone contacted Peter's parents? Maybe she's over at his house having a sleepover." She cringed uttering the word sleepover. Lani knew the difference between right and wrong and even at her age, there were no such things as sleepovers with boys.

"She's not there. I already called. Some brat with an attitude–probably Peter's brother–told me she's not there. The cops are on their way over there now," she sobbed. Aunt Betsy could hardly finish her sentence. Her voice bubbled through the phone as if she had fallen off a pier. Penny could hear the poor woman straining to speak and gagging through her phlegm as she gasped for air.

"Bess, please calm down. Listen to yourself. Lani is twenty years old, for heaven's sake–an adult. She'll be fine. Have a cup of tea and go to bed." The words that came from her lips made her feel better. "My daughter will probably be back in the morning." And hopefully, so will my husband, she wanted to add in an effort to reassure herself. *The comfortable things we rely on can unravel quickly,* she thought, before whispering, "Bess, we love you, now go to bed. Please."

"I hope you're right Penny." She sniffed. "Goodnight, tell my brother I called."

The call disconnected. Penny felt a sort of evil rush descend around her, as if a large black vacuum had sucked the life from her body. She crumpled onto the mattress and had nightmares until six in the morning. In her first dream, John had an affair with a gorgeous Ukrainian woman. Thick, wavy, lightened hair enhanced high cheekbones and almond shaped eyes. Looking statuesque, in red, patent leather, four-inch heels, the catlike seductress had slim legs and perfectly manicured acrylic nails.

In the nightmare, this woman rode up the employee elevator to find John hammering nails at the Magnifique. Her silk dress, also red, caught the desert breeze, revealing long, sculpted expanses of alluring, well-toned thighs.

This female vision had voluptuous, round breasts and plump lips like a pin-up girl from the forties. 'Oh John,' she murmured with an obvious accent, 'I have been looking everywhere for you.' John approached, and when he put his lips to the stranger, the dream vanished, switching to a different channel.

In the second dream, fog had made navigation difficult and Penny ran towards the sound of

Lani's voice. 'Mommy, where are you?' she cried. There were other noises like trucks, helicopters and airplanes in the background. "I'm here, baby. I'm right here," she said aloud, waking up, out of breath, in a pool of perspiration. The refriger-ator made a small hum and the white noise of the town that never went to sleep buzzed from below. Even surrounded by two million residents and millions of visitors, Penny realized a person could end up alone.

Chapter 22

In the morning, Ray banged on the door like an incarcerated maniac wanting freedom.

"I'm coming," Penny yelled. She swung the door open and looked at his three-piece suit. "Hope you don't mind, but I didn't dress up." Wearing jeans, an old tee shirt and tennis shoes, she was ready to paint. *Telling Ray to leave because Lani and John were missing could ruin everything. It boiled down to keeping her stylish apartment and her job until she mustered up the courage to collect Dan's generous gift. They'd probably laugh her out of the bank. Until then, she had nothing, and she didn't want to get her hopes up, in case the inheritance turned out to be a complete fraud.*

It wasn't the first time in her life that Lani went missing. At age eleven, she hid herself in a cabinet at a furniture store before the place locked up for the night. Fortunately, they knew the owner and he let the two of them back into the store, before it became a huge search and rescue operation. Easily distracted, her daughter had a library book with her, and she wanted to finish reading it. When the lights went out, the exhausted child stepped out of the cabinet and wandered around the store, falling asleep on a couch. Sadly, this time would be different.

Her husband would have to make some fast decisions about love and loyalty. How could he leave? She felt like staying at work overnight for the rest of her life. At least they had walls needing her attention.

"You look fine, doll. Now get a move on, chop-chop."

Once at work, she noticed workers trimming evergreen bushes and carpenters installing crown molding. Loud, modern classical music blared from built-in speakers. A walnut reception desk with gold-embossed filigreed trim stood in the foyer.

The first room Penny worked on happened to be the one farthest from the front entry. It needed a dynamic, impressive mural because it looked like a room that could be large enough to pass as a ballroom. She drew Bacchus on the wall. Wearing sandals with beige ties winding up fleshy legs and a blue toga, he sat on a mound of grapes, next to a waterfall of red wine. Seductive looking goddesses would swim under Greco-Roman columns adorned with vines and clusters of delectable fruit. The massive room didn't have much ventilation, but it had air-conditioning. She stepped back to imagine her color-scheme and looked around for the paint. Maybe she could borrow a fan from somewhere to circulate the air, once she began to paint.

Wandering down to the front, she noticed the receptionist sitting at the new desk. "Wait, don't I know you?" Penny inquired; certain she recognized the young woman.

The lady at the desk immediately stood up and smiled. "Yes, yes, I'm Mirage. You and your husband rescued Cleo and me, during a flash flood in the desert. What's your name again?"

"Penny," she answered, recalling the strange events of their anniversary and thinking about the irony of John leaving last night. "How's your adorable baby?"

Mirage's eyes twinkled, and her smile broadened at the question. "Cleo's fine. She's learning to walk. Right now, she's with her grandmother. Approaching footsteps sounded loud on the marble floors and when Penny turned to look, she noticed Ray making a hideous face. When he passed, she returned his sneer with a smile. He walked fast towards Julian's office, as if he had an important message to report. Penny held up an index finger and motioned to Mirage that she'd be right back.

"Ray, wait, I need to know where the paint is located."

Without turning, he pointed up and loudly exclaimed, "All the paint you could ever want can be found in suite E. Now be a good girl and run along. Get back to work before Julian notices you're not doing anything." He marched on, his leather soles echoing in the hallway. A few seconds later, a door slammed shut.

Disappointed in her ability to ask for a fan, she turned back to Mirage and shrugged. "Hope they don't mind if I go pee." Embarrassed by Ray's obvious disdain, she giggled and headed for the restroom. "By the way, can you point the way towards room—I mean suite E?"

Mirage pointed upstairs, towards the west end of the building. "Honestly, I've never been up there, but it's probably next to suite D," she replied with a smile. Mirage stood and walked around to the other side of the counter. "So, you're the new artist who's going to breathe some life into this place?"

"Not sure about life, but yes, I'm the artist. I really need to go. Hold your thought." She could tell the girl wanted to chat, but she couldn't hold it any longer. Penny rushed to the restroom. Before relieving herself, she inhaled and let out a long sigh. Afterwards, while washing her hands, Mirage burst into the restroom.

"I can't wait to see your artwork," Mirage squealed while washing her own hands. Julian told me you're really good."

"He did?"

"Yes, when he hired me he told me he's only hiring the best for everything."

"I think he likes my ideas about mixing the theme of wild hedonism with relaxing spa. He wants everything romantic with an element of magic surrealism. I'm already having fun designing the ballroom." Penny pulled a towel from a dispenser and dried her hands."

Mirage leaned toward Penny whispering, "You do know this isn't going to be a spa, don't you?"

Penny paused, wondering what Mirage had meant. She looked questioningly into the young woman's eyes. Why did she whisper? If it wasn't going to be a spa, what else could it be? She stared into the beveled mirror to adjust a wayward curl. Her mind raced around a track, landing on the answer. It had to be a resort hotel. As she reached over to throw the paper towel into the trash, Mirage caught her wrist.

"I think you should know... this is going to be a brothel. It's going to be the world's biggest, most luxurious whorehouse."

Chapter 23

At four o'clock, Ray offered to take Penny home. Thoroughly exhausted, she slumped in the back of the limo thinking about John. It certainly wasn't their first fight in twenty years. She thought back to the times he had stormed out, only to return a couple of inebriated hours later.

Ray kept typing things into his phone and since she looked sweaty and wore old casual clothes, he didn't seem interested in striking up one of his intimate conversations. She murmured a prayer of gratitude and found herself in front of the apartment building. "Thanks Ray," she mumbled, slipping from the leather seats onto the curb.

The apartment windows sparkled in the late afternoon sun. Zoned out, she gazed at them while wondering what to do. A cheerful couple bumped into her and brought her back to reality. What she decided to do is to walk the five long blocks to The Magnifique and find her wayward husband. Along the bustling sidewalks, she passed elegant tourists, drunken fraternity brothers on their first trip away from home, and grimy men handing out business cards advertising cheap sex. By the time she reached John's workplace they had placed a barricade in front, with warning signs closing off the area. When she asked around, they told her the foreman had left for the evening.

Disgusted, she wandered into a nearby casino where sad looking souls fed twenty-dollar bills into penny slot machines. Tentatively, she sat in front of a video machine portraying smiling devils and sexy angels. Though the odds looked promising, she lost a five-dollar bill in less than five minutes. She had one more five in her wallet and considered taking a chance, when her cell phone rang.

Aunt Betsy's voice sounded sharp and serious. For a woman who ordered miniature stuffed animals from an online auction and baked scones to match her Special-Edition, Wedgwood platter, this sounded unusual. "Penny, it's me and I'm sorry but I can't reach John. The cops told me the truth about Peter's brother. He sells more than drugs and he's into something very bad."

"I have no idea where John is right now. What do you mean very bad?"

"Well he lures young girls into situations," her voice dropped to a reluctant whisper.

The clang of the slot machines made it difficult to hear Aunt Betsy. Penny decided she'd go back outside. "Hold on, I'm not sure I can hear you. Wait a second." She quickly stepped onto a people mover, hoping the shoppers and gamblers would keep walking, to make progress towards the street. It reminded her of a grueling, salt-water taffy pulling machine, as the conveyor belt contraption shuttled people from one casino to another. Slowly, like a turtle moving in hot tar. Holding designer shopping bags, the exhausted sightseers appeared to be superglued to the moving rubber mat, chatting amongst each other or reading messages on their phones. "Excuse me," she said, trying to get around a heavy-set man and his petite girlfriend. "Excuse me," she repeated to a frail old woman desperately holding onto the side, so she wouldn't fall. In front of her, a family of six with luggage made her stop. Stuck like old chewing gum on a worn-out shoe, she strained to hear John's sister. "I'm trying to get to a quieter place, so I can understand what you're saying." "What do you mean situations?"

"The police said Tyler is into pimping, pandering and prostitution. They also said they wouldn't go searching for Lani because she's not a minor."

Aunt Betsy had some things to learn about their daughter. Is that all, Penny wondered, almost feeling relieved. "Lani would never be involved with anything like that. Don't worry your sweet heart about it. Our baby is not that kind of girl. Besides, isn't Tyler sixteen?"

Still speaking in a stern voice, unlike anything she had ever heard coming from John's happy go-lucky sister, she continued, "Penny, listen to me and listen to me good. They sent a female officer out here who informed me that girls brought to Vegas are exposed to 'the life' within forty-eight hours. Tyler is apparently into what's called human trafficking...."

'The life'? Penny cut her off mid-sentence. "Betsy, I'm dog-tired and demand to know what you are talking about. Vegas? Trafficking?" Suddenly self-conscious, she hoped the elderly woman standing behind her had poor hearing. "Lani is not that kind of girl and I think you know we brought her up right."

Almost tripping from the transporter to the hard surface of the Earth, she followed a crowd towards an outdoor shopping center.

"Of course, I know that—but…"

"But what?" She stared into the window of a French luggage store in an upscale mall. Colossal, Italianate courtyard fountains and blooming roses decorated the outside areas. Extravagant shops and art galleries lured rich tourists from all over the world. The luggage beckoned, as if to tempt Penny's once adventurous soul into running away. *Moments like this made her feel like moving to some exotic country or island. She could change her name, but then what? She knew leaving could not be an option. Where would she go? What would she do?* Twenty years ago, when she tried a similar trick, John, his father, and people from work were on her trail faster than a Coonhound on a rabbit.

Why, she thought, *do in-laws think they know more about your own kid?* On the verge of a sarcastic comment, she bit her lip. *After all, Aunt Betsy had never raised any of her own children. All she had were cats and that pathetic little dog Bentley.*

"Apparently she's on her way to Vegas with that Peter guy."

The fashionable luggage and the far-off dreams vanished, becoming irrelevant. The empty suitcases reminded her of the opposite. She considered them bulky, unimportant symbols of greed, packed with vainglorious articles of clothing that weighed her down. The window display made her think of the intangible, irreplaceable things that she couldn't schlep around the world. "Oh Gawd," she sighed. "I'll give her a call and find out what's going on."

"You can't, her cell phone is broken."

Chapter 24

Penny remembered the police van that had stopped near the Magic Carpet a few weeks ago. She had held onto John for dear life thinking they might corral her into the back too. Women of various ages had been handcuffed and pushed violently into the cargo hold of a government vehicle, before being hauled off to Clark County Jail. A young girl in a short pink dress kicked off her heels, making a mad dash into a nearby casino. Penny heard the officers laughing about the 'rabbit' with 'happy feet' going south. They also had called her a 'frequent flyer,' meaning they had recognized her and remembered she had spent time with the police before. Having their hands full with twenty women, they didn't pursue her, perhaps thinking they'd catch that bunny next time. They were the law. The bravado made them feel as if they were making a difference. At the time, Penny secretly hoped 'the rabbit' would be okay. But now she had a new perspective and the memory almost made her vomit. That fleeing 'rabbit' had been about Lani's age. Maybe, the memory of that girl in pink explained some of her depressing night-mares.

Penny and Lani had always had a great re-lationship. They were more like sisters than mother and daughter. They shopped for the same type of jeans and squabbled over who had the best taste in running shoes. Mothers have a gut instinct about these things and right now, Penny was certain that Lani needed her mommy. She had to find John, and she had to think of what to do, fast.

Yawning, as she pushed open the door of their apartment, she couldn't believe her sore, tired eyes. Blinking to make sure, she rubbed her eye-lids and mumbled a prayer of gratitude. There on the bed, her slumbering carpenter filled the room with the comforting sound of sawing logs. As a responsible husband, he had miraculously turned up when she needed him most. She'd recognize those dusty work boots hanging off the end of the queen-sized mattress anywhere.

Sprawled across the bedspread wearing filthy work clothes, he had pulled a pillow over his face. "Hey, glad you're back," she said as loud as possible, hoping to wake him. *After her sleepless night and what he had put her through, he had the audacity to sleep? Well sleep wasn't going to happen until she straightened out a few things.*

"Hey," he moaned. "I'm so tired. Sorry, hon. I'm really sorry but I need to take a nap. This job is going to kill me; totally wiped out. Can we eat later?"

"Eat? Who said anything about food?" *Do people learn to be arsonists or are they born to burn things down?* At that moment, the fire in her heart felt like exploding into a pyrotechnic extravaganza that would be the envy of a Chinese firecracker factory, and unlike anything, John had ever witnessed. One moment he vows to leave forever, the next he acts as if he has amnesia? "I'd love to snooze right along with you, but we have a serious problem. Wake up," she shouted, gently pummeling his chest with tiny fists.

"Ouch. Would you stop it? I already said I'm sorry."

Men can be so infuriating. "John!"

He pushed the pillow aside, mumbling "What? I hope this is important." He sat up, squinting and angry. A sunburned face seemed to accentuate the bagginess under drooping eyes. His haggard face appeared more tired than she remembered in twenty years.

"It's Lani. She took off with that Peter fellow—which wouldn't be that bad, except his brother's in a gang."

He rubbed his eyes and brushed some wayward locks from his forehead. "Didn't she say she loves him?"

Penny nodded, crossing her arms in front of her body. "But listen to this: your sister called and told me that his brother's in a motorcycle gang and sells girls into prostitution." She waited for him to speak and watched him squinting at the light. The refrigerator hummed in the background.

"How would my sister know anything about that?" Slowly, he formed words and Penny could tell he needed coffee before he could have a decent conversation. She went to the small kitch-enette and put water in the glass carafe.

"I'm making you a pot of coffee because you have to be awake."

"You told me about guilt by association. It doesn't mean Peter's involved in any of it. You're the one who taught me about how people should not judge one person by another person's actions just because they know each other or are related. My sheltered sister Betsy has never seen a pros-titute in her life. My sister said this stuff? She's like the oldest virgin in California." He blinked and rubbed his eyes again, smiling inwardly at the idea that his prudish sister enjoyed playing detective.

Meanwhile Penny, though tired herself, seemed animated and full of energy. His com-ments relaxed her, making her feel less nervous. The simple act of having John there, to discuss these delicate issues, made her feel better. As far as Aunt Betsy went, she had never thought of his sister's sex life. Ever.

A vision of Aunt Betsy pole dancing in a tight-fitting corset flashed in her mind's eye. "Thinking that she's **not** a virgin is hilarious, but can we not dispute Aunt Betsy's racy or boring past?" she asked with a smile. "And let's not get off topic. You know how easily I get distracted. Anyway, it's not Aunt Betsy you should be worrying about—it's the cops, John. The cops are digging into this stuff while Peter and Lani are heading here to Vegas. You'd have to be a moron not to know that selling sex and women into 'the business' is huge around here." She lifted her arms and put quote marks into the air when saying 'the business.' Remember those girls we saw being arrested on the sidewalk in front of the Magic Carpet?"

"Of course, but I still don't see what that has to do with our Lani."

"John, it's like an epidemic and it's all over the place. Once you notice it, you'll see it everywhere. Even my work isn't what I thought."

"Huh?"

Penny rolled her eyes. She sat on the bed, her fingers traced the pattern of stitches on the coverlet. "Found out my murals aren't for a fancy hotel, but for a deluxe chicken ranch." A loud, defeated sigh escaped her lips.

John chuckled. "You're not serious?"

"Don't laugh. Yes, I'm serious. Remember Mirage? That girl we rescued on our Anniversary during the desert flood?"

"Is she a hooker?"

She couldn't blame John for snickering. Normally it would be somewhat funny. Normally, they'd share a laugh and crack silly jokes about 'working girls' or massage parlors; but this felt entirely too close to home. All of a sudden, nothing seemed normal. "No thankfully she's not. Right now, she's only the receptionist, and she told me everything." *John's question suddenly made her wonder.* "Who knows? Maybe someday she'll get a promotion and be Madam Mirage. It does have a nice ring to it."

Yawning, he kept asking himself whether he had missed something. *He couldn't grasp why Lani's own mother thought their sweet, innocent daughter had anything to do with streetwalkers.* "Whoa, that's the second coincidence I've heard about today."

"John, this is not just a coincidence, this is horrible. We need to do something." She went to fill a cup and handed it to her tired husband. "Black coffee on an empty stomach will wake you up."

Sipping on the hot liquid, he appeared dizzy and lost. She felt like a salesperson waiting for a buying sign from a prospect, needing his commitment and wanting him to understand the severity of the situation. "We will, we will do something," he said, but to her it sounded like empty platitudes. "Are you still mad at me for leaving?"

She felt enraged at something—almost everything—but it wasn't John. She scooted closer and put an arm around his neck. "No, my handsome knight, I knew you'd be back." Gray hair at his temples and creases around his eyes only made him look more distinguished than ever. "I love you, but don't do that again or I'll have to do something drastic."

"Murder?"

"No, I probably wouldn't go that extreme, but only because you've had my back for a long time. There's something to be said for consistency." She snuggled closer, aware of sawdust and sweat.

He returned the embrace and gave her a weak kiss on the cheek. "Penny, I can't live without you."

"I know that, silly," She forced a smile, keeping in mind that they were both in huge trouble, but glad that he would be on her team during difficult times. "So, what's the other coincidence?"

"Guy called Mac." He finished the coffee and set the cup on the nightstand. "Remember Father Charles at the church?"

"Still Scottish, I suppose?" She tried mimicking the pastor's brogue.

"Hey, you told me that's disrespectful."

"Sorry. What about him?"

I spent a lot of time over there last night. By the way, they have the worst coffee at that church. Anyway, he introduced me to another priest called Mac who used to fly helicopters in Hawaii."

Bewildered, Penny shook her head from side to side in disbelief, staring into John's eyes before breaking into raucous laughter. "A priest? No way, it has to be another Mac."

Chapter 25

She had sketched the large design of Bacchus and now began to paint from the ceiling on down. The largest of all the murals, she wanted to make sure it stayed memorable, so she could take a good photo of it, and apply for a job at a respectable place. The idea that her work would remain on the walls of a house of ill repute, no matter how stately and glamorous, tarnished her earlier enthusiasm. Right now, she knew they owned her. Making any hasty moves would give her nightmares about the future. For now, she maintained a calm exterior and she had to keep showing her passion for art. *No one she associated with would be doing tricks off Fremont Street for a sleazy pimp, especially not her Lani.*

Ravel blared through the newly installed wireless speakers while she teetered on a twelve-foot ladder. Approaching footsteps reminded her she needed to ask Ray for some sort of flexible scaffolding system, but the repetitive cadence of the music drowned out the squeaky steps of Julian in his kidskin, Italian slippers. He stood beneath her, clearing his tobacco infused throat, holding a stinky cigar.

Looking down, Penny observed his gray, balding head. He swung his cigar around, using it to point at things while speaking, keeping his other pudgy hand on wide haunches. "I love the Bacchus guy. Reminds me of me," he said with a grin, noting the flabby belly and bushy eyebrows. "Great, this is just great. The fairies feeding him grapes are terrific, but those nymphs in the fountain are covered by too many splashes and vines." He stabbed the air in front of an image of a voluptuous blonde who appeared to be reaching for a turquoise colored towel. "Can you show us more of her ass?" Enthralled and clearly impressed, he chortled with amusement, but still managed to be critical.

Penny sighed, blowing bangs off her forehead. One hand held a paint brush, and another held the ladder. The music swelled to a crescendo, "Of course, no problem," she replied, thinking that

Bolero had to be the most annoying music on the planet. On and on, the notes of the rhythmic, classical piece thumped repetitively. Sensually drumming and weaving throughout the long hallways, the music filled the gigantic echoing spaces with sound, competing with what Penny thought of as the much more pleasant sound of hammers, drills and saws in the background.

"Good," Julian nodded, perhaps thinking about how the quicker she finished this room, the faster he could begin making some profit. "At least we can fill this room with furniture. Maybe they can deliver most of it Friday."

She took a few steps down the ladder and looked at her work. Not wanting to suffer any strange or painful consequences, she had to be honest. "Actually, I thought maybe the middle of next week. I want it to be perfect."

"Very well," he said with a cough. "Carry on," he added with a small wave before leaving the room. "Don't forget to add more skin."

The word 'more' reminded her of her days at the newspaper where they always wanted more. More white space or more contrast all in an effort to make more money. Her cell phone rang. "Mrs. Murray?"

"Yes."

"Police from California-we're working on Lani's case."

Trying to remain cool, she couldn't help being defensive. "She has a case? My daughter didn't do anything. Is she all right?"

"Truth is, we don't know. Her friend Peter's brother, is in a gang that trades girls for drugs. Have you ever heard of human trafficking?"

"Of course, I'm living in Vegas, but... I can't imagine my daughter being involved with anything like that," she said with a confident, firm tone to her voice. Suddenly she became aware the music had changed to something softer, and her voice carried around the massive, empty room.

"Your daughter told her Aunt Betsy, that the two of them—Lani and Peter—were going to Vegas. That town happens to be a mecca for prostitution, because there are areas nearby where the sex trade is legal. Once she's given drugs and loses her inhibitions, it doesn't take much to portray a lavish lifestyle."

"Forty-eight hours?"

"So, you *do* know about this?"

"Betsy told me what your department or rather some detective told her. I didn't realize the problem is so immense," she hollered over a new and equally annoying piece of modern, classical music.

The officer must have felt sorry for her because he began to give her a mini-course on local trafficking 101, while she stood, near the top of the ladder. "Unfortunately, it's huge. Weekly, thousands of girls apply to the legal places I just mentioned, near Pahrump. Those "ranches" promise six-figure incomes, medical insurance and free meals. Unfortunately, it's a legitimate business. They get lured in and from what I've heard, it's hard work trying to please all the paying customers. Some girls like the benefits and try to sock away the pay, but it's not that easy. These aren't great circumstances due to illegal drugs, alcohol and violence. Not to mention, the possibility of disease; once they get seriously sick, they're out. I'm sure you can imagine, these Johns, don't waste time transporting any of the girls to chemo or rehab."

"The ones that don't get hired have the crazy notion they'll work on their own with a pimp. How old is Lani again? Ma'am?" He noticed silence on the other end of the phone as Penny listened to the officer's horrific synopsis. "We try and do everything we can, but it's an uphill battle."

"By the way," he continued, "Some of these whorehouses also try passing themselves off as massage parlors or spas." Between the static and the loud classical music, she had trouble hearing his voice. Her mind had drifted into a mother's worst nightmare. Gripping the ladder, she looked at her red knuckles and clung to the hope that all of this was a cruel joke or some colossal, low class prank.

"Excuse me?" She asked, her voice thinning out and her hand trembling. She needed the name of this officer. "Hello? I'm standing on a ladder, painting a mural and sometimes your voice cuts out. Hello?"

She attempted to increase the volume, but the phone slipped from her fingers, crashing to the stone floor. The smashing sound mingled with the irritating blare of symphonic cymbals blasting from the speakers. Her phone shattered as if she had forcibly pushed a porcelain doll onto marble. After stepping down from the ladder, she picked up the plastic fragments and thought about the next forty-eight hours. Lani can't come to Vegas. Penny had forty-eight hours to do something before her sweet daughter would be brainwashed into selling her body and losing her soul.

Chapter 26

Like a peppermint filled herb garden, his warm minty breath invited her in, luring her deep beyond his lips. He flicked his tongue against her teeth, filling her nerve-endings with desire. He teased and played with her gasping mouth with artful kisses while massaging her shoulders.

"Lani," he murmured as he moved to her earlobe. "I've never felt like this about anyone," Pete whispered.

Panting as if she had run around the block, she finally took a deep breath and said, "I know." *Moments earlier she had felt cold, but now heat coursed through her veins, burning circles onto her cheeks. So, this–might be the critical moment she had held back from—during all her tempting, teenage years? This heated entanglement, could be the magic moment, surpassing all those long forgotten make out sessions at high school dances, prom and after school football games? This could be that big-cherry popping, fireworks storm her mother had warned her about so many times?*

Mom had told her it didn't feel right without love. She had said that all the hottest sex in the world wasn't worth a cold, empty bed in the morning. Her head filled with stories about the birds and the bees and weird movies from sex-Ed class. When Peter unhooked her bra, a tingle shot through her legs giving her goosebumps. He yanked her shirt off and stuck his face into the right brassiere cup, inhaling her fragrance before hooking the bra over his head like a necklace. He then returned to burying his head between her small shapely breasts. "Oh Peter," she moaned. "I think I love you."

Peter pulled his head back and looked straight into Lani's beautiful, hazel eyes. The gold hair on the top of his head had a military-type, short style. One piece however, stood up straight, giving him a roguish, naughty look. Lani inhaled and squeezed one hefty bicep before pulling him back to her bare, heaving chest. *So much man to cover in one afternoon,* she thought, enjoying every second. Continuously kissing his neck, she planned to work her way back up to his luscious lips when he replied. "I love you too. I'm crazy about you. Will you marry me?"

Soft rock emanated from the radio and Lani didn't quite catch the muffled words. Or maybe she did, but she didn't want to hear them. They were having fun. Why did he want to go and ruin the moment? Did he really ask? She pulled away wiping spittle from her lips. "Huh?"

"I said, 'Will you marry me?'"

That's what she thought he had said. Lani sat up straight; straighter than a Marine in basic training. She grabbed her tee shirt, placing it in front of her chest like a shield. She pushed him away and a tear rolled down her face. "That's not funny. Don't make stupid jokes right now. I don't know much about sex, but I think you just killed the mood."

He looked up at the ceiling and tried pulling her close, but he could tell she seemed upset and angry. "Lani, I wasn't joking. I'm serious."

"Are you? My mom told me about guys who say things like that, for the sole purpose of getting lucky. I'm not ready to travel down that road. Not yet anyway. I thought we were having a good time." *Love made people say, and do, the craziest things.* "You already know how I feel. Maybe I'm not strong enough to deal with all of this yet."

"But we are." He grabbed a hold of one of her hands and held it tight. "I joined the Navy, almost finished college, and now, all I have to do is find a full-time job. If you'll have me, I want to give you my heart forever." He pulled her bra off his head and threw it on the bed. Then he took one of her hands, placing it above his muscular abs, where she felt the rhythmic pounding deep within. "We don't have to have sex if that makes a difference. I want you Lani, to be my other half."

Pete had a sensitive disposition. Even Lani could see that his heart ached when she pulled her hand away. "I'm getting dressed," she sobbed. His facial features looked horrified. He hated seeing the love of his life splashing tears onto the couch.

"You can't even afford a ring," she said, feeling *hopelessly in over her head. He was so tender with her and always nice, not to mention intensely good looking.* "Why does life have to be so difficult?"

"It's not, when we're together." He stood up, grabbed his shirt and pulled it over his head. "I love you and I mean it. Whether I ask you once more or a hundred times, I hope you will some-day tell me yes. No matter how long it takes, I will prove my love. But, if the answer will always be no, then maybe we shouldn't see each other anymore, because it will definitely destroy my heart."

Lani went to the window and looked outside not knowing what to say to this gorgeous man, who usually made her smile. He knew so much, about so many things.

Peter came up behind her and put his arms around her waist.

"Well, on second thought, I'll take a chance," he whispered. "Like a lime-green praying man-tis standing alone on the side of a whitewashed house. He's banking on making it home, where his true love awaits. Meanwhile, he hopes the California Gnatcatcher won't swoop down from the sky and make him lunch." Peter imitated the cadence of a sports announcer, trying to make her smile. "Does he score? What are the odds, will he make it? In other words, I'm asking again." Placing his head above hers, their eyes looked outside, past the trees. A rumbling noise approached. "Will you do me the honor of marrying me? Or at least turn around so I can get on my knees or something?"

The thundering roar of two motorcycles sped down the street and turned into the driveway. Tyler knew his mom wasn't home and he decided to have an impromptu party with some of his gang member friends. Three more Harleys with girls riding on the back, parked in front of the garage. Flashes of leather, denim and bandanas mixed in the haze of smoky exhaust fumes. The reverberating sound of the engines shook the walls of the house.

Excited hollering filled the street. Peter knew he had to get Lani out of there, and he had to do it fast. "We gotta go," he said, grabbing his shoes. "My brother's here."

Lani turned to give him a quick kiss. Her head bobbed up and down with an affirmative answer, while she searched for the right words. "But wait. I will, I will Peter. You know I love you. I will marry you, but don't compare yourself to a praying mantis. Didn't you learn anything in biology class?"

"What?"

"She eats him while they make love."

"Wow, promise me you won't do that," he said with a straight face.

Peter pulled her into the hallway and out the kitchen door to the backyard. They escaped through a side gate leading to the park. His fine-looking face showed not only fear, but also anger. Lani *wondered what had scared Peter more: his brother and his dangerous friends or her comment about the praying mantis.*

Chapter 27

Penny ran to the front and asked Mirage if she could make a call. Holding up a piece of broken cell phone, her face portrayed a crooked smile. "Here, no problem," Mirage handed her the receiver and accepted the damaged bent metal. An audible clunk meant the phone now rested in the bottom of a trash can.

Penny tapped her toes and waited for John to answer. After what seemed like twenty rings, he yelled into the phone and didn't sound happy about receiving a call. "What's up? I'm balancing on a beam–high above the Strip—on the sixtieth floor. It's like a windstorm up here. Can this wait until I get home?"

She looked around, realizing she couldn't talk openly, while at work. "I had to tell you that I dropped my phone and it broke. Can we meet at that church tonight?"

"Sure, what's up? Another confession?"

She heard a snicker. *A little humor might save them,* she thought. "Very funny, this is much worse. Right now, I'm going to leave work to run a few errands. I also need to get a new phone. Don't worry, I'm fine, but say a prayer."

"I can get there about six."

"All right, love you."

"Me too."

She handed the phone back to Mirage and asked her to call a cab. Her first stop was at a bank. Finally, under extreme circumstances, she had mustered up the courage to get the money from Dan's safe deposit box. Whoever said that desperate times called for desperate measures, must have had a daughter. The time had come full circle, or perhaps Dan's evil curse had come to fruition. She'd soon find out. The crumpled yellow envelope at the bottom of her purse held the magic key she needed for saving Lani.

What she imagined would take hours, only took fifteen minutes with the bank manager and some signatures. First, she inhaled and produced two forms of identification. What she had thought of as bogus, became reality when she opened the box. After transferring the huge amount into a personal account, they treated her like royalty. They offered her mints, free checking and a nice pen. After all, in Vegas they have banking down to a science. Now she had plenty of money. She planned to rescue her daughter at any cost. *Miraculously rich beyond her wildest dreams, the incomprehensible idea of having money, would take days, maybe weeks to absorb. But at this moment, she could only think of her child's future.*

After the transferring of funds, she also took care of the mortgage on the house. This took longer and required a massive amount of paperwork. When done, she exhaled a huge sigh of relief. Her knees shook. A padded chair near the exit offered comfort. For a few minutes, she relaxed while considering her next steps. She mumbled a prayer of gratitude while asking for guidance, madly stuffing the paperwork into her purse. *John will be thrilled, she thought.*

Fortunately, the mobile phone store sat a stone's throw from the bank. She glanced at her watch before noticing a line snaked around a central display. Once she reached the front, a lethargic representative acted as if time consisted of gelatin.

Sloth-like but clean, he explained all the fancy new features and benefits of the latest model phones. All right, all right, she wanted to yell. She understood that it came with everything except running water. Her only desire centered on keeping her old number and her California area code. In her mind, these seemed to be small details, but for some reason, these two very important things tripped him up, making him appear confused.

Then he had a problem with her brand-new bank-check. The blank checks were all she had in her wallet and would be the only way she could pay for her new phone. Though she had an ATM card attached to their family savings account, one with an excruciatingly low balance, she didn't even think of transferring money from one account to another.

This money from Dan had a purpose. It couldn't mingle with regular money. She needed to use it to save Lani. As far as their regular credit cards, they had shredded those back when John had lost his job.

What should have taken an hour at the most, took almost three hours. 'Nathan', it said, on a shiny gleaming name tag that matched the gel on his head and the diamond stud in his ear. Maybe she'd give him a bad online review as in: 'Hey everyone in Vegas: Make sure to avoid Nathan, unless you have all bleeping day!' But of course, not being vindictive, she wouldn't do that, and since he had a decent job at a nice store, the manager must believe in him. The manager believed her anyway, and authorized the payment. *Slow ineptitude is not a crime or a sin.* By the time she left the store, she felt sorry for Nathan.

Calm down, she told herself, after hailing another cab. First, she needed to formulate a plan. *Breathe.* She pulled up the online yellow pages searching for Ron and Tina Parrish in Henderson, Nevada. Bam–the name came up immediately. There, they were, residing on Rose St. Tina answered on the first ring. "Tina, it's Penny. How are you and Ron?"

She listened to Tina squeal at the sound of her voice. Then Tina went into a long litany of medical problems the two of them had suffered throughout the years. Tina filled her in on the indelicate parts of getting older, including details she didn't want to hear. Ron not only needed physical therapy and all kinds of medication, but salves for chafing caused by inactivity.

"Basically, we're fine. You remember we had issues with Ron's health last time we met. Don't you?"

"Of course, but that was quite a while ago. Wasn't it gout or something?"

"It started with his feet and then went to his legs. Now it's much worse."

"Are you still at the local paper?"

"No, I got a buyout and Ron retired."

That woman had all the luck, Penny thought. A buyout would have solved so many problems. Probably would have helped keep them in California. Nonetheless, every minute counted towards helping Lani. She had to be quick. "That's great," she said, before realizing she sounded a tad insensitive. "I'm having some trouble too and thought maybe you and Ron can help me out?" She inhaled and continued, "We live in Vegas now and this situation has to do with Lani."

The question hung in the air for a few seconds. "How is our little Godchild?" She heard her name as Tina turned to tell Ron everything. She also heard some sort of game show in the background blaring from the television. Penny's imagination made her envision various categories. '*I'll take Human Trafficking for four hundred dollars, Alex.*'

She sighed, "Not so little anymore," realizing it had been ages since she saw Tina or Ron. Suddenly embarrassed, she felt flustered and hot. "Did I call at a bad time?" Her mind reeling, '*I'll make it a true daily double.*'

"Oh no, not at all—I'm about to throw something into the microwave for dinner, but we're so glad to hear from you and we'd love to help with one of your adventures. Especially if it's a tropical destination," she said, with an insincere sounding laugh.

A grumpy voice yelled, "Speak for yourself, darlin'" but Tina must have motioned for him to shut up. Penny could hear Ron going on about how she almost had both of them killed.

"Never mind him sweetie, you tell us where to meet you and we'll be there, tropics or no tropics. Okay, Hon?"

They were making fun of her and she knew it. Life, she felt, looked like a random game of chance. Sometimes, the game appeared delicate and refined, but that didn't make it any less of a game. Attractive women wear long white gloves and ball gowns to play the game. Tuxedo clad men hold onto cool, slender trophy wives, while ogling the curvaceous, warmhearted hostess. Other times, it's an ugly game of chicken, street racing and dogfights in dark alleys. Sometimes it's the chance one takes crossing a busy street or getting a mammogram. The more she thought about the odds relating to the game of life, the more it haunted her. Everyone knows it's a game of chance when couples marry. There are better chances at a roulette wheel. Sadly, even giving birth is a game of chance. Will the child grow up to be a distinguished Senator or a person addicted to meth? Will they reach his or her entrepreneurial dreams, write poetry, become an oil tycoon with a fleet of yachts or become a brazen prostitute?

The cab drove up to the entrance and the meter kept running. "Sounds good, I know I could count on you to help." She had to stop talking and return to painting. "As far as when, I'm not sure, but I promise to call back." She ended the call and paid the driver. She had to work this out in her head before burdening Tina with details.

Strange how a lovely resort could look so different when it hid behind cunning lies. Even the song birds had conspired by flying off somewhere, replaced by the shrill squawks of yellow-eyed, black-feathered Grackles. Their glossy sheen reminded her of Nathan's hair and the reason she now felt overheated and late.

No, she said to herself, as her mind rambled on about forgiveness. It's not worth holding onto that feeling–let it go. The desert heat felt like an oven after the air-conditioned ride in the taxi. *Poor, poor Nathan, has to live in this hellhole state for the rest of his wretched life.*

Exhausted and worried about Lani, she returned to work as if nothing had happened. But somehow, as she walked through the wrought iron gates and looked around at the Italian cypress trees, it seemed everything had happened. Everything had changed.

Chapter 28

The sun filtered through Peter's bedroom window. This time his brother wasn't there and Lani continued to surf the web on her Smartphone.

Though he didn't want to interrupt her endless scrolling, something important weighed on his mind. "Hey, don't you think you should call your mom and tell her we're coming?"

Lani looked at Peter and smiled. "It's supposed to be a surprise silly. Wouldn't be much of a surprise if I tell her all about it, right?" She went back to her phone, checking her emails and doing searches. "Great, we just received a confirmation from the Polynesian Wedding Chapel. I think mom and dad will be pleased to re-live some of their island memories."

"That's what you're doing online?"

"Well someone has to plan this wedding. Besides, I tried calling mom and it said her phone had been disconnected."

"Lani, check your voicemail. Maybe she tried calling you at the same time. By the way, did you get a call from a detective?"

"I think so, but I deleted it. Figured it had to do with Tyler and I'm not answering anymore questions about your whacked-out brother." She kept staring at her phone, texting, emailing and sending tweets, finally landing on a site advertising wedding gowns and tuxedos. "Ooh this is gorgeous, look at this Pete?" She held the phone an inch from his face.

"Nah, I love you baby but I'm not wearing a tux. Didn't you say it's a Polynesian chapel? How about, I wear a nifty Hawaiian shirt?" He gently pushed the phone away but held onto her other hand. This is a big moment for both of us. I told my parents and they are super happy. Don't you think it's cool that my mom said we could have grandma's ring? Maybe you should at least tell your aunt, so she doesn't freak out."

"Betsy? All she cares about is her stupid dog and her stinky cats. When I'm there, her sole purpose in life is to feed me as if I never eat or some-thing. Maybe she thinks I'm one of her rescued pets."

Peter growled like a young pup and smiled. "Some people equate food with love. I hope you plan on learning to cook someday."

Lani put her phone down and sat next to Peter. Her mom had told her cooking is easy, if there is love. With love everything is possible and even the plainest meals mysteriously tasted gourmet. "Mom used to tell me dad would eat plain baked potatoes with nothing, but salt. She swears he always appreciated every morsel."

"Not even butter?"

"Nope."

Peter rolled his eyes and laughed. "That saintly stuff will only give us regular guys a bad name–which reminds me—we have to get that ring sized."

'With love, life is delicious', her mom used to say when serving her meals. "I think it's super adorable that you're worried about my cooking. Of course, I'll feed you, but in the beginning, you'll have to survive on my juicy wet kisses."

"Juicy wet kisses, huh? Like Bentley? Maybe you *are* like a rescued pet," he returned her kiss, wiping a bit of dribble off his chin.

She pecked his nose, before moving back to his lips, but felt his hand gently pushing her away.

"Wait, this island wedding won't have Elvis impersonators, will it?"

"No," she whispered, but it might have a top-less hula dancer or two."

"Topless?" Peter asked, with a concerned look on his face. He raised an eyebrow hoping this conversation wouldn't end up all about Tyler and his ridiculous friends. The fear that Tyler could ruin their nuptials made him toss and turn all night. Right now, however, he needed to convince Lani to talk to her mother. He loved Lani and couldn't wait to marry her, but this business of not telling her mother, weighed like filled sandbags on his mind.

"I'm hoping for coconut bras. Don't forget we're talking about Sin city."

Chapter 29

John sat in the dimly lit office waiting for Penny. Pictures of the Pope adorned one dark paneled wall, and various celebrities posed with Pastor Charles in a framed collage. Diplomas and letters from the Vatican were matted and hanging in gold-plated frames. A small bookshelf held bibles, religious books and a collection of binders. The chairs were uncomfortable. Without the incredible pictures, the office could have been anywhere.

The battered desk held a large pile of weekly bulletins on one corner. A sliver of desert sunshine slipped under a small curtain-lined window, bathing an exquisite porcelain sculpture of the Sacred Heart of Jesus in vibrant rays of light. It drew John's eyes away from anything else.

"So, you see our work here, in Las Vegas, is never done." Father Charles had given John a brief rundown of his weekly activities which included a lot more than feeding the homeless. In fact, the discussion took him to places he never wanted to go. "Have you seen those topless nuns on Fremont Street?" He asked with a small chuckle. "It's that groundhog story on a never-ending loop."

Befuddled, John looked back at the priest and blushed. He had heard some vague comments about semi-dressed women wearing nun's habits in the old part of Vegas. "You've seen them?"

"Of course," the man of the cloth nodded with a thoughtful expression. "They've been dressing like that for years. One of them brings her kid to our school. She insists it's an honorable way of making a living." He sighed. "She even jokes about how the oldest profession has been around longer than the priesthood. At least she's physically clean and usually wearing some sort of blouse when she makes it over here." The old priest crossed himself and chuckled. "The way she sees it, she has to make a good impression on her clients, because, listen to this, she's afraid artificial intelligence will be replacing...." He shook his head and looked down at his desk. "I'm praying for that day."

The sudden pout on Father Charles and his incomplete statement went right over John's head. "What day?"

"Someday—soon—men will have robots or sexbots. They kiss, cuddle and will be programmed to do just about anything. They will provide pleasure for a fee. The positive side to all of this is that actual women won't have to be involved. AI doesn't have much to do with it. To me anyway, intelligence implies something is cultured and wise, not downright pornographic."

John looked and felt more puzzled than he had a few minutes ago. "That sounds bizarre," he answered, even though he didn't have the foggiest idea what the priest spoke about.

"Yes," the man of the cloth nodded in agreement. "But artificial intelligence, in the form of sexual robots, is the wave of the future. In some places, it's already available. Don't worry, we pray for everyone, but we can't be naïve. Some of my wilder or I should rephrase that, more open-minded, sophisticated churchgoers keep me in the loop. Plus, there are many engineers who attend our parish. They read those scientific journals. Supposedly, men will have the ability to order a programmed, supermodel-looking, detailed, android with various physical, genuine human-looking attributes." When John made a face, Father Charles added, "Personally, I see many positives associated with this technology."

John wanted to gag. "Yuck".

"They'll be able to choose a blonde or brunette with blue eyes…"

Wrinkling his nose at the thought of it all, John interrupted him. "So, you're saying, this could wipe out prostitution and human trafficking?"

"Possibly, but it depends on the outcome of some top-secret scientific trials. I certainly hope they use it for positive applications. They also want to use the robots to save the lives of soldiers in battle. I saw them marching on television. War is never an option, but if necessary, at least a droid is better than losing a human life. Of course, you know our church is aimed at preserving life."

John bobbed his head in agreement but slumped a bit in the uncomfortable chair. *Though he agreed about the soldiers, he wasn't sure how he felt about the sexbots. He felt strange discussing a taboo topic in front of a statue of the sacred heart of Jesus.* "That whole sex thing sounds gross."

Never mind," Father Charles replied with a disgusted look on his face. He shooed the air away with the back of his hand, as if the entire subject represented a big black fly sitting on the feces of life. "Anyway, I can't talk sense into most parishioners working on Fremont, but we have a team that doesn't wear clerical collars and they work on saving those souls. It's not easy, but we've made some progress," he smiled.

"In fact, that woman, the pretend nun, just this week, found another job. I was delighted to hear that she promises to attend our support groups. One of our teachers, Sister Josefina just asked the children in class, what their parents did for a living. John, you'd be amazed at the little things that make a difference."

John looked relieved when Penny rushed through the door. Later, he told her that most of the conversation had made him nauseous. "Sorry I'm late. Hello Father." She sat on a metal chair next to John and grabbed one of his hands hoping she could calm him. His defeated posture and deep breathing made her wonder what had gone on before she arrived.

"Your husband mentioned you had a fight. From what I can tell, this man is crazy about you, Miss Penny."

Penny swallowed, looking around at the pictures on the wall and back at Father Charles. "Yes, yes," she said while nodding. "But that's not why we're here." Tightening her hold, she grasped John's fingers in what some would describe as a death grip.

John looked confused. "But I thought...."

"No John, listen. Let me talk." She inhaled deeply and began to talk about Lani being involved with a gang. John looked at her as if she had lost her mind.

"What?"

"For goodness sakes, just listen to me. This is a matter of life and death. Father Charles, we need your help." She squeezed John's rough fingers harder. After decades together, he had a pretty *good notion that she was as serious as a myocardial infarction. Or more like his dad's coronary thrombosis? Either way, the blood supply to the heart is cut off like the blood supply in his throbbing fingers.*

Her eyes darted back and forth, trying to look into both of their faces, as she continued her story. "That boy Peter, the one she likes, his brother, is into finding young women. He sells them to brothel owners in Pahrump, where prostitution is legal. If the place isn't hiring, then he sells the girls to pimps. John, I have already told you the place I'm working won't be a spa hotel. There's a lot more to it, but I'm concerned about Lani. She's on her way to Vegas and I heard it only takes forty-eight hours."

"Forty-eight hours for what?" her bewildered husband asked. He wanted to rub life back into his numb, red fingertips, but his subdued eyes drifted back to the sculpture that seemed to thump along with the bleeding organ inside his chest. Penny had been acting strange lately and right now, she had started a scene that looked like it might end up being a train wreck. "Do you think that Peter...?"

Father Charles held up a hand to answer his first question. "It takes forty-eight hours before a young woman is introduced to facilitators who run a circuit of girls into the business they call 'the lifestyle'." When he said the words, 'the lifestyle', the priest made quote marks in the air.

"Yes," Penny exhaled as if she had blown up a giant balloon. Tears rolled down her face and she squeezed John's fingers even harder. "We have to do something John. The police won't do anything if a girl is over eighteen."

Father Charles nodded. "That's true. They assume girls over eighteen are participating in consensual relationships. Why don't you two wait a moment, while I introduce you to someone who can help? We have a task force headed up by our own Brother Mac. I'll get him to talk to you, and while I can't promise anything, I firmly believe he's performed a few miracles lately."

Chapter 30

When Father Charles left his office to summon Brother Mac, Penny turned to John. She reached for his other hand, so she could hold both tightly. "John? Look at me." Shaken by her words, he slowly faced his wife. "Do you remember when I told you I had a dream about us changing the world?" *He stared into the twinkling eyes and wondered why sometimes, perhaps not as often as in the earlier years, she seemed to be from another planet. What used to be dreams and a wild imagination he thought, could be morphing into dementia.*

Under her alien-like spell, he blinked and nodded. What was she doing? His face looked overwhelmed and his slouching posture made him look beaten. As a carpenter, he thought of himself as a simple, uncomplicated man. These types of things were too much for him to handle. Carl, Penny's dad used to tell him that he could learn something new as soon as he forgot something old. No wonder men like his dad used to carry white handkerchiefs, he thought, looking around for a way to surrender. Though Penny could handle almost everything, he knew that if things were too bizarre, at the very least, he had the faith and fortitude to offer his troubles to the Lord.

"Well it's time to change the world, right now," she continued. "It's our destiny and I'm glad we have each other because it won't be easy." The door opened and a man wearing a black shirt with a white clerical collar stood next to the desk. Though the buzz cut had turned a flashy shade of silver, he had a facial scar Penny would never forget. "Brother Mac?" Her mouth wouldn't close. It hung surprised and in open shock like an unhinged, broken barn door flapping in a storm. In a skeptical tone, she asked, "Aren't you a helicopter pilot or wait," she blinked several times in disbelief, "aren't you supposed to be in jail?"

When she said the word jail, she pulled her hand away from John and clasped it over her own mouth. "Whoops, sorry," the words came out and she wrinkled her nose and cringed.

John nodded, grunting towards the man, glad to have the circulation back in his fingers.

Mac smiled, shook his head and pulled up another folding chair. "I served my time, got out early for good behavior and then I signed up for the seminary. Trust me when I say they need all the hands they can get. Believe it or not, if my Irish luck holds out, I'll be ordained in two months. Right now, I'm Brother Mac Downey, but soon I'll be Father Mac. Sorry, but what's your name again?"

"I'm Penny and this is my husband John."

"Penny. Oh, man. This is where I'd usually cuss up a squall about stuff in the past. Thank God I'm rehabilitated and remorseful." He looked up at the ceiling as if listening to a reprimand from the Almighty before greeting Penny with a handshake. "I remember you as the girl I left on the forbidden island of Niihau. By the way, you look the same. I was genuinely sorry and I'm still sorry."

"Oh, forget it, that was over twenty years ago." The evolution of time had morphed her current problem into something disproportionate, compared to the insignificance of being set down on a gorgeous, albeit forbidden island. Like kumquats and oranges or a wombat going into battle with a tyrannosaurus rex. The past didn't compare with her moment.

"Guess if God forgives you then I can too." She couldn't believe her ears, or her eyes and her emotions flowed around in her body making her movements erratic, as she gesticulated with her arms. Once again, she clasped John's aching fingers. "Not sure how you can help us. Our daughter is a runaway and I'm worried she might get into the wrong hands."

"Wow, forgive me for saying this sounds like Karma. I sure hope I can help." Concern crossed over his face and he took a deep breath. "I head up a task force for human trafficking. Law enforcement has a good group of officers who work independently on the same problem and they recently received some funding." He scratched his head as if thinking about what to say. "There are many different groups headed up by lawyers and another one spearheaded by a famous actor. Every group is making some headway, but it's a complicated, hot mess. While the groups are all on the same page, I'm sad to say, not everyone being rescued wants to be saved."

Penny squeezed John's fingers harder while Brother Mac continued.

"Unfortunately, we only have five unpaid volunteers. Even with five of us, we're making some inroads. The volunteers try to get me in front of the girls for ten minutes. If I can talk to them for ten minutes, I might be able to change their minds. I remind each girl that there is a real family here that cares. We provide counseling and make sure they are placed in either a group home or some sort of safe environment. Building back their confidence is important. It's an uphill battle, but without a huge support staff.... I'm sure you understand that most of the church contributions go to feeding our large homeless population. It boils down to priorities."

Penny thought about her own priorities and then her memory flashed to the Bulgarian girls she had met in Ray's limo. "What if they don't understand you?"

"You mean because they are on crack?"

"No," she replied sounding exasperated. "I mean don't some of them come from other countries?"

"We have translators who speak almost every language, in our database." Pointing at the bookshelf he said, "Good thing there are computers these days because Father Charles would have me log everything into his binders." He had a kind smile and could tell that Penny still felt flustered about asking about his prison term. "But your daughter speaks English, right?"

"Of course, but I've met some girls in town...." *She didn't want to talk too much about her work, because it could open a new can of rotten anchovies. Julian and Ray, she suspected wouldn't treat her too kindly if she spilled the beans on their operation. They'd kick her to the curb and in a heart-stopping instant; they'd send her packing, right out of the luxury high-rise. She thought of the seedy rooms at the Magic Carpet motel and though she had never seen the rooms inside, she imagined they came with a plethora of critters in various sizes. At this point, she needed to focus on Lani anyway.*

"Can anything be done? How can we stop this crisis? How much would it cost?" She fired off staccato questions like encapsulated bullets.

"Fixing the crisis itself, would cost more money than there is in this town, maybe the world. We need more shelters, safe houses, billboards, transportation, beds and of course more counselors. But don't worry; I intend to find your daughter."

Stubborn and empowered, she let go of John and pulled out her new checkbook. "How much?"

Mac smirked. "Miss Penny," he glanced over at the wax-like statue of John for male support, but the tender-faced husband had fallen into an intense trance by continuously staring at the Sacred Heart sculpture. *At least he appeared to be breathing, thought Mac, who wondered if the guy might be praying.* "Eight million dollars wouldn't put a dent in this. It's a world crisis. Regrettably, Vegas is a rather large part of it."

"I can see that. Would a million help?"

She began to fill in the lines on the check. Now Mac lost the hinges on his jaw. He watched her delicate hand quiver as she signed a check to the church. "Can I have a receipt?" she asked, handing it to Mac.

John felt like he had somehow become a mute button. What could he add to this entire discussion? What could he say? Focused on the piece of marble decorated with ribbon and faux drops of stone cold blood, he silently murmured continuous, repetitive prayers under his shallow breath. Some of the prayers were for Lani, but most of them centered on the sanity of his wife.

"I'll ask Father Charles," Mac answered in slow motion, as he stood to exit the office."

Chapter 31

John appeared to be meditating. His eyes were closed, but he felt Penny's hand reach for his arm. Anger from the other night had left him paralyzed. He racked his brain trying to recall the amount of her long-lost pilot's gift. "So now we're broke again, right?" He asked in a monotone voice. *Life, breath and every human emotion, he felt, had been slurped from his soul by an industrial vacuum. When she squeezed his forearm, he felt like a hollow man; irrelevant, unimportant and empty.* When she leaned over to give him a kiss on the cheek, he opened his eyes.

"Not quite," she answered, "but isn't that what you wanted?"

"Not exactly, you'd have to be crazy to give them everything." His gaze darted from the sculpture of the Sacred Heart to Penny's flashing green eyes.

She nodded. "I know you're right, but we're talking about our Lani. I should have offered more."

Biting his lip, and trying not to look surprised, he asked, "We have more?" He took a deep breath, as if preparing to dive into a giant pool, before returning her kiss. Though he loved his wife, and never expected a landfall of money, the kisses felt bitter. The unknown wealth a short-lived fantasy, now doused by the fact that he worked in Las Vegas, a city filled with the hype of unattainable riches. She must have thought he didn't want an answer. Maybe she thought it rhetorical, and she felt his question seemed unimportant. Annoyed, he asked a different type of question. "What does it feel like to write a million-dollar check?"

"I didn't give it much thought. Dirty money anyway," she rationalized. "We're fighting fire with fire. Besides, by donating it to the church we get out of paying enormous taxes. These people can help us. If they can't, well at least we'll have some money tucked away for other options. Don't worry," she patted his arm. "You'll love this. I called our mortgage company from the bank manager's phone and wired them money to pay off the house."

"Seriously?" He shook his head in disbelief. The flames surrounding the heart in the sculpture were made of stone, and yet, he felt a warm feeling of relief in his chest. "My magical wife does it again. You are a genius."

"Awe, don't forget, this dude was eaten by ants. Maybe we should pray for his miserable soul?"

"Probably a good idea," he said, sounding cheerier. "What was the guy's name? Captain something?"

"Just say Dan. God will know who you're talking about."

Then he bent near her ear and whispered, "Which reminds me…don't forget, this Mac guy let you down once before."

"He's older now. Look at him—three months from now—he'll be a full-blown priest. I think we're safe."

"You know I love you." A ton of bricks fell off his back and John felt free at last. With a paid off mortgage, he felt free to smile and to share sweeter kisses. A giant burden lifted, like a wooden cross returning to dust. Love had never left him, but an abundance of it came flowing into his body, filling the hollow man from head to toe with joy and gratitude.

When Father Charles and Mac returned to the office, they stopped to watch Penny and John who were smooching like teenagers.

Father Charles cleared his throat before speaking. "Mac, I see you're getting better at marriage counseling. Good job." He winked and sat down at his desk. Amused, he watched Penny wipe her pink lipstick off John's face. "Your generous gift is much appreciated, and Mac will supply you with an itemized accounting of everything he needs."

Penny shuffled her feet, straightening up in the metal chair. "Can we find Lani before it's too late?"

"That's what we intend to do," Mac answered. "The generous funds you gave us might be able to stop planes before they get to McCarran. Most flights from California don't have Air Marshals anymore, but we'll be checking all passenger lists, hotels, buses and even the gas stations. It takes a little bit of undercover work and espionage, but in your case, we have to act fast. Unfortunately, and this is a hard pill to swallow, there's a support structure in place such as facilitators who encourage and pay off traffickers within the legal system."

"How do they get away with it?" John asked, with a revolting look and what felt like the beginning of a stomach ache. Today, he had learned more than he had ever planned on knowing about the raunchier underbelly of greed. Today, he had learned why he couldn't survive a minute without God and a day without his brilliant wife who wanted to save Lani from disgusting traffickers. That evening, right there, midst all the typical day-to-day highs and lows of life and marriage, he surrendered everything in his soul to the Sacred Heart of Jesus.

"John, the obvious answer is that it brings in tourist dollars. There's a longer much more depressing answer, but that will only make you mad. Let's concentrate on finding your daughter."

Chapter 32

The following evening in the quiet of the limo, the bustle along Flamingo Road seemed miles away. During the short-lived silence, Penny could think about how seconds were turning into hours. She had to help Lani as soon as possible but felt like a fly caught in a giant web. How would she extricate herself from Ray and Julian long enough for them not to notice? What would be the consequences she'd have to face if they found out that she knew about their operation? Peter's brother had to be involved with the same group.

The obnoxious ringtone on Ray's phone made her think of out of tune salsa music played by drunken mariachis. When someone called, Ray dived on the whistles and castanets before the call slipped into voicemail. Though loud and irritating, it had one benefit. The ringtone reminded

Penny of the exact opposite, that these moments in her life had nothing to do with a party. These were serious times, and when the music stopped, her heart felt like it had stopped as well. She imagined Ray standing above her, ready to swat her like a fly. Instead of his cell phone, he'd have a giant flyswatter in his hand. Let him zap her like a bug. Her baby came first.

Penny watched the the neon lights flicker along the crowded Strip. Buses and cabs advertised a gentlemen's revue with scantily dressed dancers as they passed naked Greco-Roman sculptures and lit-up fountains. Everything in Vegas seemed over the top, excessive and sexually suggestive. Though it never seemed to bother her before, the last few days had made her feel old-fashioned, prudish and suddenly, over the hill. On top of everything, the last few hours were making her physically sick.

Ray spoke into his cellphone, "Julian, I meant to tell you about the flight from California." Penny didn't mean to eavesdrop, but a few things caught her attention. "I'll stop at McCarran around one thirty." *Another fuselage full of young, hot women were landing and coming to* work at *Julian's devil inspired spa?* She wanted to scream, but swallowed her anger and tapped her practical, short-clipped nails on the leather-upholstered door.

She needed to call Mac to tell him about that flight. Her stomach lurched when the driver came to a sudden stop, making her fall forward. A tourist had run in front of the limo and the jolt brought Ray's head close to Penny's face. She wanted to gag after inhaling his Italian after-shave and thought it anything but sexy. *She imagined the lurid ads for that particular men's fragrance were splashed with photos of mating buffalos.* "Sure," he said into the phone before disconnecting his call and grinning at Penny like some sort of animal about to pounce on his dinner.

"What?" Penny asked. To be on the safe side, she smiled back, but rolled her eyes like Lani did, when things were unexplainable. She watched him reach into a pocket for a small tin of mints.

He looked her up and down. "Just you doll face—you're adorable. I bet you hear that all the time. Do you know you have blue paint on your knee?"

She *shrugged, knowing she had paint on her shoes and in her hair too. Made her wonder why he stole good lines from nineteen forties movies and made them sound lame. Seriously, doll face?*

He held out the tin after popping one into his mouth. "Want one?"

"No, thanks." Though he had thick dark hair and high cheekbones, his demeanor and personality negated any trace of what most women would consider good looks. It went beyond the regular bad boy swagger, as if he had practiced for a part as a classic gangster, the ones in gray suits, filmed before the invention of Technicolor.

He tucked the metallic container back into his pocket and reached a hand toward her knees. "I'd like to take you home and play with you. Maybe help wash the paint off." When his fingers brushed her flesh, Penny gently pushed him back to his side of the coach. He stuck an index finger in his mouth and moaned in a suggestive manner. "Delicious."

Though goose bumps appeared along her legs and arms, she had the confidence of maturity on her side. *He'd be surprised to know she could almost be old enough to be his mother.* "Stick to

those younger girls, Ray. I'm one of the employees–the mural painter, remember?"

"I think you'd like it," he said, grabbing his silk
covered crotch and laughing like a set of chomping, plastic teeth sold at Vegas souvenir shops.

*Why did Ray have to be gross on top of every-
thing else? Her stomach swirled, and she thought
it would be great to throw up all over him, and his
fancy suit. Unfortunately, she couldn't force herself to puke on command.* "Was that Julian on
the phone?" She asked. Her apartment building
came into view and she couldn't wait to run upstairs and fling herself onto the safety of her bed.

"Yes, sweetie that was Julian."

Avoiding his eyes and looking out at the orange hued twilight sky, she said, "Next time you
talk to him, can you tell him I need stilts or some
basic scaffolding? The rooms have high ceilings,
and my arms are sore." She had spent all day tip-
toeing on the top of a large ladder and her calves
were throbbing, not to mention the ache she had
developed in her lower back.

Multihued splashes of paint were everywhere,
not just on her knees. Splotches of paint were all
over her clothing and up and down the back of

her arms. Perhaps the time had come to revise her idea of dream jobs to match her age. None of it mattered. Only Lani mattered, and John of course. Either way, she'd have to find another job soon.

She didn't see the sad face Ray made but could tell he mocked her with his tone. "Poor baby—I'll tell him."

Chapter 33

Mayor Judy Vasar-Martin deleted massive amounts of email while sitting behind her expansive, hand-carved desk. While palm fronds hit the window, the mayor added a windy swoosh to each click on her keyboard. She lifted her dark blue eyes above the monitor and frowned. Outside, the swirling desert sand created a dust storm that blocked the sun, the sky and most of the light. She couldn't see her car in the parking lot and thought about how the expensive car wash, earlier that morning, had been a major exercise in futility. Irritated, she logged off and answered her buzzing phone. "What?"

The receptionist had called to tell her she had a visitor. "Sure, send him in, I'd love to see him," she replied with a sarcastic tone, adding, "I can't believe he came out in this dust storm. It must be important." She hung up. Mac walked through the wood-paneled door, took three steps towards her desk and handed her a small bunch of un-wrapped daisies.

"Well, well, is Satan cleaning house or something?" She sniffed the flowers. "Last time you brought me flowers was Darin's funeral." Her stoic, businesslike demeanor made it clear that a small bunch of flowers didn't impress her. She also didn't have much time for small talk.

Mac smiled, dusting off his suit. "It does look like the end times out there today, but as you know, I work for the other side now." He looked at her elegant manicured fingers, expensive hot pink suit and styled, highlighted hair. Jail and seminary had done everything they could to make him forget what classy women looked like–and though his heart and soul were now dedicated to his church–he couldn't deny his vir-ile eyes. Of course, few would debate that the Mayor of Las Vegas, happened to be one of God's most gorgeous creations. "Judy, in case no one has told you, you must be the most beautiful widow in this entire state."

"Very funny," she grinned showing bright, whitened teeth, "considering most of this state is desert. Besides, I don't think seminarians are supposed to notice."

The wind howled, and the branches screeched along the glass outside, pulling their attention towards the window. "Any man with a pulse would notice you, but I didn't come here to flirt."

"I know. I know. You're here about the task force on human trafficking. I got your email." She pointed a flamingo pink nail at the computer monitor on her desk. "Do you have any idea what I inherited?"

"Sure—I can imagine it might be worse than what I've heard. May I sit down and talk for a few minutes?" He sat, facing her in a comfortable overstuffed chair, crossed his legs and continued. "Amazing what you've done near Fremont East."

She looked down at the flowers. "Do you mean the alley project or the red-light district?"

"Both. I remember getting off a bus when I came to town. Those murals on the buildings are a nice touch."

"Doesn't mean there are no more homeless camps off Main, or that people don't still get high off Ogden. We do what we can. The art project helped, and so did the public parking structure."

She turned her swiveling chair and tossed the flowers on the counter behind her desk. "Come on Mac, why are you here?"

Leaning forward, he lowered his voice as if wanting to discuss some sort of conspiracy. "The way I heard the story is, that the previous mayor had a twisted dream to make Vegas a brothel destination for rich men from around the world. I know all about it. I'm sure Metro knew all about it too. Don't worry, you're not alone. It's as if he wanted to fight the natural order of things with some hellish plot. Can you update me on any progress?"

"There's only so much the vice section of Metro can do to make a difference. I'm also sure, half the folks in this area would argue with you about the natural order of things. Saving women from prostitution is an uphill battle if I've ever seen one. It's like that guy Sisyphus who rolls his stone up the mountain only to have it roll right back down again. The cops work hard in this city, but there needs to be education in place to raise awareness. They have to hold these per-petrators accountable, without themselves being killed. I'm getting tired of meeting actual politicians and businessmen who think these women are not victims."

Mac shook his head and swiped a hand through his thinning flattop. "Even the ones who don't think they are victims are victims."

"I know that but try telling that to the owner of a massage parlor." She tapped her nails impatiently, hoping he'd get to the point of his visit. "I have words for some of those guys, but I can't say them in front of a man of faith. Besides, I need to watch what I say, because there are legitimate and sincere masseurs."

Mac blushed and changed the subject. Though she had a point about the legitimate businesses, it made him think of the young men he had counseled, who said they bought centerfold magazines to read the great articles. "Excellent billboards by the way... Do you think any of the fundraisers, calendars, wine tasting events and conferences are helping?"

Her eyes narrowed, and her face looked tense. She shrugged and shook her head. When he mentioned wine tasting, she figured he might be making fun of her efforts. "I'm not sure Mac. But we have some donors who want to help, and the task force earned enough money to put more billboards on the 15 freeway."

Mac had heard enough. He had to get to the reason he came out in a dust storm. "More billboards?" The whole thing sounded like a ludicrous nightmare. Billboards were not helping; not much anyway. At least not on the streets, he had come across lately. "Judy, listen. I need your approval to shut down McCarran from noon until three o'clock tomorrow."

Suddenly her business-like exterior turned familiar and wild. Darin had once told him she was a great catch, but a fiery one. That had been a long time ago. It's no wonder he died. Mac wanted to die or at least crawl under his chair when he noticed he had pushed her to the edge of her patience. Her eyes shot out figurative, flying swords, outmatched only by the bright colored lipstick on what quickly transformed into a screaming mouth.

"Are you crazy?" she shouted. "I'd have to notify the NSA, the NTSB, not to mention the FAA and TSA. I'm sure you know this town can't afford to stop any flights. Forget it." She inhaled, pushing a few stray hairs behind her ears. "What's this about anyway?"

Mac brushed his hands through his crew cut again and stared into scary looking eyes that only moments before were alluring and beautiful. "Judy, this is very important, and you're the mayor. There's a flight coming in from California with some victims."

"Mac, I can't. Seriously–no way–can't do it." She shook her head like a bobble head doll, except instead of up and down, her head went side to side and she pursed her lips." There are lots of flights, and lots of underage children in jeopardy." Her tone louder, "Why don't you tell me something I don't know?"

He looked outside at the wind and thought about the passage in the Bible that said, 'The Lord is slow to anger and great in power. And the Lord will by no means leave the guilty unpunished. In whirlwind and storm is His way, and clouds are the dust beneath His feet.' The storm in her eyes matched the storm outside. To Mac it felt like a direct message, but he thought he'd use a different tact—maybe a political one.

"Judy, I'd say your thirteenth amendment needs tweaking."

"My thirteenth amendment, huh?"

"Well, are you going to allow slavery in your own town, when it supposedly ended in 1865? Abraham Lincoln is probably turning in his grave. It's not just sex around here. Domestic servitude, forced labor, and even forced marriages at those dingier little drive-in wedding chapels."

"You're being unreasonable," her voice rose higher. "Mac, you were Darin's best man, and I'm sure you know, that I think the world of you. I also know, that before I met Darin, and married him, both you and my husband had a few tough times. But what you are asking for is impossible. It's beyond the scope of my duties."

"I don't think it is–because everything helps. I have to admit that even the fact that you posted that hotline around town makes some difference. Hear me out. Yesterday we received a huge donation with hopes to save the contributor's daughter. It seems their daughter got tangled up in of one of those California gang networks. You know the type preying on vulnerable girls, before they drug them and bring them here?"

The mayor's wheels were turning. Biting her lip, she looked out the window and back at Mac. "We could use some of your donor's gift for mental health treatments, medical services, legal assistance, safe housing, childcare, counseling, substance abuse and clothing. Do you want me to go on? Don't forget, I'm a mayor. There are more important things to worry about in Vegas than some stupid people who want to sell sex."

The more she spoke about needing money, the calmer she became. "Just think about the basic things we have to take care of around here. There's graffiti on Maryland Parkway and litter throughout downtown. Not to mention the homeless population."

"Judy, don't be unfair, you know we're trying to help the homeless."

"You mean your church?" She rolled her eyes.

"Of course," he answered, wondering how this firecracker of a woman had become Mayor.

"There are at least fifty churches trying to help, but that still doesn't solve everything, now does it?"

He hung his head and looked at his worn shoes. "If I knew the magic words, I'd say them right now." When he raised his head, he couldn't believe the transformation. Her face animated, her anger gone, and a smirk on her lips.

"Either that, or you'd be performing on the Strip. I can imagine your name up there like those two lion tamers or that famous magician I had the pleasure of seeing last week. Father Mac Downey, Illusionist." She held up an arm, imagining his name in lights, painting a picture with her hands. "I had fun going backstage last week. They showed me how some of the props work. The talent around here is incredible."

Mac didn't know what more to say. He winced when she called him Father Mac before his consecration ceremony. He had pleaded his case. She preferred to be adamant in her thinking, and unexpectedly distracted. "Judy, I implore you."

"Begging is good. What happened, have you stopped praying?" She asked with a tinge of cynicism. In a gentler voice, almost a whisper, she added, "Maybe it's been a long time for you Mac, but don't you realize that people have *always* come to Vegas to have sex? It's a desert getaway, like Palm Springs used to be for the Hollywood crowd. Except this place is growing faster than the hair on my head. It's not just a romantic hideaway, but an escape for everyone; good-bad-gritty and in-between."

When she mentioned her hair, he looked at the exquisite layered cut, and thought about all the money that privileged women spend on hair and nails. Mac knew that Darin had left her so much money, she didn't even need to work. Mac also felt, that deep inside, Judy was a kind woman who wanted to make a difference.

"At least you still have a sense of humor hidden under that perfect hairdo. Look, if you stop that plane, I'll make sure some of the donation money comes to the coalition too."

"I'm listening, but not sure I can help. By the way, tell me more about this 'huge' donation?"

"It's a long story. Listen; did Darin ever tell you about that Operation Penny fiasco over in Hawaii?"

"Of course, he told me about 'Operation Penny. I'll never forget that name. That little hard-ass bitch Penny, caused his arrest."

Mac raised a hand to stop her from continuing. "Yes, she uncovered a giant smuggling operation, and thereby saved the city of Hilo, where they think of her as a Good Samaritan. In fact, they think of her as a goddess. And Darin's friend Dan, you remember Captain Dan? Well he left Penny an enormous sum of money. Since she can't afford the taxes on it, and needs to find her own kid, who happens to be the victim by the way, she donated the money."

Shocked, enlarged eyes penetrated his psyche. "You're joking, right? The person who had you and Darin put in jail?" Thin lines suddenly appeared between neatly trimmed eyebrows, as her face took on the flabbergasted look of disbelief. "The same exact woman? The crazy young woman who beats up tough guys and ruined Darin's dealership? That Penny?"

"Yes, the very same one, except she's not that young anymore. I know it's a strange coincidence. If nothing else, do this for Darin's memory. Look Judy, remember the news last week? They had ten girls from Eastern Europe fly into LAX, transferred here, to our town. You know as well as I do, that even the hound dog media brushed that scenario under the proverbial rug. This hits a lot closer to home. You don't need any more negative publicity. We have to do something. Plus, you must have done something right, because now…." He stood for dramatic effect and smiled an arrogant smile. "You even have God on your side."

"Oh my God. I knew it. Get out," she threw her head back and laughed while pointing at the door. Worried, she'd pick up a paperweight and toss it at him, he moved to leave. "Just go," she repeated, pulling a sticky note from a snazzy leather holder to jot something down. "I have actual work to do. Call me with the flight number."

Chapter 34

Peter gnawed on Lani's pink lace thong. "You naughty boy," Lani whispered." Can't you chew a little faster?" Restless, she sat up, pulling him near, placing her lips over his hungry, wet mouth. He kissed her but wanted to return to munching on her lingerie. "Wait," I can pull them off, silly."

He held up a pointing finger indicating that she should keep her motor running while he undressed. Meanwhile, he softly began reciting lines from a poem. "And the sunlight clasps the earth, and the moonbeams kiss the sea—what are all these kissings worth, if thou kiss not me?" She watched him gasp and dramatically pull his shirt off.

"Who are you quoting now?"

That's from Percy Bysshe Shelley's poem called Love's Philosophy.

"Philosophy, huh? Sweet. I can counter that with lines from The Philosopher by Edna St. Vincent Millay. "And what am I that I should love/So wisely and so well?"

"Touché, my sweet, geeky girl." He kicked off his jeans and moved Lani's pelvis under his chin. "Now let me get back to chomping on this lace."

She laughed. "Are you aware they make edible panties?"

He looked up with a wet smile and wiped his mouth on the back of his hand. Pink threads had lodged in his teeth and he pulled them out. "Yes, but how does my innocent and sweet Lani know anything about stuff like that?"

"I don't know," she replied with a small shrug. "Probably Cosmo?"

"Of course," he said with a wink. Taking a deep breath, he returned to chewing like a badger.

But Lani wasn't becoming aroused. She had a wedding to plan. Her mind swirled with ideas about wedding gowns, shoes and types of flowers. Besides, they spent too much time preparing for sex. It all amounted to a combination of religious guilt and the voice of her mother yelling at her in the back of her mind. 'Hold out for true

255

love Lani. It can happen to you too,' her mother would say. 'It doesn't happen when we expect it.' And 'there's no one as hardworking or as patient as your father. You do want someone like your dad, right?' It went on and on like some old newsreel playing over and over again. A sort of mantra of hopelessness, because if no one matched up to her dad, then what was the point, anyway?

While she enjoyed kissing and making out with Peter, it still seemed like they needed to do other things too. She hoped once they got to Nevada they could go shopping for souvenirs, maybe take a helicopter tour after the wedding, or go hiking in Red Rock Canyon. She had read up on all the fun things to do around the area and kept planning it out in her mind. They not only had helicopters dipping into the nearby Grand Canyon, but burro rides and white-water rafting trips. The desert tortoise habitat off Highway 159 sounded desolate, but awesome. So, did the horseback adventures, off-roading with a rugged jeep, and the idea of exploring canyons with hidden pools. These were all activities that her nature-loving parents adored.

Peter on the other hand, liked books. He had no interest in ecology, nature or stargazing. Staying home made him happiest. Though he liked cooking for Lani, he didn't even enjoy shopping for the ingredients. His ideas were ethereal and in the clouds. In fact, in this one area, he reminded her of his mother, but in a good way. His heroes weren't rich captains of industry or even comic book caped crusaders but dead poets like Whitman, Eliot and Shelley.

Peter coughed and sat up hacking like a two-pack a day smoker. He sounded like he might gag on her lingerie. Lani wondered whether they were cotton or nylon lace, and she also worried they could make him sick. Maybe she should have a package of the edible ones sent to his address using overnight shipping. After a swig of water from a bottle on the nightstand, he continued his quest.

"Pete, I bet they are available all over Vegas. She picked up her cell phone and did a web search for edible panties in Vegas. "Thirty-five stores in Vegas and the surrounding areas, carry them. Do you like fruit flavors or bubblegum?"

"Lani," he moaned. Her thong fell away. He had reached a goal.

Finally, he felt a twinge of a response, but he wanted her entire body and soul to be fully engaged.

This decisive moment demanded attention. He came up gasping. With pleading eyes, he asked, "Can you please put that miserable phone down or at least call your mom and tell her we're coming to visit."

"What are you mumbling down there?" Lani asked, still gawking at her phone but moving her hips. Her breaths were shorter now and her face appeared red and aroused. Peter kept on nibbling and licking while moving upwards towards her navel.

He lifted his head again and said three important words, "Call your mom."

Lani dialed her mother's number but screamed and dropped the phone when Peter tickled her. "Oh God."

"What?"

She jumped off the unmade bed searching for the phone, but Peter, fast as summer lightening, snatched it up from the floor.

"Gimme my phone," she stammered, upset because she had heard her mother's voice. "Mom, if you can hear me," she yelled before Peter could turn it off. He held up the phone, so she could shout into it. "Tomorrow I'll be on Southside Airlines flight 422." Peter pushed the power button on her cell to the off position and Lani watched him pull open a drawer. "You're horrible. Now my mom thinks I hung up on her."

"I'm sure she's aware of the fact that you're constantly texting, focusing too much on social media and staring at your phone. You should be enjoying life. Don't worry about anything. We're simply storing it, nice and safe, right here in the nightstand." He dropped the phone into the open drawer next to a brand-new box of condoms, before slamming it shut. "Now forget the phone please and get back on the bed. Besides, I'm proud of you for calling. At least now she knows we're coming."

"Do you think she heard me?"

"Seriously? I think they heard you behind the rings of Saturn. You can belt it out girlfriend." He knelt next to the bed. With a shaking hand, he held up a small box that he had secretly removed from his nightstand. It wasn't the box of con-doms, but a hinged, dark leather box with golden scrolls. She had wasted so much time search-ing for edible panties, he had lost track of time and worried his brother might show up with his whacked-out friends. For some inexplicable rea-son, his eyes grew misty and his hands shook. "Lani," he said choking back saliva and tears. "Will you?" Will you?" he kept blabbering, im-mensely aware of the severity of his imminent question.

"Of course, you dummy," she answered, reach-ing for the box. "I already said I would." Her jaw fell open when she opened the box. "When did you have time?" An antique ring that had once belonged to Peter's grandmother twinkled in the late afternoon sunlight.

"Grams, remember?"

Though the curtains were pulled, a sliver of light allowed colorful rays to bounce off sparkling diamonds that glittered around a larger, pear-shaped center diamond, set in fili-greed white gold. Tucking loose hairs behind her ear, she looked up to see him blinking back tears. At that moment, she knew with an intuitive certainty that she had met her soul mate. "Wow, baby, this is gorgeous. I love you."

"You're the gorgeous one," he mumbled, watching her slip the engagement ring onto her finger. "Prettier than any diamond," he whispered behind her left ear. He spread kisses around her nape, working his lips to her right ear and back again until she giggled, falling back down onto leaf-patterned sheets. She was the poet's muse he had longed for all his life. She added a cadence to his iambic pentameter and a rhyme to his steps, even clarity to his thinking. "Can't imagine we're going to be able to do this for the rest of our lives, can you?" he asked. "This might sound like an old cliché, but I love you so much."

Chapter 35

Penny had heard Lani scream over the phone about flight 422. She called the airport and found out the flight would be coming from Ontario, California. It would land in Vegas at two in the afternoon. After that call, she tossed her paintbrush aside and dialed John, who didn't answer. Seconds later, she did a search on her phone for Christ the Redeemer Catholic Church. Afraid she'd hyperventilate; she waited and waited for Father Charles to answer the phone. While waiting, she took several deep cleansing breaths. When a machine came on, she thought she'd faint.

She went to the door of the big spacious room where she had painted a series of vines that would eventually connect to vines in the smaller rooms, keeping with the overall château theme. Outside the room, Ray and Julian were discussing furniture placement. Making sure they didn't notice her, she leaned towards them perking her ears, in order to hear the discussion.

"Ray, where did you get this hideous red velvet couch? It screams whorehouse. Remember I said understated elegance?"

Penny didn't see Ray nod, but she heard his reply. "Didn't you want some pizazz up here? I even thought we should have slots and arcade games on this floor to keep people busy while they wait. You know, so they don't get bored and leave. Don't forget, we're only going to have—ahem–paying guests on this floor."

"The slots will only be downstairs and don't try arguing your point. As far as these go, how about green velvet or blue satin? Did you get some kind of deal on these?"

She heard Ray's annoying chuckle. "Well yeah, kind of, remember that Ukrainian dude with the store on Commerce?"

"You're kidding, right? You mean that son of bitch with more ink than brains and red beard down to navel? I wouldn't have his shit in my outhouse." A thud careened off the empty walls. Julian must have kicked the sofa.

"Which reminds me boss, can you come with me tomorrow?"

"What, to the airport?"

"They're Polish girls. Don't you speak Polish?"

"No. You are so stupid."

"Ouch, you know I take care of whatever you need. You had a good time with Sonia in Geneva, didn't you?"

"Of course, but you're idiot. You didn't listen in school. Polish is not like Russian language. I go with you. What time?"

Leaning over, feeling unbalanced, and glad she wore practical shoes; Penny almost fell when she heard Ray's answer.

"Two."

"Okay, now call someone to help remove this ugly couch. I hate it."

Julian turned around and headed for the stairs, while Ray followed and dialed the furniture store.

Penny crept back into the room she had worked in all morning. She continuously pushed the redial button on her own phone to connect to Lani. Over and over, she dialed and redialed her daughter's number, receiving no answer. She left a few messages for Lani to return the call. Perspiration dripped from her forehead. After a few frustrating minutes, she called Aunt Betsy.

"Any word from Lani?"

Usually chipper, Aunt Betsy sounded robotic and sad. "No, Hon." Bentley barked in the background as if he had a lot to say.

"We'll find her. Aunt Bess, please don't even for a minute think it's your fault. I tried her phone and there's no answer. Earlier, our phones were disconnected. She yelled something about a Flight 422, and then the call ended. There's something strange going on. I heard a man's voice. And, since she had to shout the flight number, I'm crazy with worry. When I called the airport, they told me the flight is coming from Ontario California." She wiped her forehead with the back of her hand. Either the air-conditioning had gone out or some sort of stress-related hot flash had taken over her body.

"That's the nearest airport to our house."

"Yeah, Oh God, Betsy, my baby sounded unhappy."

"Have you told the cops about the flight number?"

"Not yet. I wanted to talk to John first, but he's super busy and I can never get a hold of him. Plus, we have a guy at the local parish who's trying to help. If this flight is at two tomorrow, then I'm going to need all the help I can get. I'm calling that church guy next."

"What can I do, dear?"

"Stay home. Stay close to the phone in case Lani calls or comes home."

"No problem," Aunt Betsy chirped like a sad little bird about to fall off her perch. "Oh, my worried dear, don't forget she'll always be your baby. Most important, remember that Lani is a grownup girl now. To tell you the truth, I'm more worried about you."

"You know I'll be alright. I'm sure my dad told you all the wild stories about me." Penny wiped tears from her face, but the thought of her dad made her smile.

"He sure did. I bet your dad would know where to find Lani."

"Sorry, Aunt Bess, I know you and John had a great dad too. I miss mine every day."

"I understand. Carl had a golden personality. He should have run for office. Right now, he'd be reminding us to pray."

"That's a good idea. Bye Betsy, I better go."

She disconnected the call and dialed Mac's cellphone. "Brother Mac?" Penny asked tentatively?" She still had trouble thinking of the man who had unintentionally sent her to jail as a priest. Since her actions had also sent him to the slammer, she reasoned, they were sort of on an even keel.

"Yup, that would be me."

"This is Penny Murray. I have some news about the flight, but I'm at work and can't talk. It's Flight 422.

He wrote it down. "I understand and I'm on it. Call me tonight when you get back to your apartment."

Chapter 36

The large sign said, "Tours departing daily for the West Rim. Ask us how you can save $90 per person." Mac went up to the reception desk, inquiring about the manager.

"He'll be back soon," the woman answered with a smile. "Please have a seat." She pointed to a leatherette couch and a coffee table with magazines. Mac pulled out one of the sightseeing company's brochures and reminisced about his days running tours on Kauai. He stared at the pictures of the impressive red canyon and imagined dipping down below the edge. The nearby helicopter experience, he figured, must be similar to Waimea canyon. The more he looked at the photos, the more he compared Hawaii with the local area. An arid desert and a lush island seemingly have no connection, and yet the various rock formations and layered boulders filled with oasis-like vegetation and rushing water, created a connectivity and oneness he felt were rare outside of church. Something in his gut told him he could be on the right track. A glance at his watch made him sit up straight. If Lani happened to be on that two o'clock flight, he needed to hurry.

"You were looking for me?" A guy in a red baseball cap holding two or three small packages wandered in through the front door. He also had mail under his arm. His mannerisms made it obvious; he wanted to catch his breath before engaging in a conversation with a stranger.

"Are you the manager?"

The man sighed and replied, "Yeah, hold on. I have to dump this stuff behind the counter."

"Is this a bad time?" Mac hoped not. He needed to talk to this guy now, and even though he didn't wear his clerical collar, he still wanted to be polite.

The man hurried to unload the packages and turned back to Mac. He dusted his hands and introduced himself without giving away too much personality. In fact, Mac thought he probably played some poker in his day. "I'm here for another week. Malaysians—they bought a bunch of the hotels, and this place. I'm being demoted, so I might be outta here soon. You know–here today–gone to Maui. Better talk fast, cause you never know. What can I do for you?" Good lines, almost funny even, but delivered without a trace of a smile.

"Name's Mac," he shook hands with the manager. "Speaking of Maui, I used to fly helicopter tours over Kauai. The man listened and nodded, appearing interested in whatever Mac wanted to share. "I'm hoping I can borrow one of your birds for a couple of hours tomorrow."

The manager stepped back and grabbed the brim of his cap before erupting into boisterous laughter. "We're busy in the afternoons–super busy. Besides, our choppers are not for personal use. Where did you get the idea...?"

"Wait, please don't laugh," Mac had to cut him off and plead. "This is serious and you're the only one who can help me."

The man calmed down but stared at Mac as if he had lost a few marbles along the road of life. Maybe he had. Jail had a way of doing that, but Mac had a mission. He also had a grasp on the meaning of perseverance. Several tourists were milling about, approaching the cashier. The friendly woman Mac met upon arrival filled out forms and rang up sales. Planes were landing outside, and traffic noise made it difficult to speak softly.

Perhaps a rebel at heart, especially with his job on the line, the guy asked a leading question. "What do you need it for?"

Mac pulled some ruffled papers from his pocket to show him a picture of himself in uniform. He stood next to a Sikorsky UH-60 Blackhawk during Desert Storm. "I'm actually with a church now and don't even have a license anymore–but this is an emergency." He laid the paper on the counter and dug into another pocket to produce a colorful tourist brochure showing his smiling mug standing next to an Island Tours helicopter.

The manager looked down at the picture on the brochure. It showed a buffed out young man with short hair. He had a helmet in his hands and looked to be saying 'cheese'. The manager looked at the picture and back at Mac, perhaps noting the prominent scar, on the rugged cheek. In the photo, he wore a khaki shirt with a reverse pattern of white pineapples and the tour company logo emblazoned on his breast pocket. "That's you, huh?"

"Yeah, a while ago."

"Dude, you've got to be crazy. Even if you had a license, I couldn't just give you one of these for a few hours–any idea what they'd do to me?"

Mac cocked his head to the right like a listening dog with persuasive eyes. *What would they do? He envisioned the man shoved onto a frigate, bound for Malaysia. Once he arrived, he'd be pushed into a torture cell, against his will, and subjected to caning. Fortunately, this guy lived in the U.S. of A where the Constitution and the laws of the land protected employees from vicious, unreasonable bosses. Whatever happened, he'd get a fair trial.*

When his head straightened, Mac looked the manager directly in the eyes. "You just finished telling me you might quit." Then in a softer, business-like tone he added, "I have a few friends who can help you get situated in Hawaii. That's if you're interested."

"Shit, Mister, now you want to bribe me?"

"I'm serious." *He felt sorry for the sucker. Pushing forty and running this tour business on the Strip in Vegas would be fine, if he owned the place. Mac kept thinking about the caning. He hoped the guy couldn't be lured onto a cruise ship heading for the South China Sea either.*

Something about fast-planning and knee-jerk reactions gnawed Mac's gut. Flying helicopter tours over Kauai seemed like a world away from his current reality. Worried, he mumbled a Hail Mary to himself, because getting this guy, or anyone in trouble, had not been part of his quickly devised plan.

The man looked flustered, and his face turned the shade of his Red Sox cap. "You still haven't told me what you need it for?"

Bingo, and thank you Mother of God. The red face meant Mac had the upper hand. Maybe even a Royal Flush. Mac inhaled and continued to go for broke. "It's probably better that way. Don't worry," Mac said gently. I'll return it unharmed. The Mayor is a friend of mine and can give you a reference. Want her direct line?"

"No. I want you to leave before I call Airport security."

Mac didn't flinch. He didn't care for abso-
lutes, but an undeniable thing Mac had learned
throughout his years as a soldier, a pilot, a con-
vict and a seminarian, involved one persistent
sad fact; the fact that everyone, outside of Jesus, had their price. "Let's go back to that bribery
idea. How about I pay you twice what it costs to
take a tour through the Grand Canyon?"

"That's not enough, but if you're willing to pay
more, a lot more, I'm listening."

*I knew it, I knew it, I knew it. His thoughts
jumped up and down like a jackpot winner with
triple sevens. Mac exhaled in relief, but quietly. He
didn't want to show the other guy that he had won,
even though the word 'winner' kept flashing on and
off inside his mind.*

Chapter 37

Later that evening, a weary Mac looked up from the metal serving container of noodles. Tony, a gruff white-haired fellow from New York waited for a scoop of whatever they'd ladle onto his plate.

"What's up Brother Mac? Got any Osso Bucco or Puttanesca back there?" Tony had come out west to dance in a show, but after he injured his back, he ended up living in an underground tunnel. Hundreds lived under the city in a strange collection of drainage water pipes. The subterranean shelters were temporary, due to rare, dangerous rainstorms that could show up in an instant, flooding out the homeless camps with flowing water and leaving massive levels of debris in the channels.

"No Puttanesca here. Today's special is Mac's spaghetti with Marinara sauce" He dipped a ladle into the sauce and poured it over the pasta. "There's a shaker of parmesan at the end of the line."

"Sounds good Padre, I like your soulful style."

Mac winked, knowing that Tony appreciated every morsel he could get. Gratitude oozed like melted cheese from thankful, expressive eyes. Mac wore an old baseball cap he had found at a thrift store. "Need a hat?"

Tony laughed. "You're kidding, right? I wouldn't wear a Yankee cap if it were the last hat on Earth."

"But you're from the Bronx?"

Tony shook his head. "Queens brotha. I'm a big Mets fan."

"So no hat, even if it's raining?"

"Rather wear a bag," he chuckled, starting to shuffle away. "My stuff got flooded out from the last rain, but things are better now."

"Need anything right now?"

"Nah, I'm a pack rat anyway. I got me three blankets, a jacket and two pairs of shoes. Pretty soon I'll need a shopping cart."

Mac placed a roll onto Tony's tray. "You come to me if you need anything."

Tony shook his head and smiled up at Mac. Parched, tan skin lit a sparkle in his eyes. "Grazie, like I said, you're all right." He went to sit on an aluminum bench with an attached table, outside the food window. The line appeared to go on forever.

* * *

That night, Mac waited for Penny's call. Exhausted and needing a shower, he wanted to wait until after eleven before he made the call himself. Finally, at ten-thirty, his phone rang. "Mac, it's Penny," she sounded upset. "I'm sorry I was short with you, but I overheard Julian and Ray talking about girls that are coming in tomorrow at two. I had to cut it short in case they caught me on the cell. All of this is making me go wild with worry."

"Hey, relax. I don't mean to spew platitudes, but how about a little faith?" A few seconds passed. "Well?"

"Didn't I trust you once before?"

"I told you, that was the old me. Things are different now—a lot different."

"I'll give you that."

"Did you say you have a group of friends who can come to the airport? The more bodies the better. I have a way to get onto the tarmac, avoiding security, but you and your friends have to meet me outside of the Grand Canyon Tours Office tomorrow at one."

"Bodies?"

"As in: an armada of people who want to stop a plane. Like protestors who stop traffic for equal rights. Activists. You know what I mean."

"Right, okay, but it's not like a huge amount of people." She counted Ron, Tina, John and herself. Is four or five enough?"

He wanted to sigh, laugh or cry but worried she'd hear him. He had hoped she had collected thirty or forty friends at least. What they really needed were hundreds of anti-human trafficking picketers with signs, banners and the works, but they didn't have time to arrange all that at a moments notice. "Better than nothing," he quipped, wishing his optimistic reply meant it could work. *Wrangling up a few dozen homeless folks could help his crowd situation, but then he'd have to get Fr. Charles involved. Either way, he had to be the voice of reason. He had to stay cool or his plan* to save Lani would burn like cheap incense. Penny couldn't lose confidence in him. Sensing her hesitation, he had to make sure she felt comfortable, secure in the fact that he had her back. "I'll do my best to stop that flight and get Lani off of it. You see Penny, the pilot might be aware of what's going on and since he's in charge of the plane, he could turn the plane around and take off again. Remember some pilots work for the wrong side."

"Oh no," she mumbled, cringing at the thought. "You'd think I would know better, after everything…." *Pilots were the lowest forms of humanity, in her opinion. Outside of that one who cleverly landed on the Hudson, none of them should be trusted with anything. In her view, everything a pilot did on a plane should be inspected daily. Every bag a flight attendant or pilot carries should be searched. Camera equipment should monitor the boarding passengers and even the employees at all times. She wouldn't trust a good-looking, or even a not so good-looking pilot again, for all the money in the universe. Right now, however, her daughter's life depended on trusting one of them, and it drove her bonkers.*

"Don't get the past confused with the present. Of course, it doesn't mean things are easier now. People worship money around here more than they do God. I've heard they'd sell their souls for a few more turns at the roulette wheel. Your daughter is worth a lot to these scum buckets, but don't forget, her value to the Almighty is priceless. Remember Penny, He knows how many red hairs you have on that lovely head of yours. Things might be tough—and from everything I've heard about you—you can do this."

"Thanks for the compliments. I appreciate your help. Once Julian finds out I know all about his charade of a spa he won't think I'm such a perfect employee."

"True, you'll need another job."

"He's world famous, and once the media picks up this slimy story, I don't want to be dragged into it. But, I don't think I'll have a choice. He has these tough guys that work for him. There's this golf putter next to his desk. I don't think he plays golf. Let's just say, it's not just my kneecaps that could be in danger. He might go after John or Lani. He'll make the cover of all the magazines as the bad boy who keeps getting worse. The tabloids will love every sensational morsel. Fortunately, there's a light at the end of my Sin City tunnel that has freeway signs leading home to California."

"Don't be naïve kid. If they are as bad as you think, they're crawling all over Socal like roaches. Humans are being trafficked at epic proportions. Anyway, keep up your cover as long as you can for Lani's sake. I'm going to make sure the cops hear about girls arriving at two o'clock. They'll probably send out the local task force, maybe even some SWAT units. I'm hoping the Feds will come out. My friend Judy the Mayor is supposed to help us too. She'll have the authority to suspend a few flights, at least for a few minutes. That's about it. Man, I'm zonked. I had better get some sleep. You get some rest too because tomorrow is going to be a long day."

"Goodnight Mac. I'll see you tomorrow."

"Wait, I know John's busy, but is he coming?"

"Oh he'll be there. We'll both be there at one."

"Good. Sounds like a plan. Try to remember this verse from Romans 8— "'If God is for us, who can be against us?'"

"Thanks." *She repeated it to herself. 'If God is for us, who can be against us?' She'd make it her personal mantra. Words she'd say to herself repeatedly for the next few days.*

* * *

He had to make one last phone call before taking a shower. "Judy, Mac here," he said into the Mayor's voicemail. "Southside Air from Ontario—flight 422—at two. I'll be there between one thirty and two. Anything you can do to help, will earn you special mention in my upcoming novena."

* * *

Meanwhile, Penny dialed Tina's number. "Hi, it's Penny. Sorry, I know it's late, but remember you said you'd help me with my project?"

"Of course, anything you need. By the way, it's not that late. We stay up for the comedy shows. What can we do for you?" Tina seemed delighted to hear from Penny.

"Can both of you meet me at the Grand Canyon Tours office off Sunset Road and Paradise? You know–the one near the airport?"

"Are we going to the Canyon?"

"Not exactly, but your presence will make a huge difference in my life and a bigger one in Lani's life."

"No problem—we love Lani and can't wait to see you."

"Tomorrow at one then–okay?"

"Yes, we'll be there."

Chapter 38

After thirteen hours on turbulent international flights, three transfers, recycled air and bad airline food, Olga had had plenty of time to think about her situation. This was no ordinary predicament. It called for drastic measures. Tall and lanky for seventeen, she survived thus far by using her head, while the other girls seemed to have left their brains in Warsaw.

Of course, Olga couldn't blame the girls. They had heavy-duty indoctrinations that included the promise of vast American riches. They showed them pictures of elegant gowns, jewelry and luxurious swimming pools. If they disagreed or caused any problems, they were given pills for airsickness. But Olga could tell they were lying. It wasn't going to be easy, but she had come up with a risky plan. Part one consisted of using the lavatory, but the minute she stood up, the old woman they traveled with, noticed, and tried waving her back to her seat.

In broken Polish the old woman said, "Olga, hurry back, we're about to land." Averting her eyes, the teen looked into her black cross-body bag to search for her last stick of chewing gum.

Trying to appear obedient, she nodded in the affirmative and knew that the old woman's eyes would follow her down the aisle. Olga wanted to slip behind the curtain separating economy from first class, but instead, she slipped into the nearest restroom. After securing the door, she looked in the mirror at her simple dress adorned with a fake hibiscus flower pin she had purchased at an airport souvenir shop. The loud ding of the seatbelt sign made her realize she had to hurry. She turned on the hot water and kept it hot until it fogged up the mirror. In the steam, she wrote a universal word: SOS–and then she ripped a petal off her bright pink flower and stuck it to the mirror with the chewing gum. The seat belt sign rang again. A flight attendant rapped on the lavatory, reminding people to take their seats. When Olga swung open the door, she watched the ground and hurried to her seat. The Captain came on the loudspeaker telling everyone aboard Air America, flight 339 from Los Angeles, how he prepared to land at McCarran Airport in Las Vegas.

Many of the passengers had also transferred from lengthy overseas flights that connected places like London, Paris and Warsaw with Los Angeles. Many were connecting on a short, last-leg of their journey, to Vegas. Olga knew her *alleged* boyfriend had told her many things that were untrue. It had taken her too long to figure things out, but all the hours in the air made things clearer. He probably made a hefty profit selling her to whoever ran these types of sex slave rings. Somehow, deep in her heart, she felt, that in the end, she would have the upper hand. That is, if they didn't kill her first.

She had left behind her homeland, her parents and everything familiar. What she did have, put the rest of these idiotic, cheap adolescents to shame. None of them knew she could run. Like a cross between a gazelle and a greyhound. She had almost made the Olympic trials in Bydgoszcz by running sixty meters in seven seconds. She had also qualified for the Summer Youth

Olympics in track and field sprinting. She didn't drink alcoholic beverages and other than the drugs her lowlife, make-believe boyfriend had snuck into her soft drink, she had never taken a drug in her life. Her biggest mistake consisted of believing in love. That crazy shyster she met at a music festival had lied, when he had said he loved her. In hindsight, it seemed obvious to her that filthy men preyed on girls at concerts and music festivals.

The flight attendant who had knocked on the door entered the washroom to wash her hands. When she stepped inside, she noticed the SOS still dripping down the mirror and found the pink piece of silk petal. Quickly, she snapped a photo with her camera phone and went to find the Air Marshal disguised to match passengers in first class. While most local flights from LAX didn't have Air Marshals anymore, Air America flights that connected with overseas carriers still had a few.

Most of the time, these professionals were ex-Navy Seals or retired Green Berets. This particular FAM, or Federal Air Marshal Service member, lived outside of Vegas, in a quiet suburb. After a long tour of boring flights, he looked forward to seeing his family. Trying to blend in with the crowd, he wore a navy-blue business suit and stared at his laptop. The flight attendant nudged him gently, showing him the photo. She covertly handed him the piece of faux hibiscus. Finally, she whispered a description of the girl that had walked out of the bathroom, while fluffing his pillow. "Thanks for flying Air America," she said aloud, in case anyone detected her stealth movements.

After the plane landed, Olga reached for her carryon which contained a pair of lightweight gym shoes. When everyone stood to disembark, Olga kicked off her four-inch heels and rubbed her toes. "My feet hurt; I have to change my shoes," she stated in Polish to no one in particular.

"Not now Olga. We have important people waiting." The old woman looked disappointed. "Please Olga. You are so pretty with nice shoes," she said, sounding agitated. Olga hated wearing fake patent stilettos but felt that the burgundy lips and green eyeshadow kept her disguised enough anyway. No one would guess her real identity, because at all the track and field events, she had her hair pulled back and she never wore makeup.

The passengers began to file past Olga. The other girls waited for the old nana to finish reprimanding the tallest one in the group. "Success depends on first impressions," the woman told Olga. "You are like showgirls." The other gullible girls listened, while they combed their hair and retouched their lip-gloss.

As they exited the plane, the Air Marshal scanned each passenger until his eyes flew to the flower pin on Olga's dress. He noticed she was part of a large group of girls who weren't communicating in English.

At the end of the long corridor leading into the terminal were three men wearing dark suits. The heavyset, pockmarked man looked familiar from television. The one in the middle looked swarthy and dangerous and the one on the right had a scowl on his angry-looking face.

The Air Marshal walked up behind Olga and tapped her on the shoulder. When she turned around, he asked a simple question, "Have we met before?"

She didn't understand the stranger and looked away. Without a uniform, he could be anyone. Ray, Julian and the limo driver immediately noticed a strange man trying to communicate with Olga. Ray shouted, "Leave the girl alone."

"Who is that?" Julian asked Ray. "Can you imagine that pervert moving in on my property?" They took a few steps closer, but the crowd of passengers kept them separated.

"I don't know who the fuck it is but he better get lost." Ray shouted in a booming voice, right at the exact moment when the Air Marshal displayed his badge. Olga noticed the commotion and dropped her carry on bag. She ducked down, darted among the throngs of people, racing like a pursued fox in the crowd.

Poof. She vanished like a stage magician's rabbit into thin air.

The old woman began to scream at the other girls in Polish about how they must stay close to her. George the limo driver tried to run after Olga, but he tripped on her carryon full of shoes. A tired group of jaded passengers had gathered around to watch the excitement in Terminal B.

When the Air Marshal called for backup, Ray pulled a handgun from his jacket.

"Drop your weapon," the Air Marshal yelled. Literally within seconds, four uniformed officers arrived, grabbing Ray, Julian and George the driver. Moments later, the law overpowered the three evil traffickers. They were handcuffed and taken to jail.

Chapter 39

Father Charles looked overwhelmed and frail sitting between tall stacks of paper on both sides of his desk. "Sorry Mac, I'm not letting you bus our homeless people out to the airport, so you can save one adult woman from prostitution. Forget it. Don't you think these destitute individuals have had enough?"

Mac looked down at the scuff marks on his leather loafers. "All right, but that generous donor gave us enough to feed a bunch of them, and I figured they'd enjoy going for a ride." He thought of poor Tony, his friend from New York, who gave up everything to dance in Vegas, only to end up sleeping in underground tunnels. Mac could think of at least twenty people off the top of his head that would jump at the chance to help. These were people who relied on the church, and felt they needed to pay things forward. Good hearted souls without a penny.

Father Charles shook his head and looked at the bulletins and folders on his desk. "You figured wrong. What part of no, don't you understand? I'm baffled that you'd want to use those miserable suffering souls in this way. It's not right. In case you didn't know, but I'm sure that hard head of yours has some idea, a large portion of all our donations will be used for repairing the wind-damaged roof, the potholes in the parking lot and for adding new pews near the side entrance. On top of that, when we report contributions, everything we do is disclosed in a transparent manner to the public, and the Bishop. Good luck trying to sneak a busload of homeless past our Bishop…You'll be ordained in two weeks, boy. Unless you want to work across the street as a bartender, don't jeopardize everything with some last-minute tomfooleries."

Mac didn't need reminding about the two weeks. He had worked hard, and more than anything, he wanted to help as many people as he could in this life. As a full-fledged priest, he felt doors would open and people might listen. "It's not like it would cost us anything besides a gallon of gas."

"Mac, it's the principle of the thing. You should know better." Father Charles wagged an index finger at Mac, as if scolding a child.

"I understand." Mac stood to leave.

"Do you? Sit down–right now–and explain to me why that Penny woman keeps on calling and leaving frantic messages on our voicemail? We told her you'll help, but there's a limit to what we can do." He cleared his throat. "I need to know whether you've crossed the line."

Mac sat back down and rather than make eye contact with Father Charles, he focused on the statue of the Sacred Heart. "Her daughter Lani is coming in on a flight this afternoon. Penny recently heard the people she works for talking about some young women whom are landing this afternoon. Apparently, Penny, don't forget she's our donor, thought she worked for a spa resort, but as it turns out, it's a front. Well you know the rest." Mac waved his hand through the air as if shooing a fly. "Anyway, she also received a call from her daughter, who verified that she's flying in this afternoon. That's when she tried locating me, but she called here instead. Lani has a boyfriend whose brother is tied to some very bad gang activity. If we can unearth the sources say at the roots, we might be able to squelch some of the trafficking. I made a promise to Penny that I'd save Lani. End of story."

"Except, you left out the most important part and I'm sitting here on the edge of my desk-chair in anticipation. I'm still wondering why you'd need a bus full of tired looking homeless folks? Come on Mac. Something smells fishier than our Friday Fish Fry, and that's not good."

Mac turned his head to look at Father Charles. "You know, that's a good analogy. It's like the fishes and the loaves. More is better," he said with a smile.

"What are you talking about?"

"I thought a crowd would be better at stopping the plane."

Fr. Charles stood up, made the sign of the cross and looked at the ceiling before he pointed to the door of his office. "Did you say stop a plane?" A look of confusion appeared on his old, haggard face. "Mac, please stop. I don't think I can take much more of this nonsense."

"Either I'm on this taskforce or I'm not. I think outside of the box, and right now, we have a crisis. All I'm trying to do is fix it. Isn't that what Jesus would do?" The sound of church bells indicated that Mass would soon begin.

"Loaves and fishes? Is this where Jesus wins an Academy Award?" He shook his head in disbelief. "Mac in case you forgot, back then, there were no airplanes near the Sea of Galilee. No airport and no bus either. I realize the seminarian life can be mundane, but it sounds to me like you've got some blockbuster movie on your mind rather than the Gospels."

Mac stood and pulled open the door. He did have a lot on his mind, and his friend Father Charles had a point about the homeless having suffered enough. More importantly, he didn't want to end up working at Hooters. "I'll go get my robe and help with the readings and the Eucharist."

"Wait Mac—you have to understand this one concept before you leave." Mac turned back to face the elderly father figure, someone he respected with all his heart. "When you're a priest it will seem clearer, but it boils down to that box you mentioned, and thinking outside of it. Whether you're here, or relocated to a parish in South Africa, you won't be alone in that box anymore. And since your mind is in the clouds anyway, why don't you think about *that* during my Homily?" Father Charles chuckled, whispering something about Jesus and a busload of homeless stopping an airplane. "Good heavens, you're a funny guy Mac."

"Okay, okay, I'll think of something else."

Chapter 40

"Flight 422A to Tower, do you read?"

"Yes, 422. Good afternoon, you're clear to land on runway two."

"Roger. 422A, preparing to land on runway two. There's another plane taxiing to the right on that runway. Am I clear?"

"Copy, it will be clear. Flight 339, please turn right towards terminal. Flight 422A now approaching runway." American Air flight 339 turned to exit the runway, moving to park in front of the terminal. The ground crews waited to attach the disembarkation ramps. With not too many desert breezes in the forecast, the hot weather created perfect landing conditions. It seemed like a good day to be at work in the air conditioned tower at McCarran.

"Tower, what's with the helicopter?" the pilot of 422 asked with a professional and calm demeanor.

The air traffic controller turned to the man sitting next to him and then returned his eyes to his monitor. "Bob, hurry up, you won't believe this," he whispered. "Who are they?" Les pointed down through the window at the helicopter landing on runway two.

A small group took a few seconds to disembark, after which, the chopper rose quickly to avoid the plane, vanishing like a desert mirage. It all happened so fast that Bob hadn't even turned to look. Les had managed to have an entire discussion with no one but himself.

"Tower to tour helicopter, do you read?" Les kept trying to find out who flew into his airspace but received no answer. "Tour helicopter, do you hear me?" he repeated over the air several times. "Those were code violations," he broadcasted to anyone listening on his frequency. "422 we may have a problem."

Meanwhile, Bob continued to assist Air America flight 339. "Nice moves 339. Welcome back to Vegas." Trying not to be distracted, he turned to his friend Les. Impatience in his voice, he asked, "What's going on?"

"Out there on runway two, don't you see it?"

Ivy League educated, Bob didn't like the condescending question. He noticed something earlier but didn't like being interrupted when planes were landing. He enjoyed working with Les because the guy seemed to mind his own business. Les had suffered a bum knee while training for Special Ops. They were both top of their class, and they both loved working in Air Traffic Control. Both men looked stunned. Les kept pulling on his mustache. Bob scratched his head as if thinking, but he had a befuddled look on his face. The anguished look a Chihuahua has when it's wondering where to take a crap. "They could be terrorists. Did anyone call security?"

The ragtag group of what they thought could also be some sort of political demonstrators, consisted of two women, a lean guy in boots and a fat bald guy with a bright red wheelchair scooter.

Choppers landed on pads provided for them on the far side of the airport. The tour company businesses stayed far from general aviation airspace. Their hangars were situated near the surrounding fences, for easy takeoffs and exits.

"Was that the Grand Canyon Tour helicopter?" Les pushed some switches, zooming in with a security camera. He focused on the people who appeared to be taking a leisurely stroll on the taxiway between the runway and the apron. He shook his head and then shook it again. His mouth open, wider than a blimp hangar.

"No clue, but if it was, those folks are not only lost, but they are way off course." answered Bob. That's pretty sad. And I thought my golf balls were the only things that were hopelessly missing. "Wait... Les, check this out. I think that's our Mayor jogging out of exit 5."

Les put his lips together and whistled softly under his breath. "Easy to spot in those three-inch heels. Yup, recognize those legs from when she worked as a showgirl at the Sands," he said with a touch of male bravado. "I guess airport security unlocked the East gate for her." They both watched her maneuver across gravel and stone, in a teal-colored suit. "Wonder how she can run in those shoes?"

Wind aside, the mayor made a dramatic entrance. A perfect sprayed coiffure, she also had an artistic Hermes silk scarf, with an abstract yellow print, trailing behind her like watercolors. Her raised arms erratically motioned to the people dropped off by the copter.

Bob returned to his microphone. "Flight 422A on approach; please be careful, there are people on your runway."

The pilot responded, "Yeah, I see that, looks like some tourists without a map."

"Once you land you'll have to wait. Do not taxi into the terminal at this time. Do you read?"

The pilot thought it funny, "Another fun day in Vegas, huh? Affirm, will not taxi in to terminal A."

Bob rubbed his eyes thinking about the weird situations he had seen at this airport. "It's always fun but safety first."

"Copy that, tower."

The Mayor kept moving, albeit wobbly, as fast as she could, out to the group. She waved her arms and screamed about getting off the runway. Minutes later, security also rolled up in a small white truck and a call came up to Bob. "Disturbance in Terminal B caused by some perps on

Flight 339. –both men and women were apprehended, and arrests are being made. Feds are being notified and they will follow-up."

"But wait a second, can you please enlighten us? Who are those people standing next to you?"

"Not sure Sir, but they are talking to the Mayor." Bob watched the Mayor gesticulating and yelling at the small group. Security continued, "It sounds like they are looking for someone on the next flight. Can you ask the pilot to verify someone on their passenger list?"

"I don't think so. There's protocol and this is bullshit. Unless those morons plan on buying this land, can you please, do what you can to get them off our runway?"

Les turned to Bob. "I have a call to Tower from the Mayor on line three."

"Tower, this is Mayor Vassar-Martin and I want to know if there's a certain passenger on that Southside plane?"

Bob chewed on a fingernail before answering. "We can't do that, ma'am."

"I know it's not the normal way of doing things, but this is an emergency and I'm talking to you using the Airport Security guy's phone.

Can you please help me? I'll send you show tickets. Any show—any time."

"Sorry, we can't do that."

"Four steak dinners at that new celebrity chef restaurant and the show tickets?"

Bob looked at Les and rolled his eyes while mouthing the word, 'women'. "What's the name?" He jotted it down before calling the pilot. "Southside Air, flight 422A I'm sorry for the delay. After landing, you should be clear to proceed to Terminal A. But first, can you tell me if you have a Lani Murray on board?"

"One moment, Tower, after we let down the landing gear, I'll take a look at the manifest."

A moment later, the pilot spoke the words he needed to hear, but by that time, Bob had a headache. The worst headache he had ever had in his entire life, and his nails were bleeding.

"Roger. Lani Murray is in window seat 7A."

Chapter 41

"We got the girls and the Feds have the criminals in custody," the Mayor yelled, approaching Penny, John, Tina and Ron. "They were on flight 339 which came in a few minutes before that plane right behind you. Can all of you please move off the runway? Please follow me." She was out of breath and glad to see the small white security truck pulling up alongside of them. The security guard had a flashing red light on top of his vehicle and a megaphone speaker telling them to vacate the premises.

"Caught who?" Penny shouted back.

"Please can we talk somewhere else? Homeland Security caught the traffickers—uh—Julian something—and they also seized a couple of other men. Are you Penny?"

"Yes, I'm Penny."

"I've heard a lot about you. I'm Darin's widow, Judy Martin. Remember Darin?"

Penny faked a grin. She had rescued a couple in the parking lot of his dealership, resulting in the biggest drug bust in the history of Hilo, inadvertently causing a little jail time for Darin. Martin Toyota had been the paper's biggest client. Darin happened to be one of Dan's deliverymen. Of course, she remembered Darin. "That was a long time ago," Penny answered with a sad look on her face. "This is my husband John, and my friends Tina and Ron."

"Nice to meet you, she said, shaking John's clammy hand." Darin admitted that your wife's talent with graphic design is what made both his dealerships a huge success. Especially the big one he had in Southern California. I can't forget her name because Darin bragged a lot about Penny and told me she's the best."

"She's a keeper," John replied. Embarrassed for having perspiring palms, he pulled his hand away. He felt like a melting grilled cheese sandwich on toasted bread, oozing onto a warm plate. Coastal breezes had brought humidity from California and it mixed with the dry desert air. The combination made John, and most everyone, un-comfortable. He marveled at how the Mayor kept her cool in the lovely linen suit and shawl.

Besides the glaring sun, there were other factors making Penny uneasy. Of course, she'd never forget Darin, and the nightmare she had faced in Hawaii, but the noise in the air made it close to impossible to speak. "Nice to meet you Judy but can...."

"Where's Mac?" the Mayor interrupted at what sounded like the top of her vocal chords. Her eyes scanned the horizon. She held a hand to her forehead to block the blistering sun, in order to look around, while flashing lovely, pink nails. "My airport terminal looks like a law enforcement convention. You'd think that Sheriffs and cops flew in from across fifty states to show off their uniforms. This all just happened moments before you arrived. Something tells me Mac might be able to explain what's going on better than I can."

"That's our Mayor," Ron chimed in, pointing a sausage-like finger at the woman in the stylish suit. "She owns all those Martin car dealerships." Ron had dressed in his finest plaid suit for the occasion. A Globe newspaper pin, resplendent with miniature diamonds, proudly sparkled from his lapel. Outside of doctor appointments, he rarely left the comfort of his house. His gleaming head also reflected the afternoon sunshine, but his pasty complexion had taken on a dangerous shade of plum. "Remember we went to Darin's dealership in Hawaii, Honeybun?"

Tina knew the name Judy Martin too well, and it had nothing to do with the fact that her smiling face graced the front page of the local paper almost daily. The haughty woman pointed like an amusement park tour guide, in her Italian designer suit and high heels. *Tina had lived with Darin eons ago. Way before Judy, the dancer and now Mayor, came along. Though Ron knew all about it, she figured this wasn't the time or place to* reminisce.

Fortunately, the noise around them made talking difficult. *What Tina didn't understand, is why they had to fly across town in a chopper and told to exit quickly in front of this earsplitting plane. Didn't seem like any theme park ride she remembered.*

Yesterday, when she had said she's up for one of Penny's adventures, she had thought adventure as in: a fruit-filled luau brunch maybe, with roast pork and macadamia cream pie. Even a humble frozen yogurt shop, with an array of delicious toppings would have sufficed. The years had altered her sense of daring. The type of adventure she had expected, had more to do with calories, and less to do with adrenalin. Nothing had prepared her for an actual hair-raising experience. But Penny hadn't changed; still a short redhead with attitude, except now older, and at that moment, upset.

John glanced around and looked up into the air. "I guess he's returning the chopper."

The Mayor felt she might diminish trouble, if she could get them off the runway. "Oh, for God's sake," she rolled her eyes. "We have to get out of here and we have to do it now." Judy grabbed the back of Ron's motorized wheelchair and attempted to push him faster. Tina, wearing tennis shoes, still had trouble catching up. Everyone, especially Ron, seemed out of breath.

"My husband can work that thing himself," Tina responded with her brassy attitude. She pushed Judy aside and grasped the scooter. The

Mayor turned back to Penny, and shrugged, explaining that she simply wanted to help clear the path for the next plane. "Penny," Tina shouted. "Can you hear me?"

Penny nodded.

"You have green paint on your elbow. Did you know that?"

"Please keep moving," Judy interjected.

Penny shook her head in the affirmative. "Yeah thanks, Tina.

Exasperated, she wondered if she had missed something. As loud as she could speak without screaming, she directed a question to Judy, the Mayor. "What about our daughter?"

"Not sure. See that Jet parked at terminal B? It had ten underage girls from Poland on it, and one old woman who rode with them as a translator."

"Thanks to you, we caught some human traffickers."

"Thanks to me? What about Lani? Where's Lani?"

"You're Lani's parents, aren't you?"

"Yes. John and I are confused because you said they caught the group with that other plane."

"I was told your daughter is on flight 422. Isn't that right?"

"I'm fairly sure that's what Lani had said, but didn't you say they caught Julian?"

The Mayor paused to reflect on the question. "Yes, they did. I remember that name specifically because it's different. He's also a big guy. I never heard of him, but the Clark County Sheriff told me he's a famous artist. I guess his paintings hang in several of our fancier hotels. I also heard it took several officers to cuff him."

Tina moved forward to ask a logical question. "Where's 422?"

The Mayor looked up and saw the enormous jet taxiing towards them. "It's right there," she replied, pointing behind Tina. Her voice shook with fear, and her dark blue eyes bulged under wispy, well-trimmed bangs. "Please let's keep walking."

"But is Lani on it?" Both planes had come from California and they both flew in at relatively the same time. *Now John wondered whether the traffickers had split the girls onto different flights to make it seem less obvious or maybe to divert suspicion. Could they be sneaky enough?* He didn't have to say anything because the Mayor knew what he had on his mind.

"You mean to tell me there's another set of victims?" The Mayor reached through the window of the white truck, yanking the security guard's phone from the young man's hand, and proceeded to shout instructions to the Tower.

Penny held John's hand as tears rolled down her cheeks. "John, what's going on? Do you think I got the wrong flight number?" The plane coming towards them slowed to a crawl, seemingly stopping yards from where they stood on the runway. Warm fumes and engine noises added to the chaos. Sirens, alarms and distress signals seemed to be approaching.

A few minutes passed, and Judy handed the phone back to the guard. "Tell Mac, I won't have any slaves on my watch," the Mayor quipped, beaming her photogenic smile. Your daughter is on that flight right there–Number 422. She's in seat 7A and she's traveling with a guy called Peter. Now, I'm sorry, but I have to get back to my office."

The Mayor had to get to her car to make a slew of phone calls. "I'm sure your daughter will be here soon. I really have to run. It was nice to finally meet you." She moved as fast as she could in her heels. She did not realize a madman had a rifle with a silencer, aimed at her back. From fifty yards away, outside in the parking lot, a man looked through his scope. The red target light pointed in her direction.

"Business is business lady and you're ruining my luck," he mumbled before firing his shot. The shooter positioned outside the fenced perimeter, pointed his assault weapon through an SUV window. Fortunately, he missed his target.

A sobbing Penny unwillingly followed the Mayor off the paved asphalt towards the concourse of Terminal A. John jogged behind her onto a long corridor of flat escalators. But Ron stayed behind and didn't move. Tina turned back and yelled, "Honey, this way," figuring he had wedged a wheelchair tire into a small pothole. The white security truck had driven off and flight 422 crept toward the gate.

"Ron," Tina yelled as loud as possible. When he didn't respond, she ran back and noticed he didn't seem to be breathing. "Help," she screamed, pushing Ron's massive body away from the plane as fast as she could. His shiny head slumped forward, he looked fast asleep. But it wasn't the warm temperatures or even Ron's hotter polyester suit, because Tina noticed blood dripping down the side of the wheelchair. She feared the worst. "Help," she kept yelling to anyone who'd listen, as the jet engine noises drowned out her voice.

Tina waved at the tower and even jumped up and down, hollering at the approaching plane. "Stop, help," she cried. Tears flowed down her face as she kept on screaming, "Someone...anyone," her words for a few long minutes seemed to be going unheard. Penny and John were now inside the air-conditioned comfort of the airport. The Mayor had left. But Ron's soul had departed from runway two. Though the medics and emergency vehicles finally arrived, they couldn't revive him.

Chapter 42

"Mom, mom, over here," Lani yelled. Her mother heard her daughter's excited voice bounce through the crowded terminal. A voice she'd recognize anywhere, floated over the melded sounds of visitors, crying babies, overhead announcements and the general melee associated with commercial airports.

Penny sprang to greet her little girl and they both fell into each other's arms. "Oh, my baby, I'm so glad you're here." But her Lani didn't look like a baby anymore. In front of her stood a grown woman wearing a cute pink tunic and black leggings. In a short time span of three months, her child had blossomed, just like her beloved zinnias.

Lani hugged her dad. She pulled an out of breath Peter over for introductions. "This is Peter."

Peter stood over six feet. He had blond hair and it looked like he didn't eat. High cheekbones and a prominent jaw made him look even thinner. *Penny's first thought was, he'd make a good male model for overpriced cologne.* He wore tight jeans and a linen shirt the color of a well-squeezed lime. At first glance, he didn't look like a criminal, but she knew from experience that looks could be deceiving.

Penny wiped the tears off her face and smiled. *What could her baby girl be running from? She looked well fed and healthy and she didn't have any needle marks on her arms.* "Lani, I'm so glad you came dear, but why didn't you want to stay at home with Aunt Bess?" A mother's intuition required persistence.

"Well for one thing, we wanted to surprise you, which didn't work, because Peter kept insisting I call you, and now you're here. Surprise! She giggled but looked embarrassed. Plus…," she held up her hand with a dramatic flourish to show off the ring, "we're getting married and of course we want you to be there."

"Huh?" Her dad asked, as if he had lost the hearing in both of his ears. Penny inhaled and practiced forming a sentence in her mind. Normally she'd have plenty to say. She choked back emotions and felt like a teething puppy, her mouth open, but hardly a breath or even a yelp moved through her lips.

Penny glanced at all the passengers who filed past and wondered what had happened to Tina and Ron. Though the air-conditioned terminal felt cool, suddenly she felt hot. And Mac, why hadn't he returned by now? Moments like this required some sort of spiritual intervention. 'If God is with us, who can be against us?' she repeated several times inside her mind.

A brochure about a burlesque show appeared at her feet. She picked it up and began to fan her face with it. Lani knew she might cause her mother consternation. "What's wrong Ma? I thought you'd be happy for me."

"Where should I start?" Penny glanced at John. "Maybe we should grab a bite to eat or something. This day is getting too weird for me. I'm starved, aren't you all hungry? I could eat a loading dock full of those complimentary packs of airline peanuts." She pointed at Lani's bag. "Did you save your peanuts?"

Two formidable airport officials walked up, asking whether she was Penny Murray. Both tall men wore dark suits, carried walkie-talkies, cell phones and probably a weapon or two under loose fitting jackets.

"Yes, why?" Alarmed, she moved closer to John and wondered how bad a day could get.

"It seems there's a problem with your friend Tina. She's in an ambulance on her way to Desert Springs Hospital."

"Oh gawd no," she responded with a stress related rasp. *Times like this, made her want to pull her hair right out of her head.* "Is she, all right?"

"Yes, she's fine, but her husband might not be. Is Lani Murray your daughter?"

"Yes, yes, why? What's wrong with Ron?"

"Lani is our daughter. What's wrong?" John asked, stepping in front of Penny.

The men flashed badges at John but avoided her question about Ron. "We have some questions for a passenger who traveled with Lani today."

Penny attempted to look John in the eyes, but he kept eye contact with the pair of authoritative men. With a pained expression, she focused on

Peter. She shook her head from side to side and shrugged, wondering if this could implicate Lani in any way. "Do we need to call an attorney?"

"Not necessary ma'am. We just need to ask Mr. Lovecraft here a few questions."

Peter looked up, displaying a perfect set of the whitest teeth. "I'd be happy to answer any questions." Lani held his hand with her right hand and with her left, she held onto her dad.

"Peter, we need you to step into our office for questioning. Sorry, but Clark County police are waiting to talk to you."

"No problem. Remember we are kites' way above the trees." He hugged Lani and turned towards John and Penny. "Don't worry, I didn't do anything wrong."

"I know Babe," Lani replied. She kissed his nose and turned to her mom. "Can we wait for him at that airport diner over there?"

Fanning herself with the brochure, Penny nodded. "Of course—come on Lani—we'll meet Peter over there." *Food would help her think clearly, wouldn't it? What happened to Ron? Why is Tina in the hospital? Why does Lani want to get mar-*

ried? The questions rolled around in her head like a pinball machine going haywire.

As the two men led him away, she heard the first question and Peter's reply.

"Mr. Lovecraft, do you speak Polish?"

"No sir, I don't. But my grandmother does."

Chapter 43

The meal felt like slow motion. The late after-noon lunch, became dinner, and though the con-stant noise in the airport coffee shop filled the air, silence languished at their table until Penny's phone rang.

"Are you okay?" She listened with concern on her face. "Oh no."

John and Lani quietly sipped on their soft drinks. A half-eaten order of cold French fries sat like wilted grass in the middle of the lam-inate table. "No, they took Peter for question-ing. They told me Ron had injuries or something. Are you kidding, me? Okay, okay, but where? We promised him we'd wait." The waitress came by and Penny flagged her down. "Yes, Mac, I got it. Call me later but be careful." Her face suddenly matched the blob of ketchup next to the fries. A sob escaped her lips.

"What's with Brother Mac?" John asked when she disconnected her phone. "He's an amazing pilot. Did you see the way he dodged that 737?"

Penny nodded, swiping her hand through the air. "Yeah well listen to this, the Mayor—um—what's her name—Judy-something-Martin. Anyway, some creepy pimps with guns and knives approached her in the parking lot. They smashed her windows, flattened her tires, even knocked her out, but Mac was on his way in to see us and he saw them. Then he, all alone, jumped them and called the cops. Those miserable idiots stabbed him in the stomach. The Mayor is alive, but she has serious injuries. They're both in the hospital. Mac found out about Ron too."

"And?" John asked. He watched Penny take two deep breaths. Tears rolled down her cheeks.

"Who is Mac?" Lani asked with a confused look. "Ron is that man from the newspaper? Do you mean my godfather?"

"Yes, they shot my old boss. He didn't make it," she sobbed. "But Mac gave me an important message. He said, we have to get out of here or we won't make it either. The bad guys know we're here. These are serious bad guys, the type you see in the bloodiest movies. Except, this is our lives, not some Hollywood set filled with blank cartridges and ketchup. Mac thinks the bullets that hit Ron might have been meant for me." She stood up and pulled her purse over her shoulder. *Stop crying, she said to herself, or maybe her mother had sent her a message from the other side? 'No tears, you need to be strong', came a voice in her head. 'Remember to have patience'.*

"Come on Lani. You still haven't told me what's going on with this Peter guy and you can't be serious about getting married."

"Mom, please don't start. I'm sorry about your boss."

"Don't change the subject, young lady."

We're both grown-ups and we're in love."

"Where does Mac suggest we go?" John asked glancing at his watch. A deep wrinkle appeared between his eyes. Fear and worry distorted his normally calm features. *If Mac thought the bullets were meant for Penny, they probably were. Had all of this happened to be taking place in a Hollywood movie, he knew his beautiful wife would be nominated for an award. In fact, she'd win best actress.*

Unfortunately, he also knew there wasn't a parallel universe filled with fantasies, running alongside this one. He had one Penny and she was a real woman, not an actress. One love of his life, and he had to do what he could to keep her alive.

The waitress brought the change and set it on the table. "Have a nice day," she said turning away.

"Wait. Here's your tip," Penny called her back, noticing she looked tired. "I bet you're ready to go home by now."

"Yeah, it's been a long day."

"Tell me about it," Penny replied, realizing it sounded as if she wanted to hear what happened. As if a stranger's insane story might make her feel better. As if topping her story could calm her nerves, making her forget the wild events of the day. As if anyone's mundane story could compete.

"People leaving Vegas never tip. It's like they run out of money gambling. They forget that other people work hard to earn a living."

Penny reached into her purse and pulled out a ten-dollar bill.

"Here's a little extra. Can you recommend a good place to spend the night?"

John interrupted his wife. "What are you talking about?"

"Thanks lady," the waitress made a weird face at John but took the money and shoved in into her apron. "Right now, I live in my car, but someday I'll get an apartment. I don't know what's a good place or a bad place. You want a tip from me?" The sloppy bun on her head had come loose and she had a wry smile. "Here's my tip from me to you: 'Don't go east of Fremont St at night.'"

The server picked up a load of empty plates and turned to leave.

"John, look at her. She looks like she's at the end of her rope. Right now, I feel the same way. Mac told me to get a room for the night. He doesn't think we should go back to the apartment. Doesn't really matter, 'cause we'll be going home soon. Maybe you ought to give your notice on Monday."

"But Mom, I thought you said you live in a real fancy place."

"We do, or…eh we did," she stuttered. "I told you I've been painting murals for a resort, but the guy who owns the place is going to jail for a long time." She looked at her watch. "We just found out. Like seconds before you landed."

"What does that have to do with Peter?" Lani asked. She wrapped up the cold fries in the wax paper lining the basket and stuffed them into her bag.

Settle down, Penny said to herself. "It has to do with that flight that came in a minute before yours did, and a group of underage girls who were going to be bought and sold like cattle." *Please don't cry again. She continued a mantra in the back of her head like a broken phonograph, repeating the same words about staying strong, remaining patient.*

Handsome but frazzled, Peter walked into the diner. "Those idiots," he shook his head and round circles appeared on his cheeks. "They thought I brought you here against your will to turn you into a working girl." He hugged Lani and tears rolled down his face. "Lani, I'm sorry, it's all because of my stupid little brother. I swore to those cops. You wouldn't believe it, but they brought in FBI agents too. I swear to all of you, that I have nothing to do with his shady business dealings."

"Oh, my God," Lani gasped. What's going to happen to those girls?"

"Lani, you can't be serious about this guy," Penny wanted to shout, but she spoke through clenched teeth, in a hushed tone, so Peter wouldn't hear. "I'm glad you're asking about those young ladies who have concerned parents, sisters, brothers and friends wondering what happened. All those girls are going to get counseling, and then they'll be sent home. Some of them won't want to go home. That's the hard part, the ones who grew up in an orphanage for example. At least that's what Mac told me."

"Mom, who's this Mac guy?"

"He's a clergyman at the church and a helicopter pilot. He's the one who brought all of us to the airport to stop your plane."

Outraged and embarrassed, she wanted to crawl under the table. "You stopped my plane? Wait a minute—you thought that–I? That's disgusting. Mom, are you really my mom?" Visibly upset, she put her arm around Peter. Her mother had always trusted her and now that trust seemed to have shattered like the Mayor's car window. "I'm not underage Mom, and in case you don't know, being a hooker is not one of my career goals. Sheesh, Dad, what happened to mom?"

"Listen," Penny said. "This is Vegas and things like that happen here. In fact, it can happen any-where. Plus, it's good to be vigilant. What was I supposed to think?" She thought about the giant debacle she had caused the airport, the airline, the Mayor, the church, and she felt somewhat ridiculous. "It's a mom's job to worry about their kids. Show me a mother who doesn't care if her daughter goes missing and I'll show you a docu-mentary about animals that eat their young."

"Oh Mom! You're so dramatic."

Peter looked shocked and devastated. He used a napkin to wipe moisture from his eyes, before whispering into Lani's ear. A second later she asked, "Did you say Mac's a clergyman?"

"Yeah, we had to stop the plane because we are your family and we love you and yes, he's a man of the cloth. What about it?"

"Well, do you think he can marry us at the Polynesian Wedding chapel? We have an appointment for tomorrow afternoon."

"Tomorrow? Young lady, you can change the subject faster than the weather in California. I've had about all I can handle regarding this. Let's go before I faint."

John held Penny's hand on the long walk to the taxis. She inhaled and exhaled loudly, doing breathing exercises to calm herself. John looked concerned. She smiled in an effort to keep from bursting into tears. *At least she learned one thing during dinner and that was not to go east of Fremont Street at night. God Bless that woman, Penny murmured to no one. God Bless her soul.*

"Are you all right?" John asked, while waiting for Peter and Lani to catch up.

"I'm fine, but I'm sad about Ron. He didn't even want to come, but he did anyway. Such a team player, and now Tina's a widow. This is horrible." Dusk settled onto the airport. "The bullet could have hit you instead. Where would that leave me?" She sighed. "In a way, there's a positive side to all of this."

"Like what? Some mad human traffickers might come after us? Our daughter's godfather was assassinated? We're going to be thrown out of our apartment? You lost your job. The Mayor of Las Vegas is in the hospital and it might be our fault? Mac has a stab wound. Lani wants to marry the first guy she ever kissed. Did I mention some thugs want to murder my wife? Oh–and don't forget we're also broke–again."

"John, stop ranting, she might hear you. We have each other. That's positive. That night you took off, I had no doubt you'd be back." They stood on the curb watching Lani and Peter negotiate for a cab among a sea of yellow and white cars.

"Not a smidgen of doubt?"

She turned towards him and gave him a kiss on the cheek. "Not until I had a nightmare about you and some woman with legs to the sky."

"Bean pole legs, huh?"

"Yes, but she looked hot."

"You must be misinterpreting your dreams. When you mention legs to the sky, I think of a skyscraper, like the Magnifique. Unless your self-image has changed, you should know that I don't think any female is hotter than you." He pulled her close and stared into her eyes. "I'm so lucky to have you in my life." His lips touched hers and they were lost in the moment, drifting back to a long-lost sunset in Hawaii.

When she opened her eyes, she said, "You know as well as I do that luck has nothing to do with it."

"Good point, but I'm trying to be positive. We're in Vegas baby, and you're my Lady Luck."

"Am I? Right now, I feel we're on a losing streak."

"Don't forget the bullet hit Ron. It could have been me."

"True, but this mess isn't over. Have any trick dice?"

John laughed. She loved to make him laugh. He had such a wonderful, honest sounding laugh. "No, but don't forget, I have you and that's more valuable than all the gold in Fort Knox." He squeezed her hand before pulling her off the curb to the waiting cab. "Onward Christian soldiers."

"Wait; remember how nothing can get in the way of true love?" Penny whispered. "Look at those two–it's like us–I think it's real."

"Do you?" John watched Peter and Lani walk around the yellow vehicle. A hybrid car zipped past them, swirling up dust and beeping like a roadrunner in the desert.

"Look, an oxymoron," Peter pointed at the annoying little sub-compact dodging around the taxis. The small white vehicle had thick red stripes running from front to back and a number three painted on the side.

"Why is it an oxymoron?" Lani asked.

"Because someone thinks it's a racecar. There's no such thing as a fast economy car," he laughed. Peter made a sweeping gesture with his arms when opening the cab door for her.

"Your coach awaits, M'lady," Peter said with a bow. "I love you Lani."

"I love you too." Once inside and situated, Lani dug around in her bag and held up Peter's dinner. "Would you like some cold fries?"

Chapter 44

The cab driver sped out of the airport on to Paradise Road, towards the Vegas Strip. Though they weren't going far, it seemed he had missed the freeway exit.

"Please slow down," Penny pleaded. She gripped the front seat, as her body swayed left to right.

"I can't," the driver replied. "Some asshole is on my tail and it looks like he has a gun pointing out his window."

"Huh?" Penny and John turned to look out the back window. They both saw a faded gray sedan moving closer, with what appeared to be a shot-gun sticking out the passenger side.

The professional cab driver seemed agitated. Photos of his children were plastered all over the dash, and up on the visor. "I didn't want to frighten you, but they followed us out of the airport."

"Have you seen them before?" The front of the gray car had tinted windows, making light reflect off the glass, thus making it hard to see the driver and passenger. Crystal rosary beads dangled from the rear-view mirror.

"No ma'am. I thought that maybe you knew who they are? If not, it's probably a hot car."

She glanced back and ducked down as much as possible, but the four of them in the back, were like a bag of squishy marshmallows, melded to each other, without space to move around. "Looks like two young punks in a stolen car. Lani, Peter, try to scoot down, way down. John, you should scrunch down too."

A bullet nicked the side mirror of the passenger side of the cab. "Ma'am," the cab driver looked like he saw a ghost. "Shit. Please squat down lower."

"I'll call 911." Penny dialed the numbers but couldn't explain her whereabouts. "I'm in a cab with my family and we're being followed and shot at. We just left the airport."

The dispatch officer had a litany of questions. "Yes, we understand, hold on let me ask the driver. She wants our cab number. I forget. Is this a white or yellow cab?"

Penny answered all the questions and a bullet ricocheted through the back window, tearing into the roof lining. "Oh, dear God, please help us." Pieces of glass flew through the cab and the driver bit his lip and began reciting some sort of repetitive incantations.

"Everyone okay?" The kind and gentle driver kept changing lanes and worrying about his passengers, while his foot sat on the accelerator. His cab flew, like a runaway elephant.

Glass fragments were in everyone's hair. John brushed some off his jeans. "We're still here—better speed up." He reached to help Peter who had shards of glass on his pale green shirt. Peter almost completely covered a quivering Lani in a tight embrace.

The dispatcher asked another question. "What's your name dear?"

"Penny Murray."

Silence. Then more silence and the annoying rustle of papers.

"Hello, are you still there, dispatcher?"

"Penny Murray? We've heard of you. You were looking for your daughter, right? Did you find her?"

"Yes, I did. She's here with me now and we're all getting shot at."

"Okay, we're on our way. Your driver signaled his headquarters. We intercepted a call from his taxi company and have your GPS."

The driver double backed towards the 215, heading for the 15 freeway. He figured he could lose the pursuers, or at least get them to stop shooting in dense traffic. "I'm sorry Ma'am, but I'm going to go very fast, so I can crossover to the carpool lane." He wove in and out of traffic into the ridesharing lane. With his clever maneuvers, he managed to position his cab so that several other cars were between them and the gray sedan. The older gray car seemed to be having a hard time keeping up.

"This is crazy," Lani mumbled from her spot on the floor. She squeezed Peter's hand. "Never a dull moment with my mom around…."

"You be quiet young lady. Try not to move too much. There's glass everywhere. Before you blame your mom for everything, it might surprise you to know that all of this has to do with you and Peter," John said with a sigh, before he launched into his personal, unspoken prayers.

Red tail lights lit up the night. Traffic screeched to a halt in front of them. The driver slammed on the brake and more of the glass fragments flew onto their backs. "Sorry," he said, staring into his rear-view mirror. "I think we lost them." After pumping his brakes, the driver looked back again, and noticed the gray car had driven onto the shoulder. A pouf of smoke reflected in his chipped rear view mirror. "Maybe they had an accident," he said, lifting his foot from the pedal.

"Could be they ran out of gas," Peter said to the driver. "You were smart for getting into traffic, looks like they couldn't handle it."

"Or maybe the car overheated," Lani added, wondering how much more of this drama she herself would have to 'handle'.

Penny exhaled. She *thought of John's silly comment about her being Lady Luck. Right now, she felt like the opposite.* "I don't know, but I'm glad they're gone." She wanted to hold John's hand, but his hands remained clasped, and his fingers entwined.

John could only murmur what he felt in his grateful heart, "Must be divine intervention."

Chapter 45

That evening they checked in to the Magic Carpet Motel. In the morning, Penny awoke to Lani
banging on the adjoining door.

"Mom, this place is gross." She swung open the
connecting door while rubbing her eyes. "Can't
we stay somewhere better? I think I just saw a
mouse."

"How do you know it's a mouse?"

"Dad, can't you do something? This isn't
funny. We never imagined it being like this. We
thought you both have good jobs and things are
looking up, but ever since we arrived, there are
cops, fire trucks and now this fleabag."

"Those are bed bugs not fleas."

"Mom, stop it."

"Well you're the one whining. Someday you
might need to know these things. What if one

day, you decide to be an entomologist? Think of this as getting hands on training."

"Dad, is mom losing it?"

"No, I don't think so, but yesterday was too much for all of us. I'm still shaking from ducking down in that cab. Lani, just so you know, your mother had to spend every last dollar, making sure you're safe. I don't think you realize how much your mother has done for you in this life. Maybe you should learn some appreciation. If you knew the amount she has spent, you'd faint. She gave it all to the trafficking task force teams, the church, a helicopter company, airport security and anything that's left is going to patch up our legal issues with the Mayor's office. I'm hoping some of it is tax deductible."

Looking defeated, Penny plopped down on the bed. "That's if the poor woman survives. Some of those bruises sound serious. Maybe we should visit her."

John took her hand. "We will. And don't forget Tina, at least we have to send flowers."

She shook her head and looked hopeless. "No fancy wreath. We'll order sensible, inexpensive flowers or a green plant in a basket with a sympathy card. Poor Ron, this shouldn't have happened. Gun violence is getting out of control. I'm still in shock."

"Mom do we have any money?"

"Please stop asking about money. It's kind of a sore subject. You know we didn't have much when we got here."

"Maybe I'm dense," Lani interrupted, "but you two work hard. I can't believe this," she shrieked.

Peter appeared in the doorway. He looked lost in loose fitting green pajamas adorned with a repetitive print of the John Deere logo. "Lani, be quiet, you are waking up this entire motel." A few hairs on the back of his head stood straight up, reminding Penny of a cartoon character called Dennis.

Lani froze in disbelief. Her mother had worked so hard for everything, and now it appeared they had nothing. The weird zombie-like crowd she had seen in the lobby gave her the creeps. She watched Peter go back to the adjacent room, knowing he wanted to sleep late. As for her, she couldn't think of anywhere she could cry.

"At least I paid off the house," Penny said brightly. Plus, we have enough for five Greyhound bus tickets to California and enough for one more night in this posh place. We're basically penniless, but your dad still has another check coming. Can we not talk about money? Please? Instead, why don't you tell us about this Polynesian chapel. Since I don't have a grass skirt, would it be *cool* if I wore a dress with tropical flowers on it?"

"Oh yes Mom," Lani brightened. "I know Dad has a shirt with a pineapple pattern."

Penny looked over at John. "Actually, that's another problem. You see we can't go get our stuff from the apartment, so we have to charge a few things at the mall."

Lani loved the way her mom used the word 'cool' because it reminded her of the mom she knew as a child; the happier, carefree artist. Her mom had been the woman who didn't have much, but acted as if she had everything.

"Sounds like a good idea in theory Mom, except I'm wondering how we'll get to the mall without having some whacked out perpetrators follow and kill us."

"What time is the wedding reservation at the Polynesian chapel?"

"Three."

Penny picked up her phone. "Hey Mirage, it's Penny. I know it's sort of late notice, but I wanted to invite you to my daughter's wedding. Thanks. This time though, we're the ones with transportation issues. Can you pick us up from the Fashion Show mall around two?" Penny stopped to listen. "The resort? They closed it down? Cops? That's good isn't it? Out of a job? Well that makes two of us. Don't worry, we'll find something. Would you mind giving us a ride? No, it's casual. From there, we're going to the Polynesian Chapel on Main. After that we're treating you to an elegant reception at the City Centre. How about on the far side of Nordy's? Yes, thanks."

Chapter 46

Mirage arrived late because she had to find a sitter for Cleo. Penny called Tina at home and invited her too, but after listening and sobbing along with Tina, she told her not to worry about coming. Even asking her to come felt inappropriate, but the call had to be made, as a courtesy. After all, Tina might have seemed like an unlikely choice for a godmother, but twenty years ago, Tina had made a big difference and had changed her life.

Later, when Lani came into the world, Tina continuously showered the newborn with kisses and cute baby gifts. When Tina held Lani in her arms, Penny noticed glistening eyes, as if Tina had wanted the child to be her own. When selected as godparents, Ron and Tina seemed over the moon with excitement. They even threw a giant baby shower, inviting everyone at The Globe.

Penny bit her lip thinking about Ron in the morgue. The classic adman in a gray suit had been a good boss. There were so many things about him that used to crack her up, not just her, but everyone in the entire department. Of course, Tina didn't feel like coming to Lani's wedding.

Mac reiterated that he couldn't officiate because he wasn't yet ordained but said he wouldn't miss it for the world, even with bandages and pain pills. Father Charles couldn't come because he had a huge night planned at Christ the Redeemer, complete with Bingo, raffle prizes and sloppy Joes. Peter called his brother Tyler and found out the little monster was heading to Juvenile Hall. Though the turnout would be small, none of that mattered to the lovebirds.

To mark the momentous occasion, they would sit around a large dinner table at a gourmet restaurant for the reception. The reception would be elegant, unlike the Polynesian Wedding chapel. The actual wedding itself had zoomed by like the Italian Grand Prix. The downtown wedding venue could have competed with a comedy club. Penny thought she had entered some sort of punk-styled reality show, where everything made her burst into uncontrollable, almost hysterical laughter. Short and to the point, the minister had looked like a Hawaiian Elvis. He wore fake-flower leis around his neck, tinted glasses and kept repeating the words: 'thank you, thank you, thank you very much.' He spoke with the booming voice of a game show host about to give away a major prize.

Mirage parked her small banged up car directly in the front, near a row of battery-operated tiki torches. They gathered inside the small chapel to snap a few pictures, before John walked his little girl, the blushing bride, down the aisle. Strangers crowded in, filling the pews. Everyone clapped, and even outsiders threw rice at the excited couple. Fifteen minutes later, they headed back to the Strip. Whambamthankyoumam—it went by in an instant.

While walking out of the covered parking structure at the upscale City Centre to celebrate, Penny's emotions took an opposite turn from the chapel. She burst into tears. Her baby had grown up and had become a married woman.

Lani looked magnificent. She wore a snow-colored dress with spaghetti straps. The understated and unadorned white, skater-style dress didn't have a touch of lace, pearls, ruffles or sheer panels to embellish and distract the eye. Instead, the dress accentuated Lani's svelte figure, with a sweeping skirt and a fitted bodice. Around her neck, a small shell necklace, her mom had brought back from Hawaii, long ago. Peter wore a new, short-sleeved shirt with shamrock green palm leaves on a mint colored background. To the average onlooker, they looked like vintage clothes, but Lani's designer dress had cost over three hundred dollars.

Penny kept calculating the expenses in her head. John had been correct about all the money being gone. Two million dollars had flown through her fingers like water in the dancing fountains, in front of the Bellagio hotel. Not one, but two million; she shuddered, knowing she couldn't have done things differently. Bad money had created something good, but intangible.

Mac interrupted her thoughts. "She's radiant." He held onto a glass of water as if it were a potent cocktail. John sat on one side, and Mac groaned with pain as he slipped into the chair next to her.

Noticing his drink and trying to be a kind host, John asked, "Can I get you something stronger?"

"No this is perfect. They gave me codeine at the hospital. Plus, I don't drink anymore. I gave up most of my vices, except coffee and the rare glazed donut." A genuine smile graced his rugged face. "That sounded humble, but honestly, I can put away four or five donuts at a time."

Lani and Peter sat across from them. They both laughed at Brother Mac and his comments about donuts. Mirage and Mac were the only other guests. Penny thought about the celebrity chef who owned the restaurant and the contemporary atmosphere. Her mind wandered to the cost of the appetizers, the exorbitant salads, the bottle of champagne and now the inflated, but worth every calorie dessert. John said, "Too bad Father Charles couldn't make it."

When the server placed the last course in front of Peter, he looked surprised and said, "That's no donut."

"It's hazelnut gelato in a chocolate bowl," Lani giggled, sticking a teaspoon into her new husband's awaiting mouth. "It's to die for."

Penny wanted to kick John under the table but thought Mac might notice. Six people at about two hundred dollars each, barely left them enough to get home. One more wedding guest, even one as kind and wonderful as Father Charles and they would be flat busted. Shut up John, she wanted to say, but instead, she kept quiet through what felt like a semi-tragic, double-edged event. Not only were they back to having no money, but her Lani had to start a life with someone she didn't even know. This wasn't the way things were supposed to happen. Still, she had to blame herself too. After all, they did leave Lani with Aunt Bess.

They shouldn't have left California in the first place. Her family life had abruptly become empty-nest-syndrome, coupled with empty-bank-accounts extraordinaire, and this tasteless realiza-tion became too much to swallow. She twirled her spoon around in the chocolate bowl, hoping her heart would warm to all the changes in her life. And as the gelato melted, she accepted it all. There they were, The Murray's, pulling each other through the threshold of a fresh new life, which included Peter as her new son-in law and Lani as his wife. Behind them, a swirling whirlpool of good and bad memories called the past.

Next to her, stood her true-blue husband John, who held her hand and listened to her wild ideas, with unmatched trust and loyalty.

"Wow that is delicious." Mac licked his spoon and placed it on a plate. "There are few people like Father Charles, probably a handful in the entire world. Pushing eighty and working around the clock to help the homeless. He's super busy and up to his ears in hungry alligators tonight. In fact, I hate to eat and run, but he needs my help."

"We understand. After everything you've been through, I'm surprised you made it. Thanks so much for coming." Penny nodded and did some fast math. One less coffee would save them five bucks.

"I have to leave too. You should see my bizarre babysitter," Mirage intoned, pushing her chair back and standing up. It's her first time watching Cleo and I'm not sure about her vision. She has cute black-rimmed glasses, but it's obvious she has horrible stigmatism. When not babysitting, she works at a strip club and loves it. Honestly, I don't think she can see her clients. I doubt she can see my baby. Can you all walk back to the Magic Carpet from here?"

Penny nodded, concern showing on her face. "Of course, you're a sweetie. Thanks for picking us up and coming to the wedding."

"Congratulations Penny and thanks for inviting me. Let me know where you end up for work. I need to find a new job ASAP."

"I know. I will. I have your number." Penny watched Mirage hug Lani and Peter and then she disappeared like the vision she was named after.

Mac turned from John towards Penny." By the way, when I talked to Judy this afternoon she told me you gave her a large donation. Thanks for pulling me out of the doghouse. I didn't want to go back to wearing peels in the block at Lovelock."

Peels? Lovelock? It took her a few seconds to figure out he meant prison. "Was it the use of the chopper?"

Mac glanced at his watch. "Yes and no. Interrupting service at the airport disrupted the money train. It's complicated."

Penny looked down into her cup of coffee. *She wanted to jump from the edge and do freestyle laps until the beating in her chest subsided. Until the day, and the week had passed, and she sat on her couch in her home, looking after those ailing zinnias.* "Well we certainly didn't think the Mayor would get hurt. Is she doing better?"

"Much better, I'm sure she'd be happy to know you asked about her."

"And you? How are you holding up?"

"I'll be fine. Just a flesh wound."

"Mac," Penny held up her cup as if making a toast. "I want you to know how grateful we are for your support. I'm glad I know you. It's hard for me to think about the future right now, but I promise that someday, we will again donate to your task force. These last few months were educational for both of us. We had no idea about the horrors of human trafficking, but you didn't miss a beat to help us. In turn, your actions helped real innocent victims. I know you'll make a great priest."

He nodded and placed his glass down. "Thank you. What you said means a lot." He wiped his hands in a cloth napkin before standing up. "Most importantly, congratulations kids," he said to Lani and Peter. "Hope your life is always filled with love."

"Thanks Brother Mac," Lani said with a smile. Peter waved and before Mac turned to leave, he dipped close to Penny and whispered into her ear.

"There's no one like you Miss Penny. Meeting you changed my life for the better. Don't worry about jumping to conclusions. You did the right thing. Take care, and may you always find favor with God."

Like a gambler flipping a coin, there were two sides to doing the right thing. One side, it could be argued, is the entire hellish matter about a mother overreacting, while the other side is to do nothing, allowing unexperienced children to learn from their own disasters. Deep within, she knew that if she had *to do everything over, not much would change. It was a bet she had to make.*

Though not the easiest route, in this case, it worked. For a while, she felt like a high roller who plays roulette. Her ball landing on red, after placing her chips on black. Her natural instinct had always been to guard her child and protect her loved ones. In this instance, however, losing wasn't an option.

Her eyes traveled to the exit where Mac took a step from the quiet, elegant surroundings into a cacophony of noisy slot machines. Back to work and back to reality. Fortunately, she didn't need to rescue Lani, and she didn't need to enlist the help of strangers, but destiny had brought her and Mac together again. He had told her that she had changed his life for the better. More importantly, she felt that now, his new position would help Mac make a real difference in the world.

Maybe, she had been the pawn or the catalyst in God's plan to help those girls from Poland. At first, she had felt somewhat foolish, when she found out, she had made a mistake. It happened to be a mistake, but it also helped the girls on the other airplane. She thought of the girls in the limo with the fancy nails and the high heel shoes. She thought that their mother would want to know where they are, and how they are doing.

Though Lani had been safe, her maternal heart felt like breaking for those other girls. Though she didn't have anything to give Mac right now, she vowed, deep in her soul, to scrape together small *amounts at a time, in order to help this important, lifesaving cause.*

"Monday, John. Please tell me you're ready to give notice on Monday. I have to go home."

John looked at Penny's exhausted, billiard table green eyes. *Maybe she didn't realize she had promised to donate money they didn't have. Of course, she's tired, and sad about Ron. The serious tone sounded like she meant what she said. They had to return to California. He also missed her home cooking. Though the wedding feast tasted magnificent, it reminded him of Penny's delicious creations.* Slowly, he pried her clenched hand off the coffee cup, whereupon he kissed her wedding ring finger. "Sure sweetie, anything for my beautiful bride."

Chapter 47

Aunt Bess had called late that evening to congratulate Lani. "Dear, let me talk to your mother." Penny had a pillow on top of her head. She nursed a bubbling champagne headache. The pillow had a distinct odor, and though the sheets were clean, something nasty had permeated the polyester filling. She couldn't wait to get home and sleep in her own bed, with her own sheets.

Lani sat down on the queen-sized bed and shook her mother. "Mom, it's Aunt Betsy. Peter and I are going dancing."

There was no use trying to fight it. The bedside clock showed eleven o'clock at night, in neon green. Lani was a newlywed and they were in Vegas. Nonetheless, it did seem way past Aunt Bess' bedtime. Penny propped herself up, moved the pillow and took the phone. "Have fun," she said to her daughter and Peter as they waved goodbye, "but don't forget, tomorrow we'll be checking out of here, so you might want to stay in touch."

Penny could hear the happy couple giggle and quote poetry. They'd often test each other's spelling and vocabulary. "Okay wait a second, smarty pants," Lani asked, running after Peter, "What's the difference between cuddling and snuggling?"

"Bye kids," John shouted from the shower.

Into the phone, Penny turned on the charm and her personality became animated, "We missed you Aunt Bess," she winked at John who came out of the bathroom with a towel wrapped around his waist. "Lani was the prettiest bride. She looked like an angel."

"Say hi to my sister," John added. "Tell her we're coming home."

Penny put a finger to her lips to silence him. "Are you kidding me?" A look of pure astonishment and anger made her green eyes flash because of something horrid she heard from Aunt Bess. "Please tell me this isn't true." She put her head in her right hand and moved her left hand through a shock of messy hair. "This is such crap.

I can't believe it." She listened for some more details and thanked John's sister for the call. "We'll figure things out. That's what families do."

John had crawled into bed, waiting to find out what had happened. "What?" He mouthed the word, his eyes round, like giant pans of pepperoni pizza.

"Yes, Aunt Bess. We love you. Goodnight." She threw the phone onto the dirty carpet as if it were a burning piece of coal.

"John, we're in worse trouble now, than ever."

"How could that be? Lani's fine. She's married and she's happy. You said yourself, you think it's true love."

"Not about that," she said, waving a dismissive arm through the air. "Of course, those two are in love. It's our money situation. We have enough to get home, but that's really it. Seriously. Do you read me? No dinero—kein Geld—None—Nada. No money, honey."

"Stop being all huffy with me, you know I'm on your side."

Penny shook her head in disbelief. "If it's not one thing, then it's another." Tears were rolling down her face. "When I got that money from

Dan, I thought we caught a break, but then you got mad at me. After I found out about Peter's brother and those traffickers, I could only think of Lani's safety. Ron died because I had jumped to irrational conclusions. My hard headed decision to save my daughter cost him his life. What if Tina sues us? I did the only thing I could do. You don't blame me, do you?"

"Don't cry! How could I blame you? Tina is not going to sue us. Some homicidal maniac aimed a weapon at you and the cops know you're innocent. You were the victim and Ron an unfortunate casualty. Even Tina knows it's not your fault." Sensing something off kilter, he looked directly into Penny's eyes.

"Wait a minute, back up." He put one of the stinky pillows behind his back. "Didn't you pay the mortgage off? I thought you said the house is paid for? We have enough for utilities, right? What did my sister tell you?"

"That's too many questions. Slow down, because my head hurts. I did pay off the mortgage. I also told your sister that we're coming home. So, she asked the tenants to leave."

"And?" He drew it out. A short word made to sound like a long winding road. He inhaled at the end of it.

"And–they moved out–but not before they took everything and vandalized our home. They ripped out the cabinets, the stove, the dishwasher, the refrigerator and whatever else. I can't imagine. It's so shocking that I can't remember everything she babbled on about… She said they poured concrete down the toilets and put bullet holes in the stucco. Oh, and there's some critters. Either squirrels or a skunk family moved in and had babies. Aunt Bess thinks it would cost about fifty grand to fix everything. We don't even have one grand. Basically, we are flat broke."

"We won't be able to live in our own home?"

Disgusted, she closed her eyes and silently began to count to ten. *Best looking, kindest man ever but sometimes he seemed to be missing a wheel.* "Catching on faster these days?" She wanted to hide under the pillow again and forget she ever came to Vegas. *At that moment, she wished she had never been born. What could she do to save her family this time?*

"We'll be staying with your sister and her fluffy dog until we figure out what to do." Penny yawned; she had lost the desire to sleep. "I'm out of answers John. I spent decades in the newspaper business always saving for our family, and now I have nothing."

"Shut up, you have me. I'm sorry but I'm not ready to live with my doting sister and I don't want us to be homeless."

"Well, I hate to inform you, but the definition of homeless would apply to our situation. I can hardly pay for this dump. Your sister's not that bad, and I don't have any other ideas right now, do you?"

"I'd rather camp in our home while I slowly fix it."

"That's if you can get a job."

"You know I will. I'll work with Hans or whatever."

"You'd rather die of carbon monoxide poisoning than live in luxurious splendor with your sibling?"

John slipped under the covers, pulling the sheet over his head. "Yes, but don't worry, we'll grill outside. Goodnight."

Chapter 48

"Wait here or I'll never find you." That's what John had said over an hour ago when he went to get his final check. The good news seemed more like a shock to the system. There were so many thoughts floating around in her mind. Lani getting married had miraculously flipped a disaster on its head. Financially, even with a colossal bequest, they were worse off than they were six months ago. Too bad, she wouldn't get payment for her murals.

Penny's stomach growled. She didn't dare leave the stool she sat on. *She had a growing notion that she, and Vegas didn't mix. All she'd have to do is wander through the casino to the coffee shop, order a latte and turn around, only to find out John couldn't find her, and she'd be lost. With her luck, she'd call him, and he'd have his cell phone shut off, and hers would need to be charged. To make sure, she checked her phone and it looked charged. She looked in her wallet, hoping John's pay would be higher than the previous week. At that moment, she had enough for the bus tickets with ten dollars to spare. The only positive thing about finances had to do with the dilapidated house in California being paid off in full.* They owned an empty wreck.

A glamorous woman in tight, designer jeans, wandered over to the stool across the aisle. It happened to be the same slot machine that had paid out the huge jackpot earlier that morning. A large diamond on her left hand and stunning highlights in thick well-styled hair, made the woman appear wealthy. Slender fingers pulled a hundred-dollar bill from a high-end handbag. She impatiently tapped the screen. "Come on, baby—give mama a jackpot." The wheels spun around, but the winnings were meager.

Even after a twenty-dollar win, the machine made a boisterous commotion of bells and whistles. "Come on," the woman repeated over and over again. "Give me a jackpot." Penny couldn't really see how much the woman had lost, but soon noticed she had slipped another hundred-dollar bill into the same machine. After a few more spins, the woman yelled louder. She kicked the machine with her pointy-toed pumps and began to curse. When she ran out of money the robotic voice of the machine said, "Please make a deposit to continue uninterrupted play."

Tired of waiting for John and exhausted from sleeping or rather not sleeping well at The Magic Carpet, she enjoyed the entertainment. Penny concentrated on the woman's fingers and how she pushed erratically, sometimes swiping her hand across the glass monitor as if to send it superstitious superpowers. The more the woman bet, the more she lost. Even when she played with the maximum amount of coins, she won nothing. After another hundred in the same machine, she became upset and angry. She flagged down a cocktail waitress and ordered a drink. Penny noticed the money went fast, because in a few minutes she only had twenty dollars left in the machine. When the drink arrived, the woman turned around, caught Penny looking and scowled. In a reprimanding hostile tone, she asked, "Haven't you done enough?"

"Ma'am, I'm sorry, but are you talking to me?"

"Yes. I know exactly who you are. I saw you on the news and I followed you here, so I can personally explain how you ruined my life."

"Excuse me?" Penny thought the woman must be nuts. She wanted to run away but didn't want to get lost.

Though the woman made a stunning first impression, upon closer examination, her thick makeup appeared obvious and overdone. "I think you're confusing me with someone else." Penny stood up from the stool adding, "Good luck to you. Hope you win."

"Sit down bitch," the woman snarled while looking around to make sure no one heard the exchange. "I have searched those caves for years and found nothing. I have crawled around among dusty stones, rocks, lizards, scorpions and spiders to find my share of Dan's loot. Dan and I used to work together. He owed me a ton of money, and then he had the audacity to die."

Audacity to die? Penny winced, thinking the woman had used the wrong word. Didn't audacity mean fearlessness or bravery? "I still think you're mistaken," she sat back down and whispered, "Dan who?" She wanted to run from the casino but worried it might complicate things. Her heart pounded. She realized this crazy woman knew exactly who she was. Worst of all, she also had some sort of bone to pick with her, for some mysterious reason.

"I knew you'd try to pretend as if you had no idea what I'm talking about, but you can't fool me."

"Who are you again?"

"My name is Doreen. Dan promised to give me half his take, but I recently found out he left all of it to you."

"All?" Barely audible, she surprised herself by asking that question.

"Yes, all that the police could find anyway. I think there's a ton more out there, under that death trap called the Mojave, but I'm tired of looking for it. Like I said, you ruined my entire life."

"Look lady, I mean Doreen. I haven't seen Dan in over twenty years. Even then, I only knew him for a few hours. He piloted the commercial jet that took me to Hawaii. I married my husband John on the Big Island. We've been happily married and together ever since. I never heard from

Dan again." Penny stood so she could escape this woman's wrath. She wanted to run right out of the casino, figuring John could call and find her later.

"But you got the money!" Doreen tried grabbing a hold of Penny's arm.

"Leave me alone. No, I don't have any money. Are you panhandling or what?" Her legs felt bolted to the floor. She had to flee, but curiosity kept her standing in the aisle.

"Dan left you the money. I have a friend who does security for the bank. He told me you came to get it. You had the key to the safe deposit box. You opened a new checking account." The woman swung her arm and pointed an index finger at Penny while speaking. Something about Dan and his old putrid lies made the woman take her vendetta out on the wrong person.

"Well isn't that special? Your security friend doesn't sound very secure. Anyway, there's no money left. We donated it to the church and to several anti-human trafficking groups. Sorry but I'm flat broke. Maybe you'll win the big one." Penny turned away, horrified at being verbally accosted in public by a complete stranger.

The woman was seething like a rabid hound, "You're lying," she yelled. Spittle flew through her teeth as she raged on about Dan and his promises, and how being a flight attendant didn't pay enough to retire on, and how her condominium sat on lease land and they were raising the fees. Seems the bank had called the loan, and now her homeowner's association wanted to throw her out. *Couldn't happen to a nicer woman, Penny mused.* Finally, a cocktail waitress came down the aisle, prompting Doreen to shut her whale-sized mouth.

Embarrassed, at all the personal information spewing in her direction, Penny turned and looked above a row of slots. Yes, that blue shirt, John's dark hair, she'd know him anywhere. Her knight in shining armor weaved through the crowd. "Have a great day," Penny said, without feeling. "Maybe you'll win a jackpot. Good luck." Her body trembled, and her feet felt numb. *Ants huh? Bullshit. This woman probably murdered Dan for the money.* She felt it in her bones. She skipped across several aisles, away from where he had left her hours ago. Her face flushed, her heart beating, she raced towards her husband as if fleeing a five-alarm fire. Doreen huh? *I'll have to remember that name.*

Chapter 49

"Hey, over here," she called, motioning to him, not wanting to say his name, lest Doreen would hear it. *She must be a sneaky one, Penny thought, imagining* the woman in high heels tripping around in desert caverns. The thought made her feel better, even bringing out a smile. There, in front of her, the man she loved waved a flag of surrender, in the form of a white envelope, as if sending a message over a foxhole. *No more, she thought, we're out of here. She wanted to sing the song, 'California here I come,' the minute his face cleared another aisle of slots.*

He moved to kiss her on the cheek. "I got it, let's catch the Deuce and take off."

"Finally. Didn't they want to pay you? What in the world made it take so long? For a while, I thought you were kidnapped by that sly looking genie painted on the lobby wall at The Magic Carpet Motel."

"You mean the one grinning down on everyone at the check-in desk? That guy could never get me. First off, his red billowy pants would get caught in everything. Then he'd have to chase me in those pointed slippers, encrusted with colorful gems? Give me a break. Plus, with a braided beard and bushy eyebrows, he'd be easy to identify in a police lineup. I don't think he'd make it as a criminal."

She loved when her husband played imaginary games with her. She shook her head of curls and tried putting Doreen out of her mind. Seeing his face, hearing his cheery voice, filled her with spa-like relief that washed through every cell in her entire body. "Yes but come on. I thought something bad happened."

"Me kidnapped? Don't forget my net worth is back at reset, hovering around zero?" His arms encircled her waist. "Don't be upset, they had all this red tape stuff—you know how it is. I had to wait for some health insurance fund I had paid into, and that took a while. Is something wrong?"

"Well you have to admit you were gone a long time."

"Sorry, didn't really notice. I guess time flies when you're waiting for money." He chuckled.

"Outside of something weird, that just happened; I had fun watching that row of slots where you left me. This morning, a lady won over twenty thousand dollars on a penny machine. You should have seen all the excitement and commotion."

"Everything's strange around here, but Baby talk to me. What's the freakish thing that happened?" He nuzzled close, burying his nose into her smoke-filled hair. He couldn't deny missing her too.

"I'd rather talk about the lady who won the big jackpot. I couldn't believe it. Even watching someone else win is a thrill." Involuntary spasms traveled around in her nervous system making her body shake. She wanted to move farther and farther away from the aisle with the wicked woman.

"Oh yeah? That sounds incredible. Wonder why we never win?"

"Well first of all, we don't play. That probably makes a difference." A cocktail waitress, with a complicated tangle of flowers and vines tattooed on one leg, asked if they wanted a drink. They said no. Penny watched her move towards Doreen.

John said, "Can't believe how busy this place is on a weekday."

Doreen continued to move around in a clumsy manner. She appeared to be coming closer. The offensive, intoxicated woman grabbed the back of a stool and moved to the next stool, almost stumbling in her heels. After a few sluggish minutes, that dragged liked hours, Doreen exited the casino. She had wobbled onto the sidewalk, allowing Penny to exhale.

Though tired, John looked better than he had in months. Both of them were thrilled with the idea of going home, even though they didn't have any money. Heck, she'd go to work. She'd take on freelance jobs, even work at the mall. John didn't deserve this type of stress anymore. While they had planned to continue to pay for Lani to finish college, at least they had one less mouth to feed at home.

"Come on," John yanked her hand and pulled her in the direction of the big glass doors to the street.

"Wait, a second," Penny said, in a serious tone, trying to stall for time. No way would she want to run into Doreen again. "We already have the bus tickets and we have your paycheck. Other than that, all I have is ten dollars for snacks. But hear me out. I thought, since these are penny machines and since we're leaving, maybe we should try our luck."

John looked nervous. "Are you serious? We've been here for months, and all of a sudden you want to gamble?"

"I gambled on you, didn't I? Besides, life is short. Let's take a chance."

"That you did." He scratched his five-o'clock shadow and pulled on an imaginary goatee. "Good bet for the first twenty years anyway."

"Good bet always." She grabbed his hand and pulled him back to the aisle where Doreen had played and lost.

"Let's try this one." Penny sat down at a pulsating machine flashing red sevens and promising a million-dollar jackpot if five sevens lined

374

up in a row. The machine with the sevens happened to be adjacent to a slot that a shouting and screaming *Doreen had filled with hundred-dollar bills. Doreen had flailed her arms, while downing several cocktails, in a failed attempt to calm her frazzled nerves. The drinks might have helped her get up the courage to pour her soul out to Penny. By the time Doreen had left, Penny thought the stunning looker had turned into a sad, pathetic drunk.*

"Penny, if the first five dollars doesn't do anything, we should try another machine."

"Don't be negative. This is one of those instances where you have to think positive."

"Do you really think that makes a difference?" He asked, watching his wife's quivering hand slip their last ten-dollar bill into a black hole.

"No, but isn't there enough negativity in the world?" She pushed the minimum bet button which allegedly would pay on several lines, costing fifty cents per spin. After a few minutes of twenty-cent wins and a dollar win, they still had six hundred credits. "I'm cashing out. We can find another place on the way to the bus stop."

Chapter 50

Lani's hands were hogtied behind her back. Peter sat behind her with his back against hers, his hands also bound. Duct tape held their legs together. Both blindfolded, they smelled a horrid stench in the musty air. "Where do you think we are?"

"I don't know, but it's not my idea of a honeymoon."

"At least we'll die together."

"Do you hear the piped in jungle sounds and the waterfall?"

"Think. That's a clue to where we are." She coughed, "but don't forget it's my first time in Vegas." A stinging sensation burned her covered eyes. "Pete, it smells like Aunt Betsy's cat around here. I hate the smell of cat."

They sat on cold stone, hidden in the back area of a rainforest display, where misty drops of dew filled humid air, amid giant palms, rubber plants and fake bird of paradise plants. "There are several island themed hotels. Push closer and maybe I can untie the knots on your wrist." That's good. "Wait," Pete sounded alarmed. "Did you feel that?"

"What?"

"Some hairy animal rubbed against me and I don't think it's a housecat. It felt big."

Lani trembled. "Do you think it's hungry? What are we going to do?"

"I don't know. They have our phones. I heard our ringtones about twenty feet away. Bet your mom is calling to say goodbye."

"Well at least someone's looking for us." The sudden, breathtaking roar of a lion silenced both of them for a few seconds. "Peete-tur?"

"Be still Honey, these are not small cats. I'm guessing lions or tigers."

"I think I peed."

"Dang, they used nylon cord," he whispered. "You have to push towards me with all your strength. I learned how to untie knots in the Navy. Oh my God, did you hear that?" The feline turned around making loud purring noises. It grunted and hissed, before lifting its leg to mark his territory, spraying all over Peter.

"Gross," I think it wants you babe."

"That's not funny," Lani mumbled, imagining she'd be lunch for a hungry tiger. "Pete, do something."

"Don't talk. You'll only upset Clarence." A voice with an obvious accent broke through the jungle dissonance.

"Who said that?"

"I don't know. Some French dude."

"Who is Clarence?"

"I'm pretty sure it's one of the lions."

Sitting a safe distance above them on a fake boulder, behind a palm tree, away from the curious gaze of visitors, sat Julian.

Tourists from all over the world lined up single file on a narrow path, to see lions in what looked like a natural habitat, behind double-paned sheets of thick, industrial-gauge glass. The lion tamers weren't present because Ray had corralled all the employees into an outside trailer. First, he made sure to collect their cell phones at gunpoint. He had threatened their lives, and the lives of their loved ones, if they made the faintest peep. After shutting the door, Ray locked the workers into the metal room with a cable tie.

Lani and Peter weren't visible to the public either. The Wild Cat Exhibit showed several lions and tigers. They rotated from a compound outside of town. The lioness and the male lion had played fetch with one of the locked-up tamers before the man tried to go home. Exhausted from frolicking and rolling around with a ball, the lions were tired and hungry.

"Better shut up or you'll upset me too. I am better than Clarence. Or should I say, more efficient, since I have a gun."

Chapter 51

Penny dialed Lani's cell phone. When her daughter didn't answer, she left a simple message. "What are you kids up to now? Call me back."

A few minutes later, she received a call. Julian held the phone to Lani's lips. "Mom? Can you hear me? Do you know someone called Julian?"

Penny's heart skipped a beat. She wasn't sure what to say. After that freaky encounter with Doreen, she didn't want more drama. She drawled out a long, "Yes," that sounded like it had several syllables. Cautious, she lowered the octave of her voice. "Why?"

Traffic noise made her push her ear closer to the receiver. She heard a scuffle. "Lani? Lani? Can you hear me?" When the phone line disconnected, she screamed. Loud—louder than she had ever screamed—but all the other sounds on the Strip drowned it out. "Help," she yelled. It sounded like the word hell. Wandering tourists may have wondered if the she had lost all her money on Blackjack, before losing her mind. Crazy people were the norm. Vacationers enjoyed seeing unusual things, they thought it entertaining.

Mouth agape, she stared at the phone when a photo attachment arrived. That's when she screamed again. "Help," she hollered like a crazy person. She jumped up and down stomping her feet, and her screeching voice became breathless. "John, come here and look at this." Truly, a manic sight, in a few minutes' time, people would throw coins into a hat thinking she's singing a type of new-fangled grunge or hardcore punk.

"Whoa settle down before you pop a vein. What's going on? I thought you were dancing."

"Not sure, but Lani's in trouble and this time it's real. Take a look." Her hand shook as she held up the photo of Lani and Peter tied together. A male lion stood in the background. The front barrel of a gun pointed at her daughter. "Do you have Peter's number?"

He loved his wife dearly, but she had to be one of the most frustrating women on the planet.

John yanked the top of his hair. "Why would I have Peter's number?"

"It seems Julian, or one of his henchmen kidnapped her and Peter. Before the phone disconnected, Lani told me he's there with them. That scumbag Julian is with our little girl."

"You have to be kidding me? Julian? The guy who hired you to paint murals...."

"Yes," she cut him off. John was a great guy but sometimes he seemed slower than a snail in an old folk's home. "You heard me scream, didn't you? Look that picture. There's a lion in the picture and a gun. I know our daughter's voice and her tone gave me the creeps. She's scared poor thing, I don't know what to do."

"Call the cops, right now. They must be holding her at one of those wild cat shows."

"Right, but then what?" She dialed 911, describing Lani's call to a dispatcher. Fortunately, a different dispatcher than the last time, answered the phone. While on the phone, they walked along the sidewalk and sat down at a decorative bench in front of one of the glitzier resorts.

"Stay where you are, and an officer will meet you there. We can track her whereabouts through GPS from your phone to hers," the dispatcher had a formal, authoritative tone that reassured Penny.

Penny began to sob, and John pulled the phone from her hand. "This is Lani's dad. Are you sure we should stay here?"

"Yes, stay where you are. There's a ton of traffic in this town. Right now, I'm pinpointing you in front of the fountains near Flamingo Road. You're both wearing jeans and your wife told me she's wearing a pink top? Is that right?"

"Yes, but...."

"And you, sir? What color is your shirt?"

"Pale blue, I guess." He glanced down at his faded t-shirt. With his free hand, he stroked his wife's blazing red hair, in an effort to calm her down.

"Do you remember what your daughter had on this morning?"

"You mean like what she's wearing? Nope can't remember. She's on her honeymoon."

"Just wait there and someone will arrive in a few minutes." The call disconnected. John stared at the yellow cabs lining the driveway of the luxurious hotel. *He imagined that with any luck, in a few hours, one of those cabs would take the two of them back to their car that broke down in the desert. But first, they had to find Lani. And before anything, he had to pray.*

Chapter 52

The dispatcher called back. "Your daughter Lani is nearby. We have identified her location. She's close to where you are. Do you see our officers yet?"

Penny looked at John and surveyed the crowd. "No, I don't see them yet. There are tons of people all over the place."

"Is Lani at this resort?"

"Yes, it seems she's at the Wild Cat exhibit."

Penny looked straight up at the neon, glittering billboard depicting roaring lions. Technological craftsman had created the blinking billboard with with red, orange and green lights. Bloodthirsty looking fangs flashed and snarled high above the ruckus of the crowds. *Duh,* she thought, *we've been sitting here all this time.* The light display also consisted of aqua blue lights which showed a man in a loincloth swinging from a rope, like Tarzan. "Visit the Wild Cat Display Today," it said, below the throbbing lights. "Dine at the Safari Lounge." The lights pulsated dramatically, against the contrasting pale colored building.

Tiny bumps on her arms began to itch like crazy. With a few more hours of daylight left, she hated to think about spending another evening in a bed-bug infested hotel.

"There seems to be a problem. Stay at that location. I'll call you right back." The dispatcher hung up.

When Penny looked down at her phone, she saw a message with an attached photo. "Oh my God, John." The message asked for one million dollars ransom. The photo showed Lani tied up at the Wild Cat Exhibit in front of a large male lion. "John our baby is being held hostage in this hotel." She held up her phone with the photo.

"Here?"

"Yes, here look."

The dispatcher called back. "There were some shots fired but your daughter is fine. The police nabbed the gunman. Right now, they're in pursuit of another man."

"Should we stay here or go to the exhibit?"

"Hold on. We have your daughter. An officer will bring her to you."

"How about her husband, is he okay too?" Penny asked.

"Peter is the young man she's with, am I right?"

"Yes, yes that's her husband. What happened?"

"That boy's quite a hero. He untied the knots and they raced out of the exhibit. That's when the perpetrators began shooting. The two cats followed your daughter and her husband, but even after dodging large cats and bullets, they are safe, I repeat, they are safe. Animal control is trying to cage the animals before we let you, or anyone come close. The casino is going to be on lockdown for a few hours."

Chapter 53

When they found Lani and Peter they were fully dressed, and standing in the middle of the heated, outdoor swimming pool, passionately embracing and kissing each other. The under-cover officer waved at them and didn't get a re-sponse. "You can come out now. They caught the cats," he yelled. Seconds later, two uniformed guards came to tag along behind the detective.

A few swimmers swam around them. One of them tapped Lani on the shoulder. "I think that guy is talking to you."

Pulling their lips apart, they swam to the edge and looked around at the small contingent of po-lice gathering near the pool steps. The eighty-two-degree water felt warm and refreshing for late winter. It also calmed Lani's nerves. "Were you talking to us?"

"Yeah. Newlyweds huh?"

Lani smiled and looked at Peter. "Sorry, we jumped in here to get away from those cats."

"Well, your mom and dad are here in the lobby. They want to talk to you. Don't worry you're safe now. It took us a long time to calm your mom down. After you talk to your parents, go see the concierge. They want to put you up in the honeymoon suite, for a week. Just tell them you're the cat hostages. They'll know what you mean."

A few minutes later, Lani ran to her mother. She had a towel wrapped around her shoulders and tears flowed from her sparkling, red-rimmed eyes. "Oh mom, it was horrible, we were tied up and blindfolded. I couldn't see anything. The man who held us hostage said he wanted you to pay for all his losses. What would he mean by that?"

"Never mind dear, how did you manage to get out of there?"

Peter ran up behind Lani. He shook hands with John who gave him a manly embrace.

"Peter untied two knots, and then he yanked off the tape, and with lightning speed, pushed off our blindfolds. He told me to run as fast as I could. By moving fast, we got the cats excited, and they ran and followed, even faster. First, we dashed into a restroom but could hear one of the lions pacing outside the door for a while. I think it got bored of waiting or something. Then they went scavenging for food," Lani exclaimed, before sneezing. "Sorry, I'm still allergic to cats." She wiped her face with the towel. "Finally, we ran towards the outside pool because we know cats hate baths."

"Slow down honey, I think you'll hyperventilate." Peter added.

"What happened to Julian?"

"Are you kidding? That guy is so out of shape. Plus, we heard him tell the other guy, that he's super scared of the cats. He had his gun pointed more on the lions than on us. When we took off, he fired at the animals. I hope the animal rights activists get him for endangering defenseless cats."

John wondered how Peter remained so calm. "Lani told us that you untied the rope."

"Yes Sir. We learned how to tie and untie knots in the Navy. Most of the time, I was on KP duty or mopping the deck. Never thought it would come in handy," he said with a smile.

"Did they catch Julian?"

Peter hugged Lani as she continued the tale. "They must have caught him and his accomplice. There was some other guy with a Jersey accent patrolling the back entrance where the real lion tamers went in and out."

Penny knew her daughter spoke about Ray. "Well I'm just glad you two lovebirds are okay." They watched in awe as a massive crate with giant metal bars, carrying a lion, rolled past them. Lani looked into the golden eyes and turned back to Peter. "I'm yours Peter, he can't have me."

Peter laughed. "I think he wanted you for dinner, but there's not enough meat on those bones." He poked her ribcage, making her giggle.

John felt his stomach rumble at the word 'meat'. "Well let's change that and get something to eat. Are you coming back to California with us? We have to catch a bus and we have enough for your tickets."

"First, they need to put on some dry clothes," Penny stated.

"Good point," Peter said. "Security guy said they want to put us up in the honeymoon suite."

"Here?" Penny looked around at the ornate decorative mosaic tile and the life-sized statues. "Wow that sounds lovely." She pulled out her wallet and handed some money to Lani. Here's enough for two bus fares. That's all we have. I have enough for our bus tickets plus six dollars. I might have some change. Do you want the six dollars for snacks?

Peter put his hand on Penny's wallet. "No, Mrs. Murray," he replied. "I have enough to get us through the week. Please don't worry about anything."

Penny shrugged and thought about Peter's statement. Don't worry, huh? *The last few days had been more than any mother should ever go through,* she thought. Nothing but killer ants in the desert, human traffickers, a fancy woman named Doreen who wants her dead, the bordello disguised as a fancy spa, shots fired at the airport, a taxi chase on the freeway, her daughter held hostage and hunted by giant African cats. Nope, she had nothing to worry about, nothing at all. "Lani dear, we'll wait right here to make sure they honor that complimentary room. Now go to the front desk with Peter while I rub my temples."

Chapter 54

Lani looked out over the Strip and sighed. "I think this is the fanciest place in all of Vegas."

"It's okay, but can we pull those curtains, and get this honeymoon started?"

Peter had his arm around her waist. "Glad we jumped in the pool. You had a good idea. I still smell cat in your hair though."

"Meow, have any catnip?" she purred, caressing the soft velveteen drapes.

"No, is that stuff even legal?" Peter made a funny face and planted a raspberry-sound on her cheek.

The bubbly sound made her turn from the window. "Have you seen the hot-tub with jets in the bathroom?"

"Uh-huh. I saw that, plus plush towels, marble floors and an enormous shower with seating for two."

"I'm so glad we waited. This is it. A real honeymoon and I'm so excited."

"I love you baby." He went to the window and drew the curtains.

"I know that. I think my mom and dad finally know it too. We sure scared them."

"It's all Tyler's fault."

"I guess, but it worked out. I'm sorry about your brother."

"I'm not. We can't pick our family members."

"That's true. You never told me why your parents didn't come to our wedding." She kicked off her shoes and sat on the edge of the bed.

"Dad has a new girlfriend and he took her to Paris. I already told you about mom." Peter sat next to Lani and removed his shoes.

"Just that she's busy with her patients. I thought she's a veterinarian."

"She is, but some Labradoodle needed surgery."

"Oh, that sounds serious."

"Are you being facetious?" Peter pulled off his pants, leaving on his boxer shorts.

"No, I love dogs, even Bentley."

"Poor Bentley," Peter said, undoing the top button of her pants. "Can I pull off your top?" He tugged off her top and undid her bra.

"Whatever, always remember that you can pick your friends and those you love." She turned to kiss him, and he slowly pushed her pants to the floor. "Hey, that's not fair. I shouldn't be surprised after the way you pulled off those blindfolds. You are so fast. How come I'm naked and you're still wearing your underwear?"

"Meet you in the shower," Peter said, dashing for the bathroom.

The luxury surrounding them went on forever. Lani skipped after Peter and grabbed a towel. "This is so extravagant."

"Only the best for my wife," he mumbled, turning on the shower jets.

"Don't worry I won't get used to it."

"You should get used to it. Drop the towel. This is serious.

There's something I haven't told you."

"What? That you wear boxers instead of briefs?"

He pulled off his shorts and watched her eyes gravitate to his throbbing member. "I know my timing is weird. But I have to tell you this. My brother's share of the trust was just re-assigned to me. Mostly because, well you know, he's being an ass. Anyway, it's a lot of money. My dad used to play professional ball. Let's just say, this bathroom has some nice features, but the one you'll have will be even better."

Lani, blinked several times, her face showing obvious approval of her husband's handsome physique. "Wow, Peter, you know I didn't marry you for your money. I'm impressed with all of you."

He laughed and pulled her into the shower. Warm water flowed over both of them. "You are so beautiful."

"Cliche," she giggled, while he massaged her breasts.

"How about, you're the loveliest virginal flower?"

"Oh please, so where would that leave me tomorrow?" She giggled, knowing his mind worked like a greyhound on a racetrack, as he went through all the synonyms for the word beautiful.

"You'll be my stunning, incredibly gorgeous wife: A glistening sunrise above fresh, powdered snow? Diamond dewdrops on flower shop rose petals? A calm sea, under a cloudless sky?"

"That's awesome, but what about sexy?"

"Oh baby, you have no idea," He gasped, clutching her so hard she thought he might crack a rib.

"Peter," she complained under the spray of the jets. "Try not to break anything. We survived those giant cats and even some bullets this afternoon. Please be gentle," she said with a smile. "On top of that, you look—um—how do I say it? Big. Am I going to live through this honeymoon?"

"Oh you'll be living through it over and over again for the rest of your life. I didn't mean to squeeze too hard. I'm just too happy. Let's go crawl into bed." He turned off the water and handed her the towel.

"Which reminds me," Lani said. "I bought some of those edible panties for you to munch on before dinner. Think of it as an appetizer."

Chapter 55

John whispered into Penny's ear. "Glad we're trying another casino. I don't think the one I worked at has any money left. I forgot to tell you something important. They are freezing all the construction but keeping the casino open. I quit at the right time."

"How can they stop building the top floors?" The two of them were close to the bus station awaiting their ride home. "Do you know we're East of Fremont?"

"So?"

"That waitress, don't you remember? She told us not to go East of Fremont street at night."

"Whatever. Fremont is busy tonight. I finally saw those topless nuns."

"You did?"

"They look kind of funny to me. It's like I want to tell them to get a mammogram."

"Right?" Penny laughed, that would be a good start. "I saw a lot of homeless."

"I know dear, but don't forget, we're kind of homeless too."

"At least if all else fails we have your sister. These guys out here look like they have no one. Anyway, tell me about your work. They don't want to finish that enormous hotel?"

"Not for a while. They're blaming the economy."

"With all the crowds and everything it's hard to believe Vegas has money problems. Sure glad Lani and Peter are going to have the honeymoon suite at that ultra-fancy hotel. Do you think they're safe?"

"Yes, dear—they don't want bad publicity all over the news. Stop worrying about Lani. That cat exhibit alone brings in thousands per day. The police and the FBI heard your story, so they will keep an eye on her better than anyone in this entire town."

"They acted like I'm right about Doreen killing Dan. I mean I just had a hunch, but they sort of confirmed it. Plus, all that hoopla about Harvester ants made me suspicious."

"Safe to say, she won't be coming after us. What made you think she did it?"

"I looked up killer ants on my Smartphone. They exist, but not in North America." She pushed a button on a slot machine and lost a few more pennies. "I think the best I can do is forget I ever knew Captain Dan Losegg."

"Sure, but it sounds like you need to forgive him first."

"Wow, I hadn't thought of that," she said with a trace of sarcasm.

"Penny, I'm not trying to make you feel guilty or anything, but I'm serious."

"You're right. That's what I'll do. Forgive and forget."

"That's my sweetie." He leaned nearer. "Let me hear it, Babe."

"I forgive you Dan," she seemed to say to the slot machine. "Sometimes we meet a person who changes everything in an instant. You, Captain Losegg, did that. Meanwhile, as things changed, I learned many things about myself." She vehemently pushed the spin button and lost more coins. "The end, sayonara, bye, bye wherever you are. Hope our souls don't intersect, ever again.

Sorry you had to die such a tragic death." The symbols didn't line up and she sounded irritated. "Now spin away and leave me alone. Bye."

John watched her and couldn't help snickering. "Wow, it sounded sincere. I'm glad you forgave him."

"Glad to be rid of the man. I won't mention him again." She changed the subject. "So, what's this about freezing construction? They're blaming the housing market crash?"

"Rumor is, The Magnifique is getting new owners from Malaysia."

Penny pressed the collect button. She had a five-dollar slip. "Can we try that big one with the angels near the door? It has a ten-million-dollar jackpot?"

"Sure. Let's go for broke."

A progressive monitor flashed wildly on the top of the penny machine. Decorated with alluring blue angels, green angels and pink angels wearing elegant robes, the graphics looked stunning. To win the grand prize, a player had to line up one of each colored angel on the middle pay line. To win a minor jackpot of five million, a player needed three pink angels. To win three million dollars, a player needed green angels. To win one cool million, a player would need three blue angels to sit next to each other on the middle pay line. A player would also need to play the maximum bet of three hundred pennies per spin in order to win any of the larger prizes or jackpots.

Penny put her five-dollar slip into the machine and pushed the minimum bet, which amounted to fifty cents. Angels swept around and around, landing on various parts of the cycle, but nothing happened. Three halos came up and gave Penny a dollar more. Harps paid one hundred coins and one angel of any color doubled the winnings. "This is fun John. Look I'm back up over ten dollars."

"Good for you. I think we better get going. The Bonneville Transportation Center is a few streets away. Doesn't our bus leave in two hours?"

"Yes, yes, we have plenty of time. Hold on." Two harps and one green angel brought the winnings up to twelve dollars. "Can't you see I'm winning?"

He snorted when he laughed.

"Watch, we'll play max bet and see what happens."

"That should go fast. What's that three spins?"

"Four, maybe more, if we win in between."

Playing along, he closed his eyes. "Come on angels!" he said, making her smile.

"You crack me up." She pushed the spin button with the maximum bet and no angels lined up and no halos showed up either. "Three more, cross your fingers." She pushed it again and now one halo gave her twenty more pennies.

"No, you crack me up." John yawned, pulling his check from his pocket. "If you want money, maybe we should go to the bank on the way to the bus dear."

Penny's face showed a high level of exhilaration. The burden of work and her worry, seemed to vanish. Her eyes sparkled, and her pink tinged cheeks looked healthy. Though she wasn't winning, the idea of colorful angels made her forget all their financial woes. "One more, this is the last spin John and then I'm ready to go." Her eyes focused on the pretty pink angels that swooshed by faster than a meteor falling to Earth.

Then, something strange happened. Her heart leapt into the air as the blue angels rolled around one at a time. First, one blue angel with brunette hair and soulful eyes, stopped in the middle. Then a second blue angel came to rest next to the first one. Penny inhaled, her eyes glued to the monitor. "John, look!" The third blue angel wiggled her way into the correct position and lined up on the centerline. It felt like slow motion. A silence embraced her, squeezing her lungs, making it feel like they were underwater. Gasping for air, she looked around before the jolt of bells and blinking lights shook the casino floor and the entire continent. A crowd began to gather. She grabbed a hold of John and jumped up and down. "Sweetheart, I think we just won a million dollars, in pennies."

Epilogue

"Maybe Vegas isn't all bad," Penny surmised on the way out of the casino. "After all, where else can you go from dirt poor to incredibly wealthy, all in a matter of minutes?"

John shook his head in disbelief. "It never works like this. It's just you."

"Me?"

"Yeah, you know I think everything happens for a reason. God wants you to have everything you deserve."

She laughed. "John, there are people more worthy. Trust me."

"Not in my eyes." He moved around and stopped to face her on the crowded sidewalk. "You're a goddess."

"Whatever," she smiled, and their lips met. "Still have that spark, Baby."

"Sure do."

They kissed again. Deep and meaningful, as if they hadn't kissed in ages. A young man walked by and whistled.

"Guy doesn't know the half of it," she whispered in John's ear.

"You mean how–I think you're sexier than a Vegas showgirl?"

"That, of course, but we're also a sizzling hot couple, changing the world with our love."

"The hottest... Now come on, my red haired angel. Let's go repossess our vehicle from the Mojave impound lot before they close. A fortune cookie told me there are major home renovations in my future." He pulled one of her hands into his and said, "Love you."

"I know, but I love you more."

* * *

* * *

Though this is a fictional story, the part about 48 hours is true. Getting that message across is crucial to saving lives.

If you, or anyone you know needs to talk about this subject, call the **National Human Trafficking Resource Center at 1-888-373-7888.**

Dear reader,

We hope you enjoyed reading *Penniless Souls*. Please take a moment to leave a review, even if it's a short one. Your opinion is important to us.

Discover more books by Eve Gaal at https://www.nextchapter.pub/authors/romance-from-the-inland-empire-author-eve-gaal

Want to know when one of our books is free or discounted? Join the newsletter at http://eepurl.com/bqqB3H

Best regards,
Eve Gaal and the Next Chapter Team

Books by the Author

Penniless Hearts
Penniless Souls
The Fifth Commandment

Penniless Souls
ISBN: 978-4-86750-069-9 (Large Print)

Published by
Next Chapter
1-60-20 Minami-Otsuka
170-0005 Toshima-Ku, Tokyo
+818035793528
7th June 2021